A Diplomat in Paris

Morgan L. Fox

© **Copyright 2024 - All rights reserved.**

The content contained within this book may not be reproduced, duplicated or transmitted without direct written permission from the author or the publisher.

Under no circumstances will any blame or legal responsibility be held against the publisher, or author, for any damages, reparation, or monetary loss due to the information contained within this book, either directly or indirectly.

Legal Notice:

This book is copyright protected. It is only for personal use. You cannot amend, distribute, sell, use, quote or paraphrase any part, or the content within this book, without the consent of the author or publisher.

Disclaimer Notice:

Please note the information contained within this document is for educational and entertainment purposes only. All effort has been executed to present accurate, up to date, reliable, complete information. No warranties of any kind are declared or implied. Readers acknowledge that the author is not engaged in the rendering of legal, financial, medical or professional advice. The content within this book has been derived from various sources. Please consult a licensed professional before attempting any techniques outlined in this book.

By reading this document, the reader agrees that under no circumstances is the author responsible for any losses, direct or indirect, that are incurred as a result of the use of the information contained within this document, including, but not limited to, errors, omissions, or inaccuracies.

Table of Contents

PROLOGUE: NOTTINGHAM, 11 MARCH 1980 1

CHAPTER 1: CONSUL IN PARIS: 02 JUNE 1942 9

CHAPTER 2: A CHANCE ENCOUNTER: 05 JUNE 1942 23

CHAPTER 3: RECONNAISSANCE: 20 JUNE 1942 35

CHAPTER 4: THE LOOPHOLE: 22 JUNE 1942 47

CHAPTER 5: THE PROMISE: 23 JUNE 1942 59

CHAPTER 6: THE PLAN: 26-28 JUNE 1942 71

CHAPTER 7: OPERATION LIFELINE: 28 JUNE-03 JULY 1942 83

CHAPTER 8: ON THE RADAR: 05 JULY 1942 95

CHAPTER 9: UNLIKELY ALLIES: 05-07 JULY 1942 107

CHAPTER 10: LOVE AMIDST SHADOWS: 10 JULY 1942 119

CHAPTER 11: THE UNRAVELING: 10 JULY 1942 131

CHAPTER 12: THE OPERA HOUSE: 15-16 JULY 1942 143

CHAPTER 13: THE CONVERSION: 02 AUGUST 1942 157

CHAPTER 14: A BATTLE OF WITS: 07-15 AUGUST 1942 169

CHAPTER 15: BETRAYAL: 03-06 SEPTEMBER 1942 183

CHAPTER 16: HIGH STAKES: 16-19 SEPTEMBER 1942 195

CHAPTER 17: EXODUS: 26 SEPTEMBER-10 OCTOBER 1942 209

CHAPTER 18: PARTING OF WAYS: 12 OCTOBER 1942 223

CHAPTER 19: THE SUMMONS: 8 NOVEMBER 1942- 9 SEPTEMBER 1943 233

EPILOGUE: NOTTINGHAM, 11 MARCH 1980 241

Prologue:
Nottingham, 11 March 1980

As a child, there was no other character that fascinated me as much as Robin Hood. He and his band of merry men, who dwelled in the forests of Sherwood, fleeced the rich and helped the poor—or so the legends have it. I used to think that righting the injustices of the world was heroic. Of course, now that I was an adult, my mind was less inclined to such romanticism. I can't say that I believed much in a fair and equitable world any more than I believed in a unicorn or a fairy at the time. It wasn't as if I had given up on my childhood dream of visiting Sherwood Forest entirely. However, as I grew up, more contemporary heroes replaced Robin Hood. The academic rigor of Oxford had not really given me much time to take a holiday either.

Finally, on a warm summer morning, I drove the two-hour journey from Oxford to Nottingham. I wanted to bask again in a childlike sense of wonder that I, a history postgraduate and now a research student, was afraid I was fast losing.

Nottingham did not disappoint. The day I reached there, I quickly freshened up and wandered around Old Market Square, where I was put up at a quaint bed and breakfast run by an ancient, friendly couple. The city was everything I expected it to be. Slower-paced than London, it housed historic buildings such as the Nottingham Castle, The Theater Royal, and splendid Victorian buildings. It was too late to gain entry passes for most of the historical sites, but I was content just watching from the outside. There was time to dwell on each of the sites, and I was determined to just soak up the atmosphere for the present.

Away from academia, my heart was singing. I was excited because the next day, I had booked myself on a tour of the country park, a part of the Sherwood Forest that was opened to the public a little more than ten years ago. I was hoping to catch a glimpse of the Major Oak, which, as legends have it, was shelter to my childhood hero and his men. I couldn't wait to see it all. Suddenly, it was as if I was ten again and reading the books in my father's study. I felt the same sense of peace stealing over me.

In the evening, I had tea and a few scones at one of the nearby cafes. As I ambled back to the B&B, I saw Mrs. Kitteredge, my hostess, speaking to a rather stately-looking man in his mid-60s. He wasn't as tall as the average European generally is, but there was something striking about his stature all the same. He was sharp-featured, and a cover of dense white hair gave him an even more regal appearance. His face was scrunched up in concentration, intently listening to Mrs. Kitteredge, and you could tell by her face that she was flattered by his attention. He was a fair man, and though his English, the little of it that I could catch, was impeccable, I knew he wasn't of European descent. It was something in the way he used his hands that gave this away. He was also dressed in a three-piece suit cut well to his figure. The only problem was that it gave the impression that the man was from an era long bygone. Nobody these days wore a three-piece suit except when they attended formal functions, and it seemed he was merely dressed up for evening tea.

After he left, presumably back to his room, I approached Mrs. Kitteredge and asked her about the easiest way to the country park. I wanted to know how early it opened too. After she supplied me with all the details, I casually asked her about the man she was talking to. Her eyes brightened as she said, "Oh, that's Mr. Farmani, our tenant who is in the west cottage. He's been here for a couple of years now."

"Interesting name," I ventured and then added, "You see, I was mentally telling myself that something about him looked a little foreign."

She beamed at me, "Yes. Mr. Farmani is an Iranian. He was the consul in Paris during the war and later in Brussels, if my memory serves right. Quite an intelligent and well-spoken man. There are rumors that he was an Allied spy or some such—that he helped save many Jews, but the man remains tight-lipped about the subject."

By now, I was piqued. "He helped Jews in Paris?" I asked. It seemed incredible that I had come searching for Robin Hood and was instead in the proximity of a real-life hero.

"That's what they say," she said as she turned to pick up a cloth and wipe down the already sparkling glasses in the cabinet behind her desk. "Quite a hero, is what people say, though he ran into trouble with his own country for his actions. That is why he is out here."

"Interesting," was all I could say, though my mind was busy at work. My own research was tangentially about the Second World War, and though I had vowed to myself not to bring work here when on vacation, I felt Mr. Farmani could be of help. Here was a man who had witnessed the madness at close quarters within German-occupied territory and probably worked with the French resistance too. My romantic mind conjured up daring escapades and adventures that he could have been a part of, and I felt half-admiration and half-envy for this serene-looking man who could tell us so much about the turbulent period he had been a part of. I knew I had to try to speak to him, no matter how uncommunicative he might prove.

***

It would be a couple of days later before I would drum up the courage to visit Mr. Farmani. I knocked on his cottage door once, fearing that he wouldn't open up at all. However, my fears seemed unfounded. He did open it and looked at me, a little perplexed.

"Hi," he said in a friendly enough tone. "Are you here to fix the gas boiler? I reported a problem to the manageress a few days ago."

"Uhm. No, I have come to introduce myself. I am David. I stay at the B&B," I said by way of a clumsy introduction.

"Ah. Oh. Sorry for being so presumptuous. David, you say?" he said at once and opened the door wider for me. He waved vaguely at his parlor, a cozy little nest with plush furniture and flowered curtains. The whole effect of the room was summery and bright. It was also spotlessly clean, and the only things strewn about were books and magazines, of which there seemed to be no dearth.

My first impression of the man was confirmed. He was merely waiting for the gas man but dressed as if he had been invited for tea to Buckingham Palace and was making his way to meet the Queen shortly. He wore a well-stitched three-piece suit, and there was a pipe resting on one of the arms of the settee, on which a newspaper had been flung in careless haste. It looked like he had been reading when I rang the bell.

"Are you here on holiday?" He asked, smiling at me.

"Yes. I am a research student from Oxford. Nottingham has always appealed to me owing to the legend of Robin Hood. When I got my first break, I drove over," I said.

"Oh, research student? That's wonderful. What is your subject?" He asked me.

I could hardly get out the word "History" when I noticed a subtle change in Mr. Farmani's attitude. He sat up a little stiffer than before.

"Let me guess then," he said. "Perhaps you are writing your thesis on the war?"

I smiled wryly, "I guess my cover is blown then?"

He did not smile this time as he said, "Let me be frank. You may have heard things about me. You may have come to get my statement, eye-witness account, or whatever. You would not be the first to have tried, and you might perhaps not be the last. But I honestly do not have the strength to narrate everything or to relive it. I think some things are best buried in the past, no? The world wars have not been the finest moments for humanity."

I was deflated, but I was prepared for this. The landlady had warned me that he was rather reticent about this subject. So I went full steam ahead, "You're right about the wars not being our finest moments. But would you not agree that there is a lot for us to learn about it? Perhaps even prevent such a catastrophe from repeating itself?"

He was skeptical. "There have been reams written about the wars. No amount of writing can undo the damage to those who have lost lives and more. I do not feel that anything I can say further will add to the subject. I do not see the point of it, and I prefer the anonymity of this humble retirement."

"But you must have been in the thick of things in Paris. Wouldn't you want your story to set matters straight? Perhaps with your homeland?" I asked.

"This land," he said, waving vaguely around him, "has been my homeland for over two decades now, and *my homeland*, as you refer to it, is a relic of the past. I no longer understand what is happening there," he ended, not unkindly. There was a faraway, sad look in his eyes.

I knew he was referring to the Iranian revolution. The Shah, who had ruled the country for 38 years, had been overthrown, and Iran had become an Islamic state almost overnight. I had kept up somewhat with what was happening in Iran, of course, but what really interested me was what happened during the war.

I turned my head to look at the room where we were sitting. By the mantelpiece, I eyed an old sepia photograph of a young, slim woman in her 20s. She was beautiful in an exquisite way. I knew the photo was an old one and that the woman in it should be at least in her late 60s now. However, it was still an arresting image, and my curiosity was aroused.

"Is that a picture of Mrs. Farmani?" I enquired boldly. I knew that this man might show me the door any moment now, and the thought made me reckless. Any information he offered was good enough for me.

My question aroused him from his reverie, and finally, there was that smile again. It was as if the sun had emerged from the clouds as he said rather jovially, "I must say I am impressed at your perseverance. I was given to understand that the British are a very politically correct and reserved nation, not given to prying into people's affairs much. But you seem not to care much for conventions, David? To answer your question, no, that is not my wife. There never has been a Mrs. Kameron Farmani. I am a bachelor."

I smiled in turn and said, "All the more reason to ask who she is then and why she occupies such a prominent place on your mantelpiece. Also, I am not British. Well, not really, I suppose. My parents and I immigrated here from Italy when I was three. We stayed in Plymouth for most of my life until I got a place at Oxford. It was the golden ticket out of the relative poverty we had always lived in. So perhaps that explains why I am more curious than others."

He laughed. "Oh, there have been a couple of nosey ones in the past. I suppose I thought you would be as easy to dismiss. But clearly, I am mistaken."

"You will help me then?" I asked, not daring to hope.

"Well. That depends. What exactly do you want from me? And what do you plan to do with the information I provide?" He asked, considering me. It seemed like he was sizing me up.

"I would like to write a book about you. If you want me to keep your name anonymous, I can do that too. I want to know your story, as much or as little as you want to say. I will honor your wishes with respect to how you want to tell your tale, from wherever and in whichever order you deem it right. But I know there is a story...," I said somewhat lamely.

Something about my demeanor must have struck him as being genuine, for surprisingly, he did open up to me. I will admit that I had thought it would take more effort on my part to un-clam Kameron Farmani, but it seemed he trusted me. Or perhaps he was tired of keeping the tale to himself. But the words soon poured out in an unending torrent.

"Everyone has a story, David. But my story started around the time of the war. All my existence till then seems to pale by comparison. It was as if everything else had only been a preparation for it. When the war started, I was only 25, and I was in the heart of German-occupied Paris in 1942..."

Chapter 1:

Consul in Paris: 02 June 1942

It was a warm day in June 1942, two years since Paris had fallen to the Nazis. The sweltering weather was indicative of the brewing political turmoil within the city. From one perspective, the Nazis seemed to have firmly entrenched themselves, with Marshal Pétain's Vichy government not having the grit to oppose them; from another viewpoint, General de Gaulle's untiring efforts to rally for internal and external resistance was gathering more momentum by the day. The French citizens in Paris, who could hardly bear to look at the red and black abomination of the Swastika flying high on every monument and building in the city, hoped and prayed for the day when they would be freed. Yet, it seemed that they would have to keep waiting for that day. Hope was slowly turning to despair as the atrocities of the Nazis kept growing to monstrous proportions.

First came the curfews, which darkened the once-gay city from 9 o'clock every night until the wee hours of the morning. This wasn't applied to certain posher parts of the city, but Parisians gathered in numbers without a valid reason could be unexpectedly arrested by the police or the Gestapo. Then came the rationing of food, clothing, tobacco, and coal. While the Parisians were cold, hungry, and miserable, the Germans were slowly bleeding the city dry. For every year of the occupation, the basic amenities were getting scarcer and more expensive. The French were finding it hard to feed themselves. Most entertainment had been suspended, and even radio channels were only mouthpieces of the Germans spewing their propaganda. Whether the broadcast was from Germany or

Vichy, it mattered not—the content was always the same. It spoke of Nazi glory and how they would soon conquer the world. Even the entertainment channels played only the compositions of German masters like Bach and Beethoven. If there was a respite from classical music, it was only replaced by German military music or songs. It seemed hopeless indeed that a country that had its roots deep in arts and culture, such as France, was held hostage in this manner.

However, covertly, the communists and supporters of Free France of de Gaulle were working inside the city. Threats of arrests, punishments, and torture did not deter these brave men and women who worked tirelessly, surreptitiously carrying messages to the Allied forces outside, waiting to recapture the country. The Nazis in the city were seething at the flagrant disobedience of these French citizens, and yet, though they could pull out a few stray leaves, flowers, and perhaps even branches of the Resistance, the tree of French nationalism remained firmly planted in the soil of France and Paris.

If there was one group of people who were more afraid of the Nazis than the French, they were the Jews, marked conspicuously by the yellow star of David on the arms or chests of their clothing. From May 1942, the Jews of France were asked to wear the star on their clothing. Though they had been treated poorly since the establishment of the Vichy government, they were openly discriminated against now. Discreet arrests and sudden disappearances were common among them. They could no longer work, be seen in public places, or hold property. Now, there were rumors that they were going to be rounded up and taken to the camps. "Camps"—a word that previously conjured up happy associations with summers, tents, bonfire nights, and leisure, had taken on a dark, sinister overtone in the last couple of years.

***

The Iranian consulate in Paris was a grand building with classical architecture. It stood tall and proud, flanked by the Seine on one side, representing the diplomatic presence of Iran in France. The exterior was adorned with intricate carvings and decorative statues, showcasing the artistic heritage of both countries. The consulate was surrounded by landscaped gardens, which, though not as beautifully maintained as they were before the war, still bore vibrant flowers and hedges along pathways that were in tolerable condition, given the shortage of the staff. The main entrance was a large double door made of solid oak leading to a spacious reception area. Inside, the consulate was tastefully decorated with Persian rugs, antique furniture, and ornate chandeliers. The walls were adorned with Persian artwork and historical photographs. The consulate's interior was decorated in warm and inviting hues—a mix of rich browns, deep reds, and golden accents. The furniture was elegant and comfortable, offering a welcoming atmosphere for those seeking assistance or refuge.

Kameron Farmani's office in the west wing of the consulate was a modest space, reflective of his diplomatic role. The walls were adorned with maps, highlighting Iran's geography and its connections to other countries. The furniture was minimalistic yet functional, with a large wooden desk, a few chairs, and bookshelves lined with leather-bound volumes. The natural lighting allowed in by the large windows flooded the room during the day so that he never had any use for the wall and desk lamps. His desk had stacks of files and documents. A small Iranian flag sat proudly on a stand in one corner of the room, symbolizing his allegiance and commitment to his country, while on the wall behind his desk hung a portrait of the young Shah, who had succeeded his father to the throne only a year ago.

Farmani finished clearing his desk of papers that were strewn all over. He sorted them into three files that were in front of him, which he had marked "Pending," "To be Filed," and "To be Checked." He sighed deeply, running his hand through his hair. He had just finished reading a letter that deeply disturbed him. It was from his father, who wrote to him from time to time. They weren't all that close, and yet, this particular letter was one of the longest that he had received from his father in the near past. After the general pleasantries, urging him to write back more often for his mother's sake, and so forth, his father addressed what he thought was most important. The letter went on to describe in detail the plight of their Jewish neighbors who had been family friends of the Farmani's for several generations. The patriarch of the Ashouri family was a doctor. He and his family had emigrated to Bonn in the 1920s because he had been offered a good position in one of the state-run hospitals in the country. Now, they had returned to Iran, having lost his house, job, and pretty much all the possessions they owned in Germany. They had barely escaped being captured, carted off to some internment camp, or worse. Using their connections and some money they had secretly saved up, the Ashouris counted themselves among the lucky ones for having made it back just in time. Senior Farmani mentioned some of the horrors that they had witnessed and narrated to him the brutality of the Gestapo and SS, as well as the plight of the Jews in Germany. People like the Ashouris were being treated worse than hunted animals, shorn of their respect and rights. Once upon a time, before their immigration and before they lost touch, Farmani had called Amir his best friend. He was moved by the letter and knew how deeply it must have affected his father for him to have written about it.

Farmani remembered sadly how he had spent many a happy summer day playing with young Amir Ashouri, the doctor's son, a boy who was only a year or two younger than him, in the large gardens surrounding his house in Tehran. He wondered how things had changed drastically in such a short span.

Farmani was almost 29, though his face was unlined and could have passed for that of an undergraduate. He was fair, and his hair was atypically dark black. It was slicked back, as was the custom just then. Thick, bushy eyebrows added to the overall boyish charm of his good-natured, handsome countenance. Clean-shaven and spruce, he was dressed fashionably in a grey suit cut to his figure. He was of average height and build, though people who met him always seemed to remember him as taller than he actually was.

Young as he was, he was now the consul of Iran in Paris, one of the few office bearers who had stayed back to complete the work here. He hadn't been appointed to this position. He had been, in fact, a junior attaché working for his brother-in-law, who was the consul. When the Nazis attacked Paris, they issued a decree warning all officials to flee before they took over. His brother-in-law, whose family had also been in Paris, did not have much choice. He had to either stay behind and face the wrath and mercy of the Germans or move to Vichy with his family. He chose the latter, relocating to Vichy with his wife and children while Farmani stayed back.

He was young, ambitious, and out to work for his country, no matter the consequences. As things stood, the previous Shah had been in the good books of the Nazis, and Farmani's diplomatic immunity as a government official of Iran ensured his safety. Most Iranians in France and Germany were safe for the present owing to Germany's trading relationship with Iran, which continued despite the political turmoil. In order to establish these ties, Germany had classified all Iranians as "pure-blooded Aryans," exempt from the Nuremberg Laws, the series of laws that the Reich had adopted from 1935 on ward to "preserve German blood and honor," as they claimed. The laws declared all Jews on German soil Semites, distinct from the German Aryans, and as such non-citizens of Germany, undeserving of political rights. The old Shah, mesmerized by German progress and technology, had readily embraced the Germans, who came into his country to build the finest

13

infrastructure in Iran. In return, much of the Nazi wealth flowed from countries like Iran.

But things were different now. Iran had been surprised by an invasion by the Soviets and Great Britain less than a year ago. Its position now was tricky, to say the least. On the one hand, it still had a huge trading partnership with Germany; on the other, the new Shah was sworn in with the blessing of the occupied Allied forces. Strategically, the young Mohammed Reza Shah continued the strict non-alliance policy militarily where the war was concerned. However, Iran's hands were tied, and it had no choice but to help the Allied cause when it was demanded. Iran did not have the military might to fight against its invaders. As long as the Soviets and the British ran the country in proxy, it was an enemy state for Germany. There was no telling when Nazi Germany would revoke its stance on Iranian ancestry.

Farmani heard the news the day before from a trusted source within the French administration. He had been expecting it, of course, but it came as a shock nonetheless. To think that people, some of whom he knew and worked with closely, would be rounded up and transported like cattle from the country to camps God-knows-where simply because they were born into a particular ethnic race was bad enough. It was still worse to reckon that there was very little he could do, even with his political and diplomatic connections. He knew that very soon, it would be too late to do anything about the situation. News pouring in about the camps in Poland and Germany was disheartening, to say the least. Worse were the rumors being relayed about the extermination camps at Chełmno, Belzec, Sobibor, Treblinka, Majdanek, and Auschwitz-Birkenau. It was like the world had gone mad and that the vortex of the madness was Germany and Western Europe, where he was stationed.

His main concern was primarily for the Iranian Jews. Despite the sway the Shah seemed to exercise over Hitler, Farmani was worried. He wondered how long it would be before the decree for the badge and roundups applied to their countrymen as well. Any well-bred man of moderate intelligence knew that what was happening in German-occupied lands was atrocious. However, being in Paris, occupied by Nazis, there was only so much one could do openly. If the Nuremberg Laws came into full effect in France, there wouldn't be much that he could do for any Jew, including Iranian ones. He sighed again—

It had been hard work to keep the French officials happy and drunk enough at gatherings so that he could glean vital information from them, even as he retained his friendship with them. This had been one of his favorite pastimes in the consular office earlier. He never missed the grand parties and functions thrown by the French and, in return, had coaxed his brother-in-law to do the same for the French officials. He had, by now, quite a large number of associates within the French administration. For the last two years, he had been trying his hardest to win over the Nazis, despite his internal loathing for the whole lot of them. This had proven to be extremely difficult, owing to the lofty attitude of the arrogant Germans and the language barrier, of course.

This particular day, he had been personally invited to a bridge party by Colonel Pierre Dubois, an old ally. Everyone of some consequence would be there. Farmani was torn. He did not want to ally himself with the Nazis by being present in the same room and breathing in the same air as the Nazis, and yet, he did not want his social absence to be taken for an Anti-Nazi stance which could have serious repercussions for his Iranian brethren. This was partly why he had to, though he did not particularly want to attend the event at the Ritz that evening.

He eyed the gold-rimmed invitation, which had followed the quick telephone call from Dubois that morning, with distaste.

He knew that Dubois was sympathetic to the Nazis now. He had been one of the first to help them to establish their base in Paris. Farmani remembered his conversation with the ruddy old colonel nearly two years ago. The news broadcast in which Pétain had all but garlanded the conquerors into the city had just been aired. Dubois had looked sad but only murmured, "If you can't beat them, join them." And that's exactly what he had gone on to do. Farmani never knew what exactly the old man's sentiments were, but he was shrewd enough to guess that, like most of the French, Dubois' fiery French national pride wasn't far beneath the surface of the otherwise cheery, food and wine-loving old man who seemed like he loved nothing better than to make merry. Farmani reckoned the old fellow had his own reasons for joining hands with the Germans.

***

The Ritz, Paris, was one of the most luxurious hotels in the world and one of the first to provide bathtubs, electricity, and telephones for every room. The hotel was constructed behind an 18th century townhouse that had changed hands innumerable times and had even been used as a lesser-known hotel. Cesar Ritz and his ally, the impeccable chef Auguste Escoffier, who had managed the Savoy in Paris, were well known to the wealthier clientele of the city in the eight years they were there. In 1897, the duo were discharged from the Savoy over the pilfering of wines worth thousands of pounds. But if the Savoy thought that that would be the end of them, they were sadly mistaken. With the help of a financier friend known to him, Ritz and Escoffier bought the old building overlooking Palace Vendôme and converted it into the magnificent hotel that stood before Farmani. They also appropriated for themselves the wealthier clientele of the Savoy. Among the sparkling regulars at the Ritz were King Edward VII of Britain, distinguished writers like Ernest Hemingway and F. Scott Fitzgerald, and the one-time queen of Parisian and world fashion, Coco Chanel, who was even now supposed to be residing in one of the suites of the hotel, pursuing a relationship with a wealthy German baron. Like Madame Chanel, the Ritz, the pride of Paris, now served the Germans as one of their many bases in the city.

As he approached the hotel, he saw the Swastika over the facade. Shaking off the moody darkness he felt in the pit of his stomach every time his eyes fell on it, Farmani willed himself through the swivel doors, flashing his invitation card at the stern-looking man who was at the desk in the foyer.

He soon found himself at the Ritz bar, which was the venue of the party. This was supposedly the world's first hotel bar and was furnished in Victorian style, replete with red velvet armchairs and a fireplace above which hung historic portraits. The men gathered were smoking, and the entire room was hazy. There was also the faint smell of spirits mixed with the tang of makeup and cologne as the women who accompanied the soldiers, officials, and administrators waltzed past. Farmani always found the dim ambiance, gay chatter, and the live music at the bar a little heady. *One does not have to drink to get high here*, he mused to himself.

Before long, Colonel Dubois came along and linked his arm through Farmani's. "Monsieur Farmani," he purred the 'r' sound as was his way. "What took you so long?"

"I had business to wind up at the consulate," Farmani said smilingly. It was impossible not to feel a liking for rotund little Colonel Dubois, with his ruddy cheeks, pointy chin beard, and wispy white hair, which was combed to perfection in a middle parting, despite the man's political bent.

"Of course you had. I'm sure you must be kept on your toes all day long, with hardly any staff left," chimed Dubois.

"We manage, do we not?" Farmani asked innocently. For a minute, Dubois seemed struck dumb before he forced himself back into geniality.

"Come, come, let's meet the others," he said as he nearly dragged the Iranian along with him.

It turned out that Farmani was to be partnered with Dubois, and on the other side were two German SS officers he had never met before.

"This is Hauptsturmführer Klaus Richter and Obersturmführer Heinrich Müller," Dubois said as he proceeded to introduce Farmani to the two men. Farmani understood enough to know that Hauptsturmführer and Obersturmführer were the Schutzstaffel equivalents for Captain and Lieutenant, respectively. He also knew that the SS, as the Schutzstaffel was popularly abbreviated, called themselves the political soldiers of the Nazi Party.

Farmani sized up his opponents. It seemed clear that Richter held the upper hand between the two men, not just in military ranking but also in stature. Müller was a short, mild-mannered man in his 20s, about whom the only thing you would remember afterward was his bushy brown hair. Richter, meanwhile, was the epitome of Aryan manhood, as the Nazis were fond of proclaiming. He was tall and fair. His blond hair was slicked back neatly from a wide forehead. Farmani could only guess that he was somewhere between 35 and 40, though, at first glance, he could have seemed younger to an onlooker. He had piercing blue eyes that were coldly calculating over a beaked nose that oddly lent classical charm to an otherwise stark face. In another life, Richter could have been an academic or an ascetic. For now, however, he was dressed in the khaki green uniform of Nazis, which offered a contrast against Dubois' grey-blue uniform. Richter was solidly built in proportion to his height. As he acknowledged Farmani, his eyes narrowed slightly. This was in lieu of a smile, Farmani realized, somewhat startled. It was only when his side profile was turned to you that you would notice it. Richter's face had a thin, deep scar that ran all the way from the outer end of his left eyebrow to his jawline. It did not seem like a recent injury, and yet it gave the man a steely edge when you looked at him from that angle. This wasn't a man to mess with, Farmani realized instinctively.

"Shall we start then, gentlemen?" Dubois was all smiles as he asked this. He had been a dedicated bridge player ever since he had learned the game in his youth. He never missed an opportunity to play with professionals, amateurs, and anybody else who would play with him. This is how he had discovered Farmani once in the hallowed portals of a Parisian club. He had latched on to the Iranian ever since as a partner for any game he wanted to organize. Farmani always complied because it was an opportunity to meet with administrative officials he would otherwise never meet in the ordinary course of his work. It was also a great way to establish relations and be seen.

The cards were already laid out on the table. Farmani and Dubois sat opposite each other, while Richter sat on Farmani's right and Müller on his left.

When the game started, it was clear from the outset that Dubois and Farmani had an advantage. This could have been owing to the several games they had already played as partners. Somehow, they seemed to have all the luck and the best cards so that they could meet their bids rather effortlessly. With every reshuffling of the cards and new game, this winning streak continued for the Iranian and French men. The game went on for a while in silence. Each one of the players was so focused at first that nobody had time for pleasantries and small talk.

It was clear that Richter was getting angrier with the game as the evening wore on. However, he attempted to conceal it for the time being.

"The Devil, take this!" he snarled as he laid his hand, only to realize that Farmani had a better one.

Dubois cheered his partner on with a hearty, "Bully for you, old man!"

Richter's mood went from dark to outright surly as he cussed something unintelligible under his breath in German. Müller, in stark contrast, seemed to get agitated, not because they were losing round after round but because he could read Richter's temper well. An amused Farmani noticed how Müller seemed to get more nervous as Richter got angrier. The fact that the other team was losing their cool made it easier for Farmani and Dubois to play their best. Once the game drew to a close, the men shook hands and decided to move to the bar for some drinks and nibbles.

Farmani could see that Richter made an attempt to appear pleasanter as they worked their way through the hors d'oevres and light drinks. He wasn't sure, though, if he liked the sneering attitude of the Nazi any better than his earlier ill-temper.

"Well, played, Farmani," the Nazi jeered. "Of course, though you have an edge, I suppose, it being that card games originated among the Jews of Arabia, is it not?" The way he said "Jews" made Farmani's blood boil. There was so much contempt hidden in that one syllable.

Farmani kept his voice low and polite with some effort and replied, "Thank you, Captain Richter. I am Muslim, though. Not Jewish. And Persian, not Arabic." Farmani deliberately used the French equivalent of the man's rank rather than the German mouthful for it.

"That is right, I suppose," Richter had a gleam in his eyes now. There was a sardonic smile playing on his lips. "I was wondering how, with the implementation of the Nuremberg Laws, you could still retain your position in the embassy here."

Farmani replied steadily, looking into the Nazi's eyes, "The Nuremberg Laws apply to Jews who are Semites. All Iranians, including the Jews of our land, are exempted from it owing to our Aryan descent. The Führer himself has decreed it shall be so."

The other man did not seem to pay any attention to Farmani's words as he said, "There is a reason why the law has been put in place. You must agree that the Aryan way is superior. Well, your Shah was eager to embrace us, wasn't he? He must have better taste than the other savages around your lands, I guess." The German nearly spat out the last couple of words, still smiling haughtily.

"Come now, what say to another couple of rounds of cards?" Pierre Dubois was trying his best to ensure the situation did not escalate into a confrontation between Richter and Farmani. He wanted to defuse the tension before it built itself up any further.

Farmani remained silent, though he was seething at the superior attitude of the Nazi. Yet, he couldn't say anymore without attracting the attention of the Germans, something he wanted to avoid at all costs. His silence was eating him up, though.

"No, Dubois," Richter intoned, "I have a busy day tomorrow. Since we were on the subject of Nuremberg Laws, I don't mind telling you that we will shortly see some action here in Paris too. We are preparing trains for 35,000 toward Auschwitz and other places. It's only a matter of time now before the Nazis realize who is who. The true Aryans will be separated from the rest as grain is from chaff." He held up his palm to his lips as he blew across it mockingly.

Then, with all the deliberation of a man who knew his words weren't an empty boast, he wore his military cap, held out his right arm stiffly, and said, "Heil Hitler."

Farmani and Dubois had no choice but to follow the lead and chant the same. In his heart, Farmani felt dread brewing. He internalized what the Nazi had just proudly said—*trains for 35,000 Jews to be taken to the camps.* He knew what was coming, and he felt his blood run cold.

For the first time, Farmani seriously thought about whether there was something he could do about the situation. It was only an idle notion for the present that gave him some solace against the anger he felt when he thought about the malevolence of men like Richter, who seemed to control the strings just then.

Chapter 2:

A Chance Encounter: 05 June 1942

The Opera House of Paris was a majestic building with its neoclassical facade and towering columns. Napoleon III commissioned it, and it was a mixture of architectural styles such as the Baroque, Palladio, and Renaissance. Interestingly, the building took a long time to be completed, and by the time it opened, Napoleon III was in exile in England and never saw the structure in person. Opulent statues carved into the exterior walls of the building featured famous artists and characters from Greek mythology. One of the main reasons for foreign tourists flocking to it in hordes before the war was because it was the setting of Gaston Leroux's 1910 romantic Gothic horror thriller, *The Phantom of the Opera*. Most people wanting to see the "lake" that was the abode of the phantom were often disappointed that the cistern beneath the Opera House, though real, was shut off from all except the janitors and workers employed by the Opera House to clean it up regularly. On this particular day, the only dampener was the Nazi flag flying above one of the highest points of the building, partially obscuring the magnificent statue of Apollo, and the Swastika banners hung at all the main apertures of the building.

Once inside, onlookers were often bedazzled. The building consisted of interweaving corridors, stairs, alcoves, and landings, allowing the crowd to intermingle during intervals in the performance. The main foyer was adorned with gilded decor and crystal chandeliers, exuding an air of luxury. The lighting was dimly lit gold, highlighting the red-maroon and green of the marble stairs that were immediately visible in front. This flight of extravagant stairs that diverged after the first landing led up to the auditorium and the balconies. The auditorium was resplendent with plush velvet seats arranged in a horseshoe shape around the stage. The stage itself was always adorned with elaborate sets and richly colored curtains appropriate for each performance, creating a dramatic backdrop for the equally captivating performances. The lighting was dim and focused on the stage, creating an intimate atmosphere throughout the auditorium. An interesting fact that most people did not know was that the stage of the Opera House was one of the largest in the world. Its height and girth would allow it to house the Arc de Triomphe with ease.

Farmani was looking forward to this evening of quiet relaxation. He had been invited to this performance by Pierre Dubois. Dubois' friend, the wealthy widow Mrs. Marie Leclerc, was organizing a charity event for the Red Cross. Farmani wanted to meet this distinguished lady himself because he had heard that she wielded a certain influence in Parisian circles. He imagined she would be a good ally should he ever need one and was determined to make a good impression on her. As he crossed the main entrance, he noticed a rather large blackboard, a hasty installation, that bore the words in white chalk: *No Jews Allowed Inside*. Similar signs were common across most public sites in the city then, and yet here, it was nothing short of profanity. Farmani walked past it with a set expression, refraining from the urge to tear down the horrid inscription.

The Iranian was no stranger to Western classical music. He had records of Bach and Beethoven in his bachelor quarters, which he often listened to for solace. His other love was the opera. He marveled at the luxurious settings and the musical talent on display and often felt that in another life, he should have loved to pursue music or drama or both. The performance that he was attending that night was a rendition of Shakespeare's *Twelfth Night,* and Farmani was excited to behold the spectacle.

As expected, the opera was magnificent, and the singer who played Viola was par excellence. She outdid every other artist onstage. She was beautiful, soulful, and elegant. There was a certain nobility to her features. Her light figure made her perfect for the role. Her love for Duke Orsino was so palpable in her music and expressions that it was almost difficult to believe it wasn't real. As the evening progressed, Farmani struggled to take his eyes off her throughout the performance.

When intermission came, he headed to the Grand Foyer, where food and drinks were being served. It wasn't long before he located Dubois and Madame Leclerc. Pierre Dubois, ever ready to play the good host, introduced Farmani to Madame Leclerc and then moved off to see to the comforts of other guests on her behalf. Madame Marie Leclerc was a woman in her early fifties. Silver-gray hair at her temples added distinction to her graceful and serene face. She was slim and handsome, and one could tell that in her youth, she must have been a woman of remarkable beauty. She was wearing a simple evening gown in dark blue, and a single diamond tiara adorned her hair. She wore very little makeup, and yet her face and neck were startlingly unlined. Except for a tiredness around her eyes and her grey strands, one could easily mistake Madame Leclerc as being in her thirties.

"Charmed to meet you, Monsieur," She smiled graciously at Farmani, who lightly touched his lips to her gloved hands as he returned her salutations.

"Madame, I am honored to be invited to this event. The Red Cross is most lucky to have you as one of their chief campaigners at a time like this," he said. It was with great difficulty that Madame Leclerc and other Red Cross workers got the sanction of the Nazis to organize this event. As the humanitarian organization was based out of Geneva in the neutral territory of Switzerland, the Nazis had to finally give in reluctantly. In the eyes of the world, Germany also wanted to look honorable by allowing funds and provisions for the prisoners of war.

"Well. These are unusual times indeed. When I first heard of the war, I never imagined a day like this," she said. She looked wistfully around at the guests who had made it and added, "I try to imagine that this is just an ordinary day from before."

Farmani nodded as he said softly, "Yes, one would give anything to forget for a moment the horror of what we are being forced to participate in." It was a bold move on his part to speak so directly, but he gauged correctly that Madame Leclerc's sympathies weren't wasted on the Nazis.

Madame Leclerc's eyes teared up as she fixed her gaze on him and said in lowered tones, "I would do anything to see French honor restored." She added with a glint of pride in her eyes, "My son, Eric, fights for his country in North Africa." She did not have to elaborate further for Farmani to know that she meant that her son was part of the Free France forces fighting under de Gaulle for the Allies.

As he nodded, a group of German officers came their way, and one among them said to her in French heavily, accented with German, "Madame, what a lovely and noble gesture to host this event. We are so-"

Immediately, Madame Leclerc stiffened, and though she was polite, there was no mistaking the frigid undertone to her voice. Cutting off the man who was still framing his sentence, she said, "Thank you, gentlemen, for coming. Your generosity means much. I must see to my guests. Pardon me." She glided past them regally to mingle and be lost in the crowd.

The officers knew that they had been rebuffed, but they knew that making a scene would earn them public outcry and censure. Madame Leclerc was a beloved figure in the city and well-known for playing a lead in several charitable causes. They knew better than to earn her wrath. They were stationed only to see to it that no anti-Nazi activities took place in the guise of a charity event. They shrugged nonchalantly and moved off.

Farmani was, on the whole, pleased with his interaction with Madame Leclerc. He knew that with a son fighting for France, she would be an amenable ally for the cause. It was harder to fathom how Madame Leclerc maintained her cordial relations with Dubois, who had established himself as a collaborator. Then again, Farmani knew better than to take anything at face value. Everything, they said, was fair in love and war. Nothing was as it seemed in times of war. Maybe the friendship was more of an attempt to retain public face or to preserve a nostalgia for past relationships. Who could tell?

As he bumped into Dubois at some point in time later, he wanted to clear up one other matter. "Who is the lady who played Viola?" Farmani hoped to sound casual and cheery.

Dubois must have been more perceptive than he imagined, however. "Ah. The beautiful Eva Klein has made an impression upon you, I see," the jolly old man said with a bright smile.

"I have never seen her before," Farmani faltered slightly in a clumsy attempt to conceal his interest.

"Yes, that is right. This is her debut performance in the Opera House. Though she has been part of the operatic circles for a little while now," Dubois clarified.

"I see," Farmani said.

"She was brought up in Paris before her folks moved away to the country just before the start of the war. Grapevine has it that they weren't happy in her choice of profession and cut her off." The Colonel seemed to be happy to be passing on the rumors as he said, "She is a marvel, is she not?"

Farmani was intrigued by this young woman who seemed to have so bravely faced familial opposition to pursue her career and persevere in performing at none other than the Paris Opera House. He did not have to strain his imagination to see why a family would oppose one of their women wanting to be a professional singer. Though more modern than several other European countries in terms of the freedom bestowed to its creatives and artists, many were still traditional when it came to the roles they expected of women. At the end of the day, most households wanted their daughters to marry respectably, raise children, and be good wives and mothers.

When the performance resumed, Farmani was struck more than ever by Eva's performance. He knew that he wasn't the only one moved by the melody of her soulful renditions, her grace and poise. Yet he couldn't help wanting to know her better. It was as if he was drawn magnetically to her charm.

Right after the curtains dropped, when the audience had finished giving the team a standing ovation, Farmani met Dubois and vocalized his intention of wanting to be introduced to the singer. However, his search for the rotund Colonel proved fruitless. The man was nowhere to be found. Farmani wasn't one to stand on traditions, though. *Nothing ventured, nothing gained*, he thought as he went in search of the singers' rooms. Eva Klein's room was one of the first in a narrow corridor on the right side of the stage. He knocked and waited a little impatiently, tapping his feet on the ground. He wasn't sure about what he wanted to say. All he knew was that he would congratulate her and introduce himself. The rest he knew would come at the right time. He wasn't a man who fell short of words generally—especially not with the fairer sex. But he also hadn't met, until then, a woman like Eva Klein.

Another woman opened the door, and for a minute, he wondered whether he had made a mistake in his haste to make the acquaintance of the singer. She was smaller and darker than Eva and had black hair, whereas Eva's had been ashen brown. The lady stared back at Farmani in askance.

Confused, he said, "I just wanted to meet Ms. Klein and congratulate her on her performance. Pardon me if I have the wrong room I was led to believe that this was where I could find her."

The woman gazed at him a moment before saying, "A minute, monsieur, I will tell her of your presence. What name shall I give her?"

He said, "Kameron Farmani, Iranian Consul to Paris."

The lady nodded and went inside. In a moment, Farmani heard the rustle of skirts, and the door was pulled wide open. It was as if he was struck in the face by the glory of the rising sun. Eva Klein was in her late twenties. She was not beautiful she was ethereal. The angels must have crafted her when in a good countenance. She was in the same red gown from the final scene of the performance. Her pale, almost golden hair was held back in a hair tie of the same color as her dress. Her short sleeves revealed the flawless fairness of her complexion. Her sparkling light blue irises were set in perfectly shaped almond eyes. She was wearing elbow-length gloves, and in one hand, she held a crumpled piece of paper. There was only one anomaly in the otherwise perfect picture before Farmani. Eva Klein had been crying just minutes ago and it was as clear as daylight. She had made an attempt to tidy herself up, but her cheeks were tear-stained, and her nose was red. It was obvious that something had upset the singer.

Farmani had intended to be charming and gallant. However, when met with this unexpected circumstance, he was

29

temporarily at a loss for words. Swallowing down the exuberant compliments he had prepared, he said, "I came to congratulate you, Ms. Klein. I simply had to let you know how much I enjoyed and admired your performance tonight. Forgive me; I see I have come at a wrong time. Is there anything that I can do to help you?"

She had composed herself well enough, and when her voice rang out it was clear and calm, even if a little forced, "I thank you for having taken the trouble. I assure you that this moment is as good as any other. There is nothing you can do for me."

The voice was pleasant, even if the last sentence was rudely phrased. Farmani knew better than to judge a person when they were distressed. He nodded at her, gave her one of his crooked smiles, and then said, "Well then, Ms. Klein, until next time." He gently touched his hand to his hat before striding away.

Eva couldn't help smiling up at the handsome stranger. There was something so positively comforting and boyish about him that she felt lighter for a minute.

She gently closed the door behind her and was deep in thought when her maid Miriam aroused her from her reverie.

"So, looks like we have another suitor in tow?" She was giggling a little.

"Quiet," Eva thundered, though there was a hint of a smile around her lips.

"But look, Eva, the man meant no harm, and you have scared him away. He only came to say he loved your performance," Miriam said.

Eva sighed this time as she said, "I am tired. It has been a long day, even without this missive." She looked at the crumpled paper in her hands and then tossed it into the waste paper bin that stood beside the desk.

Miriam looked at her in sympathy and said, "You knew in your hearts that Alexandre wasn't the one for you, Eva. You said so yourself. Even if he hadn't called off the engagement, I know that you weren't convinced."

Eva looked at Miriam with relief. "Yes. I knew that it may not work. I respected him, and I knew he loved me. I am just tired of the people in my life leaving all the time."

Miriam knew what Eva was talking about. Eva had been disowned seven years ago by her family when they first knew of her ambition to become a singer. There had been a terrible row between her parents and herself. Even her two elder brothers had condemned her choice of profession. They considered the profession no better than a common harlot's. With his noble Dutch lineage that he so proudly reminded them of, her father had always been one to value reputation over one's happiness. He threatened her with denunciation and banishment from her family home if she ever mentioned her "degenerate" dream again. Eva Klein, who was as proud and perhaps bolder than her father had imagined, wasn't one to keep quiet in the face of threat. So she had walked out bag and baggage one foggy night and applied her heart and soul in pursuing her career. Her father had told her that she would come to nothing and drag their family name into the mire with her. Perhaps it was this fire in her belly to prove her father wrong that made her succeed where hundreds of others like her had failed. Perhaps it was the beauty of her music and the strength of her performance, combined with her physical perfection. Whatever it was, she, Eva Klein, had made it. She was a well-renowned singer who would be remembered for her work and talent.

One would think that at least after attaining success, her family would have accepted her back. Which parents could resist the joy and triumph of their children? And yet, the Kleins had studiedly avoided all contact with her. The few letters she wrote home went unanswered. Before the start of the war, when the news of the invasion was pouring in, Eva finally screwed up her courage to visit them. But the old house was locked up. From a neighbor, she heard her family had moved to one of their relatives' homes in Lyon. Even the news of imminent war and possible death had not made her parents and brothers budge from their stance. She understood then that she was all but dead to them. With a broken heart, Eva finally made peace with the fact that her family would never accept her.

That was around the time that she met Alexandre Marc, a junior clerk in government service. He had been charming, gallant, and seemingly besotted with Eva. What she felt for him was more difficult to explain. It wasn't love that she felt. She liked Alexandre well enough, but she knew that what she wanted was companionship and a place to call home. So she had gone along with it. Even when he had proposed to her after three months of courtship, her heart had known that it was too early and that perhaps he wasn't the one. However, she did not want to let go of him and then feel alone again. Despite feeling unprepared, she gave him her assent.

But fate sometimes has a way of sorting out human affairs in her knowing way. It seemed that Alexandre's family did not approve of the match. They, too, considered an opera singer inappropriate for a man who could one day rise through the ranks of the government. Unlike Eva, who knew her heart well enough to withstand the wrath of her father, Alexandre was less courageous. For a couple of months, he kept dilly-dallying the inevitable. He told her that he would convince them and that things would turn out all right. She knew it was a farce, but she played along because she could not bear to think of an alternative. But even she knew from his half-hearted letters and verbal assurances that it was a doomed relationship. So she waited for the death knell to their engagement one way or the other. It came in the form of his transfer to Vichy.

That was the letter she had received and held crumpled in her palm a while ago. He was one of the last batch of government workers to be summoned. The letter he wrote her told her of his undying affection for her. Yet, it also conveyed his regret of not being able to take her with him. He did not want to prolong her agony by giving her false hopes, and so he said that though he loved her, he was setting her free from their engagement. It was worded touchingly and even passionately in certain places. However, she had been expecting it, and when it came, it brought a curious sense of freedom and relief. The tears she cried gave her the catharsis and closure she badly needed. The long wait and hoping for something she wasn't sure she wanted had been weighing on her. The uncertainty of whether she would end up with Alexandre had been more insufferable than this final letter ending it all.

It was into all this drama that a young Iranian diplomat had walked in. She was suddenly aware of the irony of it all. For her, it had been only minutes after Alexandre had walked out that another had walked in. It was tempting to see it as the work of fate. Yet, so many abandonments later, Eva Klein was not one to give in so easily. She knew that Kameron Farmani could be the one to bring a ray of Mediterranean sunshine into her bleak Parisian world. She knew that where there was hope, there was also the chance of loss and pain. With a war being waged right in the middle of the country she called home, she did not want to wager her heart on uncertain outcomes again.

Chapter 3:

Reconnaissance: 20 June 1942

It was the summer solstice, and the Nazis were throwing a fête of sorts for all officials stationed in Paris. Solstice wasn't exactly a festival in France, but the Reich considered it a celebratory occasion. It was also partly to raise the morale of the people. It would be three years since the war started, and people, including Germans, were beginning to get restless about the lack of outcome. Farmani hated these events thrown by the Nazis. He knew they were only held to proclaim their own glory and remind people how they would overtake the world slowly but surely. It was also a venue for Nazi propaganda to be freely shared and distributed. However, as always, he put on a brave face and decided to go. This would be an event where he could widen his social circle, and he considered that a minor win in between the disturbing news that kept pouring in. Apart from the stalls that would sell overpriced fare and trinkets that most Parisians would hesitate to buy, there was to be a ball at the hôtel de la Marine in the evening. This was where Farmani was headed.

Hôtel du Garde-Meuble, as hôtel de la Marine was initially called, was constructed during the reign of Louis XV in the late 18th century. It was constructed as a place for the palace chief in charge of royal furniture and tapestries that were considered to be national rather than personal property of the royal family. The building housed prized pieces and was opened to public viewership in 1772. It was thus the first museum of decorative arts in Paris. The building had a chapel, stables, workshops, a library, and apartments for the chief in charge of royal furniture. When dignitaries visited, they had their own quarters within the building as well. Marie Antoinette, for instance, had an apartment for her use.

By 1789, when the revolution was imminent, Hôtel du Garde-Meuble housed many weapons, some more ornamental than military, such as swords, shields, and ornate cannons. It was these cannons that were robbed by the angry mob and fired at Bastille, formally starting the revolution. During the revolution, the marine office functioned from this very building. There was also one other interesting point about it. The square in front of this structure, Place de la Concorde, was where Louis XVI and Marie Antoinette were executed.

After Paris fell in 1940 into Nazi hands, this was where the German Naval forces were operating from. As Farmani reached his destination, he looked with awe at this historical monument that the Nazis were now using. He shook his head, feeling a little sad that the Reich should use a building so filled with history for its dirty work. The neoclassical facade of the building presented a series of Corinthian columns and a long loggia with grand sculpted medallions on its ceiling. The building had several salons, and one such—the Salon of Admirals—was the venue for this ball. The Nazis had gone as far as to invite everyone of some reputation, including citizens and celebrities, as well as government officials. It seemed that they were desperate for Parisian goodwill and cooperation.

As Farmani crossed into the Salon of Admirals, he was stunned by the gilded sculptures and nautical-themed decorations on the walls. Shiny mirrors reflected the warm glow from the room, and the whole effect was simply spectacular. On another day, he would have loved to take a closer look at the whole building, but that would have to wait until after the war, assuming the Germans left. Nobody, at this point, wanted or dared to think of an alternative where the Germans stayed back.

As he stepped inside, a jovial and warm voice greeted him. Farmani was surprised at his own happiness to meet a friendly face. It was Pierre Dubois who was rushing toward him. If his expression was anything to go by, he was equally happy to move away from a couple of German officers he had been talking to.

"So happy to see you here," he beamed at Farmani.

"Likewise, Colonel. This venue is simply marvelous. Though I had passed by it on so many occasions before, this is my first entry within its walls," said Farmani.

"Better late than never, eh? I wish the occasion had been a happier one, perhaps," the Colonel said a little thoughtfully. Intuitively, Farmani felt that perhaps Dubois was echoing some of the same feelings that had besieged him a while ago.

As they kept moving within the salon, meeting one group of guests after another, Farmani's eyes were suddenly caught by two people almost at once at different corners of the room. One was Madame Leclerc, and the other, to his surprise, was Eva Klein, the opera singer. Both the discoveries gave him joy in different ways. One was work, and the other—well, it was too early to classify that one, but he could hope. No harm could come from hoping, after all.

Since work always came first with him, Farmani moved toward Madame Leclerc. He bowed deeply and told her, "Deeply charmed to meet you again, Madame."

Madame Leclerc was dressed in a taffeta silk gown of a peachy-golden hue, and as always, the effect was classy without being overtly showy. Unlike some of the women who accompanied the Germans, dressed in gaudy colors and revealing clothes, Madame Leclerc's dressing style was as modest as it was modern.

She smiled at Farmani and said, "If it isn't the Iranian consul, Mr. Farmani! I hope you are having fun here."

"Work and fun, madame, for me. I am, after all, a humble agent of my country. I go where she wants me to," he said.

"Of course. I did not mean to assume otherwise. How is the Iranian consulate coping, with many of your officials now being in Vichy?" she asked.

"It is tough. There is paperwork for a hundred people, with only a quarter of that number to move it along. It is hard. But then, isn't that so for everyone here?" he asked.

"Quite," she said. "One hopes every day that this day will be the final day ending it all, and yet it drags on incessantly," she added wistfully.

Farmani immediately remembered how she had mentioned her son fighting on foreign soil and was at once moved by this brave mother's plight. She had to pretend to tolerate these men whose ilk could kill her son at any time. Yet, here she was, doing what she could and canvassing for the Red Cross.

He lowered his voice as he asked his next question carefully, "I hear that your son's regiment has soldiers here as well—the brave Maquis multiplies daily." He kept his voice low and used the word for "underbrush"—the name that many Resistance groups in France went by. He did not want a passing German to hear him use the word "resistance," even though many of them were not very fluent in French.

Madame Leclerc formed her reply measuredly but not missing a beat, "Yes. That is true. I hope I can do my bit. For now, I just wish that I would meet one of them soon."

Though she did not say anything that would give her away, it was clear to Farmani that she was trying to imply that she would help if she knew whom to approach or what to do. She had to be cautious. There was the Resistance, and there were also the counter-intelligence groups of Frenchmen betraying their own countrymen to the Germans. One could never be too careful when approaching so-called Resistance groups. There had been stories of set-ups so that people wanting to help the free France movement could be declared traitorous to the Reich. Madame Leclerc would be on the radar already because her son would have been known to fight for the enemy. Farmani was satisfied because he knew that he could count on her as an ally against the Nazis when the time came.

***

His next target, Colonel Pierre Dubois, seemed more tricky. Though the two men often played bridge and socialized at events, Farmani had no clue as to why Dubois had so easily joined the ranks of the Nazis. Perhaps he had a family or property he wanted to protect. People who did not help were threatened with the loss of both. He went in search of the old man and found him cracking jokes with a group of Germans who seemed to be already high on the drinks.

With great tact and diplomacy, Farmani managed to draw the Colonel out of the group so that he could talk to him a little more privately. He ensured that nobody seemed to be taking any special interest in them and then led the conversation to the imminent roundups he had heard about.

The Colonel stiffly answered, sobering up immediately, "Well, it isn't new news, is it? It has been happening in other areas. One doesn't like what they are doing, but it is their mission. What choice do we have in the matter?"

Farmani lowered his voice and then said, "The Maquis could help. Would you help if given the opportunity and means for it? Just hypothetically, of course."

Pierre Dubois was following every word of what he was saying intently, and yet his face and stance were non-committal. He said at last, "For now, I have nothing. I must protect what is important to me. Everyone for himself or herself, is it not, monsieur?"

Farmani bowed, not wishing to proceed further or to bring up indelicate matters. What was clear was that the man had something he wanted to protect, and he believed his best bet was to ally with the Nazis. Farmani felt sorry for the old man. He was sure the man was innocent but caught up in things beyond his control. He also suspected that left to himself, the Colonel might have wanted to do more to help free the country but that his hands were tied for some reason.

A germ of an idea had taken its roots in the Iranian consul's head. He only wanted to take stock of whom he could and could not count on. Madame Leclerc seemed a win, while Pierre Dubois remained a question mark. There would be time to sort out things later. Farmani nodded. He needed more people—that was for sure, and he did not know where to start searching.

***

As the evening wore on, Farmani became more restless. The waltzes had begun, and couples were already on the floor. He wanted to meet Eva Klein and ask her for a dance if she was willing. However, every time he began to approach her, she was already talking to somebody or being requested for a dance. He was beginning to get quite despondent. It seemed to him that the lady had seen him, but she did not show signs of recognition. Was he to interpret this as a lack of interest, or was she playing hard to get?

Normally, Farmani had no trouble where women were concerned. He found it easy to weave a spell over them with his mild bantering and gallantry. But the difference was that he had never pursued anything serious with a woman before. He had, of course, had his share of flings in England and Switzerland, where he studied. Later, once he began his job, he had been so focused on his career that he had never consciously tried to meet anyone. There hadn't been anyone whom he found so fascinating. What he felt about Eva Klein was altogether novel. He knew that whatever he felt about her wasn't mere infatuation either. He suspected that if he got to know her better, it would be something more serious than a casual dalliance. For the life of him, Farmani couldn't decide if he could offer her anything more.

Finally, he got his break when after a dance, Eva walked to the side of the hall. Swiftly, confidently, he followed her and said, "Mademoiselle, if I may have the honor of the next dance with you."

Eva Klein looked at him for a while, during which Farmani felt his heart beat erratically. He wondered if she would make an excuse and refuse him. She was dressed in a peach shimmery gown, with matching gloves, tiara, and slip-on shoes. The light from the chandeliers threw a glow on her fair face and shining tresses. Farmani was fascinated by how effortlessly graceful she was. Vaguely, he was conscious of other men who perhaps wanted a set with her, throwing him dirty looks. *Her hand is worth the expense of making a few enemies*, he thought serenely.

She said simply, "It is the consul. I will be delighted to, monsieur." Farmani's heart leaped a little at that, though he hoped he did not sound overenthusiastic in his response and scare her away.

The song played for their set was "Erika," a popular German marching song composed nearly a decade ago. It wasn't a political song in the least. It was about a soldier who fondly remembers his sweetheart, named Erika, back home. What made the song political was the fact that its composer, Herms Niel, had joined the Nazi party in 1934. It was one of the most popular German songs at the moment and played at every party and event.

When they started their waltz together, Farmani noted she was an excellent dancer—light on her feet and poised. He could not believe his luck in not being turned down.

"You are a wonderful dancer, Ms. Klein," he said.

"Please, just call me Eva. Ms. Klein sounds so stuffy," she replied with a smile. Then she stopped for a minute and added, "And you, Mr. Farmani, you lead with such ease. I couldn't have asked for a better partner." She seemed to struggle with her next words but finally said, "I must apologize. I was out of sorts the other day when you came to meet me backstage. I thank you for your kind gesture and words. They meant a lot to me."

"Kameron. Yes, I could see that. Your performance was out of the world. Believe me, Eva, you are talented. I am a regular at the Opera, and I do not waste my compliments where they are not due," he replied. He did not want to push her to explain why she had been crying. He wanted to keep the conversation smooth and effortless. There would be a time for explanations, but they could wait.

She smiled slightly at this and said, "Thank you again." After a brief silence, she continued with a playful smile, "I thought you might ask me about why I was crying. Most men are pushy, or nosey, or both in my experience," she said.

He replied lightly, "I wasn't sure you were ready to talk about it. I am all ears if you do want to. Then again, if you feel you would rather not, that's okay too." He gently pirouetted her.

Catching her breath, she said, "You are an interesting one, I'll wager, Kameron," she laughed. "I don't know what to make of you."

"Is it necessary to make anything of anything? We could just enjoy the dance in silence if you prefer it so," he laughed in turn.

"Oh no! That's ghastly," she said jokingly and continued, "I hate it when partners don't talk during dancing. It is like the silent talkies! All action and no words."

"Very well then, since you are determined to have a meaningful conversation, what shall we talk about? he asked.

"Let us start with you," she said. "How did you happen to wash up here?"

"That would be an extremely long story, but I'll try to keep it short. I belong to Iran. I have a father and mother who wanted more for their son. They let me go to boarding school in England. I studied well and hoped to be a lawyer. However, the life of a diplomat lured me I suppose, and though I finished a degree in law and history in Switzerland, I ended up becoming a consul to Paris for my country," he said keeping it as brief as possible.

"So, what was life in Iran like?" she asked.

His eyes wandered above her head in an effort to remember. "Well, to be honest, there is not much I can remember. I was only eight when I was sent off to England. My mother belonged to the royal dynasty of the Qajars, who were replaced by the Pahlavis, who rule the country today. My family owns a house in Tehran—one decorated in Persian style. We had a beautiful garden out front where so many different flowers grew in bloom during the sunnier months. I remember climbing those trees and falling from them so many times that I have lost count. The dappled light of the sun through the trees was a sight to behold. It is still so clear in my mind. The garden was my friend, my refuge. I also carry memories of the streets of Tehran, so different from any that you will find in Europe. So many colors and vendors and hawkers calling out to you about their wares. Such a treat for the eyes—so noisy and vibrant—" he trailed off a little consciously and said, "But all this must be boring for you."

"I assure you nothing you have said so far is boring. You haven't spoken much of your family—" she said.

"Indeed. My father worked in the government circles, and my mother was the niece of one of the earlier Shahs. I have six siblings in all. I was the second youngest, and some of my elder siblings were married by the time I was born. I was raised at home in relative affluence by ladies who served my mother. Both my parents were kept busy by their social calls and duties. I am afraid I have no real stories to tell you of my family. They loved me, and I, in my way, love them. But we aren't a close-knit family as such," he said honestly.

"Well, that's luckier than many, I would guess. I was brought up in this city. My parents disowned me because I chose to pursue a career. My father and brothers opposed it and threatened me. My mother chose to close her eyes and to go along with them. I have had no news from them in seven years or more. Even the outbreak of the war and the occupation has not changed their mind in wanting to meet or hear from me," she ended with a bitter laugh.

Farmani had heard it already from Dubois. He said, "I believe families can be of blood or choice. Some are lucky to have the former, while some have the luxury of the latter. I don't think one's birth has to determine one's true family."

"And what if you have neither?" Eva asked. She wasn't mocking him. He could see the hurt in her eyes.

"Nobody can be that unlucky, Eva. Some people do not deserve your time or energy. If they leave, then the loss is theirs," he said gently.

She nodded and then said, "When you met me yesterday, my fiancé—we had been engaged for almost a year—had just written to tell me that he wouldn't stand up in the face of family opposition to marry me. I suppose I should have expected it, but what can I say?" She stopped suddenly, wondering if she had spoken too much to this man, who was a relative stranger after all.

"Like I said, Eva—his loss," was all Farmani said. He smiled at her, and she was transfixed by how attractive he was. It wasn't just his fair face and the dark hair swept back from his brow. There was a genteel nobility about his countenance, and his dark eyes were so kind and warm. It was unusual for her to feel moved by any man so soon after meeting him. It was exciting and slightly unnerving. She felt the warm flush of her feelings creeping across her cheeks and neck.

The ballroom seemed to come alive with the enchanting melody. Amidst the swirl of elegant gowns and tailored suits, the couple moved seamlessly to the rhythm, their bodies floating as if weightless. As they twirled and spun, their thoughts only existed within the sphere of each other.

For him, the world seemed to fade away, leaving only the celestial presence of his partner. The soft touch of her hand in his, the gentle pressure of her palm against his back, it was a heady feeling indeed. With every step, he marveled at her grace and the way her laughter resonated in the air like pure joy. At that moment, he was captivated not only by her beauty but by something deeper that seemed to connect them.

45

For Eva, the dance floor became a haven from all the despairing thoughts she had been carrying around. She clung to him as if she had come here with the sole purpose of finding him—as if he were her soul's anchor. As her feet glided across the polished surface, her thoughts inevitably wandered to the man in her arms. His strong presence and tender gaze made her feel cherished and valued—things that had seemed impossible all these years. In his light embrace, she found solace, a sense of comradeship and belonging. He understood her.

Together, they danced as if time stood still. Their bodies moved as one, in perfect sync. It was as if this dance had made them not just dance partners but confidants, supporters, and perhaps more—but that only time would reveal. For now, this night was theirs. The unspoken words between them painted a vivid canvas of beauty and joy to come. Their hearts beat in harmony, and their thoughts whispered similar sentiments. They knew that this dance was not a fleeting moment but a testament of many promises to come, though neither wished to say it aloud and break the spell of the moment.

***

The party ended too soon for both despite the lateness of the hour. On the way back to their own apartments, they could not stop thinking about each other. There was that delicious sense of promise laced with uncertainty at the beginning of a new friendship that was so tempting, even to the wisest throughout history. Who could not fall prey to its charms?

Chapter 4:

The Loophole: 22 June 1942

The American Library in Paris was one of the few to have been kept open and running throughout the war and the years of occupation. The library had been founded during the First World War as a memorial to those who had lost their lives in it. It was opened to boost the morale of the people living the unprecedented horrors of the times. With the signing of the armistice in 1919, many of the American Expeditionary Forces in France needed a literary getaway, at least. About 1.5 million books were shipped from the US under the aegis of the American Library Association (ALA) to keep them engaged when not on duty.

In Paris, a central reference library was created to house some of these books. As soon as it opened to the public, several Americans, French students, and citizens flocked to become its members. The library was financially well-off owing to the donations of British, American, and French donors who believed in the transformative power of words. Alan Seeger, the famous trench poet who had penned "I Have a Rendezvous with Death," was one of the first posthumous supporters of the library. His father donated 50,000 francs from the royalties of his son's poetry to keep the library flourishing.

After the outbreak of the war in 1939, when most Americans and foreign nationals returned home, this library served the faithful French citizens. The fiery Dorothy Reeder, who had directed the library for years, ensured that it continued its mission. It even provided books for the enlisted personnel. Rumors had it that the staff hand-delivered books to their

47

Jewish patrons despite their ban from the library premises. When the Nazis took over the city, they briefly shut down the library, only to reopen it after a brief inspection, after which it got the official approval of the Reich.

Its operations were curtailed owing to the US declaration of War on Germany in December 1941. Against her wishes, Reeder and other American staff were advised to return home. The American-born Clara Longworth de Chambrun, who had become Countess Chambrun through her marriage to Count Chambrun, was now the director of the library. It was hard on her. Unlike Reeder, who was in her early forties, the countess was only two years short of 70 when she took over. However, she was well-read and a scholar. She had a doctorate from the Sorbonne University and several books and manuscripts published in her name. Her intense enthusiasm was only dimmed by the political situation the city found itself in. The library was now cut off from American funds and was working with a skeleton crew, who, though efficient, were insufficient to keep the place in order.

The building of the library stood as a beacon of knowledge nestled in the heart of the once-vibrant city. The elegant facade—adorned with grand windows and intricate architectural details—exuded a sense of history and allure. The building's charming exterior seemed to invite visitors, even those who did not read, to embark on a literary journey, promising a world of intellectual treasures within its walls.

Stepping into the library, Farmani felt his troubles ease. It was a sanctuary for book lovers, and he fit perfectly. The serene ambiance, with its warm lighting and cozy reading nooks, created an inviting atmosphere. Rows upon rows of bookshelves held a vast collection of literature spanning various genres and subjects. The air was filled with the quiet rustling of pages and the occasional hushed conversation of fellow readers. The library's serene courtyard offered a tranquil retreat where patrons could immerse themselves in a book surrounded by lush greenery.

He had obtained special permission from the countess to be in the archives section of the library, which was located at the back of the building. She was a friendly woman, dressed in finery which had run its course of fashion at least a decade ago. It was clear enough that she wasn't dressed so out of poverty. It simply seemed a style that she was used to and liked. She was refined in manners and well-spoken. Though she was fluent in both English and French, she preferred to speak in the latter. With the US in the fray, she perhaps thought it in her best interest to downplay her American roots. It could have also been that she had been so long in Paris that she had become a part and parcel of the city. When he told her of his purpose, she shook her head.

She said, "At other times, I could have had the volumes you wanted transported from America. As things stand, I am not sure if the meager collection here will aid your work." She quickly assured him, though, "Everything here is at your disposal. I hope you will find what you seek."

In the dimly lit room with a few collections of ancient books amidst the hushed whispers and the faint scent of aged paper, Farmani was completely consumed by his task. He was immersed in the intricate world of archival research. With each carefully selected volume that landed on the worn wooden table beside him, the Iranian was transported to another era. He meticulously leafed through fragile documents, their yellowed pages carrying the weight of history. He treated each artifact with the utmost care, turning delicate pages with reverence, afraid that their secrets might dissolve if mishandled.

As he unearthed forgotten letters, faded photographs, and a few hand-written manuscripts, he felt like a detective, piecing together the fragments of a puzzle long lost in time. His furrowed brow, illuminated by the glow of an ancient desk lamp, reflected his determination and dedication to his quest for knowledge. He scribbled away on a writing pad, jotting whatever he thought might help him in the days to come. It wouldn't do to gather half-baked information for which he wouldn't have answers if questioned from various angles. His arguments had to be watertight.

The world outside faded into a distant hum as his focus narrowed on the intriguing narratives and historical threads that the archives offered. Hours slipped away unnoticed as he became the guardian of forgotten stories, resurrecting the voices of those who came before him. In this quiet sanctuary of knowledge, where the whispers of scholars echoed through the air, he found peace and purpose. He was a curious explorer, unearthing the untold stories, unmasking hidden truths, and weaving them together to illuminate the present predicament with the wisdom of the past.

Finally, Farmani closed the volumes and replaced them on the shelves from where he had taken them. His eyes were shining brightly with an idea that was becoming firmer and taking on a more solid shape. There was a slight smile playing at the corners of his lips. Massaging his jaws with his fingertips, he seemed to be lost in the depths of his thoughts. He whispered quietly, a word that would have sounded strange to anybody who chanced to overhear it. It sounded very much like "Jugutis"—a word that would have held no meaning for anyone who heard it.

***

Upon exiting the library, Farmani was suddenly seized with an idea. He walked quickly toward a house he knew in the same area as the library. Located on Rue du Général Camou, he knew Marc Dupont's house was toward the end of the same street, though he hadn't been there before. The old lawyer was an old friend whom Farmani had consulted on matters of the consul. Long ago, he had said that his house was in the area, a bit of information Farmani was glad he had held on to. He did not know how many of the new laws Dupont might be familiar with, but it was worth a shot asking him for his opinion. He knew that Dupont was staunchly French, preferring to resign from his profession rather than work with the Germans in any capacity. With Dupont, Farmani knew that his questions would be safe and their discussions would go no further than the walls of his house. He hoped Dupont would not mind Farmani's visiting him without a prior appointment. There was no time to be lost, and these were not times to wait on formality.

Locating the house did not prove to be a problem. By the gate was a large, old, crumbling board that had the lawyer's name and qualification. Farmani noticed that the garden was unkempt and that the house could have used a fresh layer of paint. However, it did seem like people were still living there. It was early evening, and some of the windows were already lit. The house, which once must have been an elegant abode, now wore the signs of neglect and decay. Its weather-worn façade reflected the passage of time, with chipped paint revealing the exposed brick underneath at places. The shutters hung askew, creaking mournfully in the gentle breeze. The roof, covered in moss and missing a few tiles, bore testament to years of weathering. The grand entrance, adorned with ornate carvings and a once-gleaming brass doorknob, now showed signs of rust and tarnish. Overgrown vines crawled their way up the walls on either side of the gate, their tendrils snaking through cracks in the crumbling stonework.

Farmani knocked at the door, which was opened by a young girl of about fourteen. He introduced himself and told her that he wanted to speak with Mark Dupont, who was an old acquaintance.

The girl looked at him for a minute and said, "I will tell Papa. Stay here." She quietly closed the door after her, leaving Farmani waiting on the porch.

About two minutes later, she opened the door with a smile and said, "Papa will see you presently. He is upstairs in his study." She waved her hand toward a staircase that was located immediately near the door.

Inside, the air was heavy with the scent of must and dampness. The once elegant furniture was now faded, and the wallpaper peeled off in tattered remnants. Rays of sunlight filtered through the dusty windows, casting a melancholic glow upon the interiors of the rooms. It wasn't a large house. It had seen better days too. However, everything was neatly arranged, and somebody had meticulously seen to it that no dust had gathered over the volumes of books and the desk in the study. There were a great deal of pens, books, and other stationary materials on the desk and on the shelves.

Marc Dupont was seated in a large leather chair behind a mahogany table. His frizzy hair stuck out in every direction possible, the same as ever. He had been busy writing something as Farmani entered. As the latter closed the door, the bespectacled little French man leaped off his chair and came around the desk to hug him. The thin, bearded man reached only Farmani's shoulders in height, though his lively attitude made up for his seeming lack of physical vigor. Farmani smiled at his effervescence. It would seem that they had been best friends rather than mere legal consultants over work. But Marc Dupont had always been so.

"How are you, dear friend? It is so good to see somebody from the olden days now," Dupont twinkled at him.

"I am well, Mr. Dupont. Work is hard, but it goes on. I came for some information, to be honest. I don't know whom else to consult on this matter. It is rather confidential, you see," Farmani said. He knew he could come directly to the point with Dupont.

"Of course, tell me what you need, and I will tell you what I can do. And you can trust me absolutely. Your matter will not leave these walls," Dupont said, almost crossing his heart. There always had been something a little bordering on the theatrical with Dupont. Farmani smiled inwardly. However, he knew that apart from his flourish, Marc Dupont was harmless enough and one who could be very loyal to you if he happened to like you. On this count, Farmani was convinced that he was in Dupont's good books. They had always shared an easy camaraderie.

Farmani went ahead, wasting no time, and explained his plan. He referred to his notes so that he wouldn't forget any vital detail that might be of use to the lawyer. He took his time, clearly explaining the political situation between Germany and Iran and the present equation the countries and their political heads shared. He finally ended with the question he wanted to ask, "Will it work? What are my chances, legally speaking?"

Dupont was cautious in the answer that he framed. He said, "Well, I know a little about the Nuremberg Laws, of course. I don't have a draft of it. You will already know that the Reich will not let lay people, especially those of other nationalities, get their hands on them. However, if what you are saying is correct and the Führer has personally excluded them from the purview of the law, then what you say could work. As long as the exception granted isn't revoked, that is. Mind you, this is my first impression. But I would need some time to verify everything I say. I hope you will keep my name out of the issue if it comes to anything?"

Farmani quickly assured the old man that he would never reveal Dupont's help in the matter.

What Dupont was talking about was the German laws enacted hardly a year ago to protect what Nazi Germany believed to be their true heritage and race—Aryan. These laws were the basis of the segregation of the Jews. It started with them not being given citizenship or political rights in Germany. Their passports were revoked, and they had to wear the yellow Star of David badge, marking themselves out. A Jew was defined as anybody who had three or more of their grandparents as members of the Jewish faith. As per the law, the *Mischlinge,* or the half-German-Jews who had only two Jewish grandparents, were theoretically excluded from the purview of the Nuremberg Laws. Though Germany started with the Jews, there were other ethnic groups such as Romas or the gypsies and Blacks who were also targeted and differentiated as racially impure or different from "pure-blooded" Aryans. In France, these laws had not been strictly enforced. There had been an attempt at roundups the previous year, but for now, the Jews had only been segregated and excluded from public places for the most part. However, this could change any time Germany decided to apply the laws to all German-occupied lands, which would include France.

"That is what I thought too. What would you suggest that I do to make my case? Where do I start?" Farmani asked eagerly.

The lawyer took some time as he composed what he would say next. Finally, he said, "Look, Farmani. Much as I want to help you, I need your word of honor that I won't be implicated in helping you. I want the freedom of France as much as anyone else who loves their country. It is why I resigned from office when the Germans invaded. I did not want any of my services furthering or helping their cause. Yet, I have a family—a young daughter, as you have seen. As a father, my love for her precedes my love for my country as a patriot. I don't want myself counted among the Resistance or any allied groups. I will give you the information because I want to do my bit for France. But I will give you the information only if you promise to keep a secret of where you received it from. I will give nothing in writing."

Farmani looked at him, "Be at ease, Monsieur. I come only for myself and have no wish to embroil you or your family in trouble. You don't have to provide anything in writing. Your advice in good faith will suffice. Two heads are better than one principle, I guess. And you are one of the most knowledgeable people I have met in your line of work." Farmani knew that flattery was Marc Dupont's weakness.

He said in answer to Farmani's earlier question, "If I were you, I would write letters, mentioning all the facts and attaching whatever proof I can add, and send them off to the highest offices here and in Berlin. The fact is, one never knows who might be working against you. If you have written permission from Berlin, then nobody can question you. You will have to work fast as the roundups are imminent." The lawyer was running his thin fingers through his beard thoughtfully.

"Letters..." Farmani repeated a little absent-mindedly. He knew his next steps would have to be a race against time indeed. Even if the letters reached the right places, the replies would be slow in coming. They would perhaps conduct their own research or verification before confirming or rejecting his arguments. Of course, the slowness did not torment him; it would also buy him time to set his plans in motion.

The French man said, "I would start with the Vichy government. The letter you send there will hardly take any time to reach. If they are convinced, they will forward the matter to Berlin. Meanwhile, you can use contacts here in Paris to argue and endorse your case. If you can somehow orchestrate the Shah speaking to the Führer—extracting a renewal of the promise, then that would also work in your favor."

"Hmmm. I see what you mean," Farmani was appreciative of all the help this man was rendering him. "What could happen if they see through it?" Farmani asked. There was a tenseness in his muscles. He knew what the answer would be, but he had to ask it nevertheless.

"I won't lie to you son. If they catch you trying to pull the wool over their eyes, they will be merciless. They claim to be the best race. Why would they want to be made fools of in the public gaze?" The lawyer was honest; one had to give him that.

Something about his calmness rubbed off on Farmani. The young man felt more at ease knowing the whole truth and the potential consequences of his actions. There was no point in beating about the bush.

"In the end, you have to decide whether it is worth it. Otherwise, you can close your eyes. Many people are doing the same. The French are betraying their own kith and kin these days. Nobody would expect you to go out of the way to do more than what is strictly your duty," Dupont said practically. There was a steely glint in his eyes as he made the last statement. Dupont did not seem to think much of his fellowmen who were currying favor with the Nazis. Though he said nothing further, it seemed to Farmani that the little Frenchman abhorred these French traitors more than the Nazis themselves.

Farmani nodded. He knew what he had to do. It wasn't faith in his religion or a God above who watched him that drove him to his duty. In fact, it had been years since he had uttered a prayer. In his mostly European upbringing, he had all but forgotten the traditional rituals of the Islamic faith. However, Farmani still believed in the power of humanity. He knew that not doing anything now would mean a lifetime of regret, and he would not be able to sleep knowing that his actions might have saved at least a few.

He replayed the last words the old man told him, "Don't lose heart. It could work with reasonable success, provided you have the right contacts. In these times, there is so much chaos with the maintenance of records that they may not have the time or spare the effort to verify your claims historically. Even if they do, it might prove difficult to establish your tale as a lie. After all, most of what you say is based on actual historical facts that can be cross-checked. If they sit on their final verdict, it will still buy you enough time to do a little good. Even a little goes a long way in these times of darkness."

Farmani had to agree. Even a little was indeed a lot.

***

As Farmani made his way to his bachelor apartment, not far from his office buildings, he was seized by a desperate longing to be rid of every serious decision looming ahead of him. He wanted to throw off his responsibilities, choices, and the decisions he must make. He was filled with loathing for the Nazis who had made this mess and for the Germans who had voted the Nazis into power. He couldn't understand how such a warped lot had been elected into power. He felt nothing but contempt for the Vichy government, puppets of the Germans who had allowed the Nazis to walk into this ancient and historically rich country without as much as a fight. He didn't know whether the world had gone mad or if he alone was unsuited to the direction it was taking. His other worry was that the new Shah might wash his hands of the matter. Not wanting to make a scene against the Nazis, what if the Iranian government failed to offer him the support he wanted in helping those he wanted to?

There were so many details to be worked out. How would the logistics of such a big operation be handled? Will he be able to find trusted hands and sealed lips in this city? How would he decide how to save them? On what priority would he list them?

How on earth was he going to make an entire listing of them in the first place? He needed support—of that, he was convinced. After all this effort, how many could he save? It seemed a futile waste of energy and time over something that would happen inevitably.

Between all this, there was another thought that was bothering him. He remembered the enchanting time he spent with Eva Klein at the German ball only a few days ago. It was imperative that none of his actions were traced back to any of his friends or family. They could all get into trouble for his choices. It was not fair that someone else should pay for his actions. Was it even wise to get close to someone at this time when he was planning a certain course of action that would affect all their fates? When would be a good time to reveal his intentions to her? Should she not know that he had plans that might get in the way of a future together?

He paused right there and reframed his question—but did she even want a future together? In addition to all the stress piling on, this particular line of thought made him feel more dejected than ever. He knew he had to sleep off these black clouds settling over his head before setting for work tomorrow. There was much to be done, and he needed his energy and his wits about him. There was no time to sit around and wonder about ifs and buts.

Chapter 5:

The Promise: 23 June 1942

It was another sultry day, and Farmani was sweating in his office. The windows of his room were wide open, letting in a gentle breeze from across the Seine. The endless paperwork was maddening. Each time he completed dealing with a batch of documentation, it seemed there was more. That morning, he had just sent his letters—one addressed to the Iranian consul, his brother-in-law at Vichy. This was to be forwarded to the French officials there. The second letter was addressed to Berlin. It was intended for Dr Walter Gross, who was the head of the Nazi Party Office of Racial Policy. Farmani wasn't sure if it would reach the doctor, but he was hoping the contents would be relayed to the department in charge of the question of Iranian Jews in German-occupied territories—if at all there was such a wing. At the very least, he hoped the department would undertake some primary research on what he was saying. The third letter was addressed to his superior in Iran, to be forwarded to none less than the Shah himself. The idea was to launch a multi-pronged discussion on shaping the question of Iranian Jews. Even if these letters did not achieve anything concrete, his suggestions might delay the roundups of Iranian Jews and give them more time, at the very least. Unless a letter revoking the previous ordinance counting Iranians among the Aryan races was issued from Berlin, he knew that Nazi officers would have to comply with Führer's stated wish to allow Iranians to leave.

Meanwhile, he had to actively try to get more people on board to help. He had to have a team of trusted members who would help the cause without revealing details. Ideally, he knew it would be best to have bit-players—people working on various parts of the operation without being aware of each other or the full picture. This way, even if the enemy captured them, there would be little to nothing of use that the operatives would be able to reveal. But this would need a dedicated staff and a certain number of them. He wasn't sure where he would find so many of them. He had a few ideas about people on his staff within the consul office. Yet it was a dangerous game, and he did not want to imperil too many lives that could also make matters worse for his country's standing with the Nazis.

There were yet more complications coming his way. There were early indications that Iran could pull out diplomats from German-occupied lands because it was now occupied by the British-Soviet forces. The occupying forces compelled the Shah to stop all diplomatic relations with Germany. Of course, this move might take more time to come into effect. The Shah was stalling as expected and repeating that his stance was unchanged and that Iran would continue to exercise neutrality where the war was concerned. However, with the Allied forces occupying the land, this was difficult to achieve. It would be only a matter of time before he would be able to do nothing. Farmani would then have the difficult choice of whether to continue unaided in Paris or to return home. But he knew that for now, as long as he was here, he had to try.

***

It was mid-morning, and Farmani had just got off a call with his superior in Tehran. He was supposed to report matters and progress from Paris every two weeks. These calls were mostly just routine discussions and were not considered much more than a formality on either side. A large number of these calls were generally lost to transmission delays as operators put them through to the right exchanges and static interruptions. But they were a part of the diplomatic protocol he had to follow.

Farmani was deep in thought. If his plan was to be set into action, he would have to withhold at least some information from the Iranian embassy head. If he were ever caught for this, it could land him in a lot of trouble later on. It was risky, to say the least. However, another voice told him that it was best not to dwell too much on the what-ifs of the situation and just go with the flow.

After all, going with the flow was pretty much how he had landed up in Paris. After his law exams, he applied for a post in the foreign service that would take him away from home. He only planned on having a good time and enjoying himself. When he heard that his application for junior attaché at Paris had come through, it was as if luck was stacked in his favor. He was only 23 at the time, and it was exhilarating to be in the "city of love"! However, with the war now, everything had changed.

He heard a quiet tapping at the door, interrupting his thoughts. It was so soft that he was beginning to think that he may have imagined it. That is when he heard it again. He quickly opened the door to find a young man around his age at the door.

Farmani smiled and said, "I'm afraid I don't have too many visitors these days. I am Kameron Farmani, the Iranian consul. How may I help you?

The young man was tall, extremely thin, and had black eyes set in beautiful golden-toned skin. His hair was curly black and seemed to define his personality. He had a rough stubble and wore no hat. He held out his hands and said in Persian, "I am David Cohen. I'm an Iranian German. I have been wandering for two days, hoping for some help. I have been directed to many individuals who, though sympathetic, will not promise anything. I came to you because I felt you might understand my plight better. After all, you come from my own land, even if you aren't Jewish."

Farmani switched to Persian and said, "I am sorry, I assumed you knew French. Please tell me how I can assist you." Farmani was curious about this young man, whose intelligent but tired face spoke volumes of his situation. It seemed like he was desperate, though he was too well-bred to beg anyone. Owing to his peculiar upbringing in Europe, Farmani had not had or cultivated many Jewish friends. However, his family had professional, business, and friendly ties with several Jewish ones, and it seemed natural that this man should assume a kinship. Farmani found himself liking the man and yet feeling a little wary. This was the task he was preparing for, and somehow, he had never guessed that a plea would come so soon.

David launched into his story. He and his family, comprising of his mother and sister, had lived in Germany for close to twenty years. They had family back in Iran and Palestine. He wanted to desperately leave Europe as fast as possible.

"How did you end up in Paris?" Farmani asked, a little confused.

"We crossed over into France, aiming for Vichy. Because we were advised that Vichy still allowed Jews to leave for Palestine. I don't know the situation right now. At the time, I was just filled with a sense of ludicrousness that Germany was closing its borders on the Jews. We were to be held captive, alive or dead, within the country. We had to act swiftly, and this was one of the few choices that we could afford. If possible, I don't want to waste too much time here in France. One never knows when—." He was about to say something, and then he abruptly broke off and said, "I wondered if it was possible to leave from here directly. I don't want our papers scrutinized or for our Jewish status to be revealed too much. I wanted to ask you. As the consul, surely you must know." The man's voice held an anguish that was hard to ignore.

Farmani deduced that Cohen belonged to one of the affluent families owing to his clipped guttural German-accented Persian. However, considering that he was wearing a frayed suit at least twice his size and a pair of boots that must have definitely seen better days, it seemed that the family had fallen upon hard times.

Farmani looked the man in his eyes and said kindly, "I will help you. But I want to hear the entire story, David. I promise you that I will do whatever is in my power."

As Farmani handed him a glass of water, he took it gratefully and said, "My family resided in Frankfurt for nearly two decades. Before the rise of the Nazi party, my father owned a textile business there, and we were pretty comfortable. My sister and I had a decent education in the same city. We were hoping to expand our business and eventually even start an exporting wing." David ran his fingers over his eyes as if shielding them from a bright past he could hardly bring himself to look at anymore.

He continued, "About nine years ago, my father passed away, leaving the business and our house in my name. As the restrictions on us increased, we found that we could no longer pursue any meaningful business. We were prevented by the laws. We were no longer citizens of Germany by the same decree. Instead, we were classified as *state subjects* without citizenship rights. My family and I stayed on a little longer, hoping that there would be a solution. I suppose we were blinded by our stupidity in assuming that no government would be so blatantly unfair and that, eventually, our home and property would have to be returned to us. But things only kept growing worse. Friends and family members started disappearing. Some of us turned up dead, and we were terrified of being the next random victim. The state took away our property and ownership rights. We had to stay cooped up in hiding, depending on the mercy of friends and acquaintances, who could no longer harbor us in public, or kind strangers who took us in for a night or two."

An involuntary shudder passed through David as he remembered the dark times. Farmani could see that the man in front of him had seen loss, death, and destruction firsthand. This was not the death of war, where men fought and could be killed in battle. As traumatic as fighting in a war was, this was even worse. People were being hunted down and killed like common vermin. Farmani was startled suddenly because he had thought the exact word the Germans had been using to describe the Jews in their state propaganda—"vermin."

David took another sip of water and then said, "A couple of years ago, we got the new decree that Jews mandatorily had to stay behind in Germany. There were rumors that Jews would be used—driven like slaves to build the Nazi empire. Of course, it wouldn't be the first time. The Torah itself talks of how the Egyptians used the Israelites to build their vast cities for years together. But this time, it looks worse. Our deliverance this time around looks unlikelier than ever. When they spoke of the camps where we would be transported like common cattle, I decided that my family would not die like animals, driven to work for those inhuman pigs. We used our contacts and were put in touch with an underground Zionist group. They helped us with travel documents and bare necessities. We left behind our house and estate. God knows what has become of them now. We had family and friends—I don't know if we will meet them again. We reached France only a couple of months ago. We believed that Paris would be slightly more relaxed in its attitude to us. However, with the Germans stationed here, I don't think it will remain safe for long. We have toyed with the idea of going to Vichy. But I simply don't know if it will be any better there. We feel so trapped and alone." Here, the young man broke down a little.

He then rallied his strength and continued, "Please. You have to understand that we have faced starvation and state brutality for almost ten years now in Germany and on our way here. My family and I have to live in poverty, hiding from people because we never know when or by whom we could be hunted down. I want to do right by my family, at least. I cannot rest without ensuring that my mother and sister cross over to somewhere—anywhere safe, where they won't be persecuted. We have seen death, destruction, and blood. So much blood that even in safety we are unlikely to sleep soundly for a very long time. The dreams that haunt us are of capture, torture, and rape. I can't live like this anymore, thinking that at any moment now, we will be caught, and I will be helpless to save my mother and sister. I dread being a witness to their torture at the hands of the enemy." David's eyes had taken on a glazed expression. To Farmani, it was clear that there was no point in pressing him further. David was exhausted by the effort of narrating everything he just had. It didn't seem that there was anything more he could say. He had said everything that Farmani had surmised.

Farmani said gravely in a low tone, "David, I want you to know that you have come to the right place. I will help you. I haven't planned everything, nor do I know everything yet. But in a day or so, you will have all your answers. I will tell you what to do. I just want you to know that before roundups start here, we will have you all safely across. That is my word. I will honor it. I want you to go now and rest. How can I reach you when things are in place? And would you be able to make arrangements for the tickets when I get the papers ready?"

"My family and I are put up with friends in the city. They stay at La Goutte d'Or. You can just send word to the Bernhardts there. Yes, tickets can be arranged via friends I know here. I only need the relevant papers," David said.

"Alright. That can be managed, David. Take good rest. We have a lot of work to do and quite a bit of action coming up," Farmani said, smiling up kindly at the young but prematurely lined man who was now rising from his chair wearily.

***

Port Debilly was a historic port. Situated along the Seine River, near the Eiffel Tower in the 16th arrondissement of Paris, the port was named after Jean-Baptiste Debilly, a French military officer who fought during the Napoleonic Wars. Port Debilly served as an important transportation hub for goods and passengers along the Seine River for decades. It was primarily used for industrial purposes and played a significant role in the city's trade and commerce.

It was also where people used to walk around and look out onto the Seine. Though constructed not more than a century ago, the Debilly footbridge was in disrepair. In fact, the president of the architectural society had called it *a forgotten accessory of a past event* just a year or so ago. The footbridge was built on a metallic framework, one of the few monuments like The Eiffel Tower to stand as a testament to the progress of metallurgy and engineering in the country. Resting on two stone quays at the riverbanks, it was adorned with dark green ceramic tiles arranged in a wave-like pattern. At one point from the walkway, one could see the Eiffel Tower a little away in the distance.

This was where Farmani was headed. It was a spot where he liked to ruminate over things. The fact that the scenery offered him a spectacular view of the Seine only added to its attractions. He was frowning into the bright sunlit day, taking in everything—the river flowing placidly beneath him and the few boats floating idly on it.

He knew that the time had come. He had to follow through now, no matter what. He had given his word and the Farmani's never gave their word if they couldn't keep their promise. His heart pounded with a mixture of fear and determination. The weight of the world seemed to rest upon his shoulders as he contemplated the pivotal action that lay ahead. The war, he knew, waged on and would wage on, casting its dark shadow over humanity. But it was the first time that Farmani found himself standing at a crossroads—of life and death, courage and uncertainty, discovery and destiny. So far, the war, despite the shelling and threat of military might, had seemed a thing far away on the battlefield. Of course, civilian life had changed drastically, but Farmani had thought of it as a hardship that could be borne. This time, it was different. He felt like he was caught in the crossfire for the first time. Though the burden of the promise loomed heavy, he also knew it was the right thing to do. Paris was no longer the city of lights he had been drawn to as a young man; it had become a city cloaked in fear and oppression.

Farmani stared pensively at the glistening waters of the Seine. The river flowed calmly, but Farmani knew of the dark and deep currents beneath the surface mirroring the conflict within his soul. He understood that helping the Jews meant defying the Nazi regime and risking his own life. The enormity of the task weighed down on him, as did the consequences of failure. But as he gazed at the river, he couldn't help but be reminded of the countless lives lost and the atrocities being committed against innocent people. He knew he couldn't stand by as an idle spectator when fate was giving him a chance to alter the course of history itself.

He remembered his father's description of how the Ashouris had returned to Tehran too. Images of David's family fleeing the state police and soldiers flashed through Farmani's mind. Though he did not know him personally, it was as if his story had finally broken through a shield in Farmani's heart. David's story was his story too. David could be friends of his family back in Iran—people who had done nothing wrong. Certainly, nobody, not even the vilest of criminals, deserved what the Jews were being meted out simply for being born into their race. Even women and children were massacred without sympathy or a second thought. What kind of men did such things? Even animals were more humane. The desperate eyes of the countless victims of the Nazi regime, filled with despair, haunted Farmani. He had heard firsthand the cruelty inflicted upon the Jews and couldn't bear to stand by idly. Even Paris, once a beacon of art and culture, was slowly becoming a battleground of prejudice and hatred. Farmani knew he couldn't let fear paralyze him; action was the only way to preserve humanity.

A breeze whispered through the sultriness of the afternoon, slowly turning to a warm evening. It carried with it the echoes of resistance and resilience. Farmani's determination grew stronger with each passing moment. He visualized himself as a beacon of hope with the potential to shine light amidst the darkness. The mantle of responsibility settled firmly on his shoulders, igniting a fire within him. He had a purpose now.

Lured by the strength of his convictions, Farmani decided that he would embark on this perilous journey. He would seek out the underground network of brave individuals committed to helping those targeted by the Nazis. The network operated in secrecy, risking everything to save lives. The Resistance members would be hard to find, but find them he must. He would find solace in their camaraderie and shared cause. Together, they would forge a path of defiance, determined to challenge the oppressors and protect the innocent.

He knew it would be no bed of roses. No doubt, there would be obstacles and danger at every turn. Betrayal, too, would lurk in the shadows. It would have to be a test of his faith in humanity. Even if adversity threatened to extinguish the flickering hope within him, he would—nay, must—persist. The memory of what happened to David's and Amir's families and countless others like them spurred him to a momentary blinding rage. He knew that there would be no stopping once he started. The lives of so many depended on his unwavering resolve.

Amidst the countless challenges, he knew he had only the indomitable spirit within himself to depend upon. He embraced the role thrust upon him, finding courage in the face of adversity. The city of Paris would become his battleground, where he would have to sieve friend from foe and establish an army of the righteous to do what had to be done now.

As the evening turned to night, the night sky was ablaze with stars. It was as if an answering voice from above was telling him that things would be fine if he did what was right. He felt more at ease. As he watched the river flow beneath him, he felt a profound sense of purpose. He was to embark on a journey that would forever change him, witnessing both the darkness and the strength of the human spirit. He would do what was required of him; god help him and save the lives that depended on him now.

He quickly walked off the footbridge and made his way home. Tomorrow would be a new day.

Chapter 6:

The Plan: 26-28 June 1942

The time had come for action. Farmani steeled his nerves, called up people within the printing division of the Iranian consul, and told them his needs succinctly but clearly. It was a minor thing to be taken care of and would in no way affect the issuance of the passports for Iranian nationals. They listened calmly to him and promised him that the new passports would be delivered within two days. He had merely asked that the passports should not contain any mention of the religion of the person carrying it. It was only about deleting a line from the documents that were in circulation.

He knew the risk he was taking. He knew they might guess why he was asking them to make this change. Very subtly, he made it seem that his orders came from the Shah. These were junior people, and they wouldn't question him. In time, he might be able to get papers showing the Shah's approval if the need arose, but for now, this would have to do. Two days gave him some time. Meanwhile, he sent word to David saying that he could go ahead and make arrangements for his and his family's travel from Paris to Tehran on the 27th of June. Not one to sit idle, Farmani decided to meet the lawyer again.

When Farmani rang the bell, the same girl as before opened it. However, this time, she had a ready smile for him as she said, "Mr. Farmani. Papa had said that you would come again. Please join him in the study."

Farmani looked at the thin girl and said, "Thank you, Eloise."

Marc Dupont was as exuberant as ever upon seeing his friend. "Ahhh. Welcome, welcome," he said.

Farmani had no time to waste on pleasantries. He said, "Were you able to find out anything, monsieur?"

"Yes and no," the little Frenchman was pulling at his beard thoughtfully. He continued, "I have enquired with friends everywhere. Nobody seems to know for certain. Yet, the good news is it seems that you are right. For now, Iranians do seem to have some immunity. Passports or paperwork with your country's ensign are being let off at borders. Legally speaking, Nazis can't hold back your countrymen unless, of course, there is something illegal in the nature of their conduct. But of course, in these times, even Führer is probably finding it hard to exercise complete control over his army and men. In effect, it all boils down to the temperament and mood of the border security personnel. If they know of the rule, they are letting them pass. If not, they are apprehending them until they can confirm matters with higher authority. Either way, unless there are sudden new changes in policy, your plan might work for now."

"Meaning, all Iranians, irrespective of their religion, can still leave Nazi-occupied lands?" Farmani wanted to hear this said out aloud.

"Yes, in all probability, most Iranians will make it across without much fuss," the lawyer confirmed. He then added thoughtfully, "However, if their passports don't mention their religious affiliation at all, especially should they be Jews, it might prove more to their advantage."

That was the best Farmani could hope to hear. He knew Dupont well enough to know that when tasked with delicate matters, he would be discreet and do his best to find out facts from every angle possible. He was a thorough man and one who could be trusted. Farmani sighed a deep sigh. Now, it was all up to fate. He had set the ball rolling, and he could only hope for the best.

On the way back to his office, he sent word to David that he could come to the consular office the day after tomorrow to pick up their papers and passports needed for travel. As he sank into his seat, Farmani was relieved. He had plunged into battle. There was no more need to agonize over what to do and where his duty lay.

***

When the passports arrived at his desk, he opened them and checked everything. There were three documents—in the names of David, his mother, and his sister. Farmani checked every page of each of them to confirm that the insignia and other details of the country were printed correctly. There was no column mentioning the religious affinity of the bearer.

When David came to collect the documents, Farmani asked him, "What about the tickets? Are they bought and paid for?"

"All done," David said, flipping through the documents the other had just handed over to him. After he had gone through each page of it, he said, "It doesn't say what religion we are."

"Iranians have immunity, for now, because the Nazis have a deal with the Shah. We don't know how long ties forged before a war will last during a war," Farmani said.

"I understand. If asked, what are we to say?" David asked.

"Say that you are Persian Jugutis of the Aryan race," Farmani said. He then clarified, "As per the standing instructions of none less than the Führer himself, all Iranians are Aryans. Since we don't want to complicate matters, we will say that you are Jugutis, a sect among Muslims who only practice the Jewish faith in private but identify more with the Islamic culture. I am sorry; it was the best I could do. I, too, hope for a day when you and your family can travel without suppressing any part of who you are."

"You have done more than you can imagine for us. I and my family will be eternally grateful to you for this, Farmani," the young man said with tears in his eyes. He had gotten up and extended his arm. When Farmani gave his hand in return, it was met with a strong grasp.

Farmani said, "I have done nothing yet. In theory, everything I have told you is true. And yet, we can only hope for the best at the border when you have to show your papers. The Nazis are suspicious, hard, and unyielding. You must set aside your fear and show that you are entitled to cross. For the sake of your family, convince them that you have the right of passage. Do not hesitate, and ensure you mention that the consul of Iran can verify your papers personally if they ask you for any further proof. I will stand by you and take care of the rest."

"Thank you. It means a lot to us. I will repay this debt to you, no matter when or where. I will find you." David's words sounded genuine.

Farmani replied jovially, "Well then, I will await your gift every day here. After all, it is very dry times here for a consul stuck in war." The two men laughed heartily, and the moment of tension was broken.

As David turned away to leave, Farmani prayed in his mind that he would never have to intercede on their behalf nor see them again for the duration of the war. Their chances of making it safely across were higher if they were cleared on the first attempt of trying to leave.

***

When a couple of days came and went by after his last talk with David on the 26th, Farmani was relieved and a great burden was prised off his chest. He assumed that the Cohens must have left. Since he hadn't received any word for further help from there or clarification from the French or German officials, he assumed that they must have been permitted to leave without any hassle.

Therefore, it was with great surprise that he saw David entering his office jauntily one fine morning on the 28th of June.

"Are you all still here? What was the matter? Did they ask you for more papers?" Farmani asked, alarmed.

"My mother and sister have left, all thanks to the good lord who directed us to you. I decided I would stay behind," David said.

"What on earth for, man?!" Farmani was irritated now. "Why would you risk yourself by staying on here? After all the trouble to get those papers prepared, is this the thanks I am to receive?"

"I am sorry. I never intended to disrespect or cause you any harm. My documents are still safe with me, and I can leave any time if you insist. But I want to work with you in helping as many of my kin as I can. When I met you, I only thought of myself. But you changed my perspective—opened my eyes. Now, I want to be part of the cause too. Please, I am sure you can use more people on your team. I would rather die trying than save my hide and not try," David said.

Farmani was still angry that this brazen, stupid lad had not saved himself while he had the chance. However, the practical part of his mind soon took over. He reasoned that it was true Cohen was trustworthy, and for the plans Farmani had, he would need extra pairs of eyes and hands. It would be only a matter of time before more people approached him with their needs. He would need people to delegate tasks, find out information, and get the paperwork ready. It wasn't like he had held Cohen to ransom. He was a grown-up who had willingly volunteered. Why should he not accept them into the ranks of the operation with open arms?

"Well, this work can be dangerous. I warn you in advance. With all the horrors that you have already undergone, wouldn't you rather go and live peacefully with your family?" Farmani asked, not unkindly.

"That's what I wanted to do. But I don't think peace will be mine wherever I go—the things I have seen will haunt me for years to come. Additionally, it would torment my soul to think that I could have helped you and that I deliberately turned my back on the chance. You, who have nothing to gain from this, are helping us, and I am turning my back on my own people. It simply doesn't seem fair," David added plainly.

Farmani knew that he could not lose such a worthy man. He said, "Welcome, David. It is my turn to thank you. You are right; I can use help. I don't know how many more I will be able to protect. But I am sure going to try my best. But you should know that I have diplomatic immunity and that my government will vouch for me should things go wrong. Well, again, we don't know how long the Nazis will help the government either, but for now, this is how it is. I can't extend the same security to you because you wouldn't be working for the government. I can't give you the papers to prove something like that. I am also Muslim, which is the other part of it. I won't be persecuted as much."

"I understand the risk that I am taking. As I said, I intend to die trying rather than not try at all. Besides, setting aside the diplomatic immunity, we are both going to bear Iranian passports without any reference to our religions. I think that rather evens out the risk. I know I can't be shown as a government agent. It would be too risky to forge papers like that. Despite the many perils, I would like to give you a hand, brother," David said.

Farmani was amazed that he should have the good fortune of having such a capable man on his team. It strengthened his resolve to work on the mission even harder and to help save as many lives as it was in his power. The men shook hands on that note before David Cohen left the office.

***

It was almost noon on the same day, and the raging fire in his belly reminded Farmani that he needed to eat. He was in a good mood after his meeting with David. It was one of those days he knew that nothing could go wrong. As if in answer to his spirit, he saw a sight to gladden his heart. As he sauntered through the streets toward the cafe where he generally had lunch, Cafe Heritage, he caught sight of Eva Klein and her maid seated outside having something to drink. Farmani thought it was a chance sent by the heavens itself. After the gala night, there wasn't a day that went by when he did not think of Eva. Since more pressing matters had to be seen, too, it was with great effort that he had forced thoughts of her away. Now was the opportunity he could renew his acquaintance.

As he reached nearer, he could see that the two women were so deep in discussion they hadn't noticed his approach. He heard a few scraps of conversation that floated to him from the general din of the cafe.

Miriam was saying, "Yes, he has been very insistent. I feel unsafe by the Herr Kommandant's..."

As Eva seemed to listen to her, Farmani could see the intense worry and sympathy she had for her companion etched in the lines of her face.

For a split second, Farmani wasn't sure whether he ought to disrupt the serious nature of the conversation. He then resolved that he would ask them politely and move off if they expressed any signs of his presence being unwelcome.

Farmani strode up to them, removed his hat, bowed to the two women, and fixed his eyes on Eva as he said with his happiest smile, "We meet again, madame."

Eva's eyes instantly lit up as she looked up at him. She said warmly, "Why, it is the consul!"

The Jewish woman looked up, and Farmani could tell she was upset that her narrative had been abruptly interrupted.

He said, "I can visit you some other time if you are busy. I happen to have my lunch here every day. That's my office building right there."

Miriam said, "No. It is fine. Please do join us, monsieur. I will be leaving in a while anyway. I have some personal work to attend to."

Eva asked him, "I was hoping that you would call one of these days. I haven't seen you around after the fête."

Farmani answered, "I have been flat out it isn't a great time to work in a political office. There is so much documentation—whether people want to stay or leave. How have you been?"

"Oh, the same. More performances. More fans," Eva's eyes held mischief as she said this.

"Fans. Yes, I know there must be quite a few," Farmani replied gaily.

"A few? Why, you do injustice to my fame. There are more than just *a few*, thank you," Eva said in a mock huff. They all laughed at that.

As Miriam excused herself, Eva's face took a more anxious expression. Farmani asked her gently, "Is everything alright, Eva? You look worried."

She said, "It is Miriam. I fear for her. There is a certain German official who has been following her around. He seems to be obsessed with her and is making overtures that are unacceptable to her. For now, he is using only his persuasive abilities. Yet I am worried. No German will tolerate a no from a Jew, and especially not from a Jewish woman. It is only a matter of time before—" she broke off here and shuddered, unwilling to complete the sentence.

Farmani knew what she meant. The Nazis considered the Jews little better than slaves. By their own laws, Germans weren't allowed to pursue a relationship with Jews, but then the Nazis always overlooked laws that prevented them from having what they wanted. What they couldn't get via arguments and protestations, they would carry off by force. Miriam could be harmed or kidnapped if the officer willed it. She would just be another Jew who went missing or was found dead mysteriously in the city. The man would get his friends to help him with the dirty deed, and the whole incident would be nothing more than an inconvenience to them. There would be no legal redress because they would take care not to leave any proof tying them to the crime. Anyway, Jews were not even legal citizens of Germany or German-occupied territories. What chance would a girl like her have? Farmani knew that he had to help her get out of the city before the situation escalated.

"Can you not ask her to leave?" he asked.

"That is what I have been advising her as well. I don't like the sound of everything she has been telling me, and Jews aren't safe anywhere. However, in Vichy, she may have access to better resources to help her out of the country. I don't know how to help her, though. I have the money, of course, but her papers will be scrutinized. I don't know how she'll get past that," Eva said nervously, twirling a lock of her hair.

"Yes, you are right; she needs to move fast. Besides, I don't know whether to tell you this. The Nazis are planning the roundup of the Jews soon. Word has it that they have arranged trains to carry twenty or thirty thousand people out of Paris alone. I got it confirmed from the French officials who wouldn't lie about these matters," Farmani said.

Eva's hands went up to her lips, and she went very pale. Instinctively, Farmani held her hand and said, "It is dreadful. But we just have to wait and see. Perhaps there could be a way out. I don't know for sure. But I will find out what I can and let you know."

Eva looked at him. She was beginning to tear up. She could no longer trust her voice not to give way. She nodded at him and gave his hand a gentle squeeze in response.

He looked at her for a while and then asked, "Where can I find you when I have more news?"

She had composed herself and said presently, "I stay in the byline on Rue Halévy. You can ask somebody there to direct you. Most everyone knows me in person as the singer."

Farmani released her hand and, looking deep into her eyes, said, "Thank you. Don't lose heart. Keep strong for Miriam and yourself."

She nodded once before she got up and left.

On his way back, he sent a small note to be delivered to the Bernhardt's residence.

***

Late in the evening, just as he was winding up his work, a tap on his door made him look up. It was David again.

Farmani said, "Thank you for responding so soon, David. I know I did not commit to including you in my work. But I may have something for you. It should be done fast. Do you think you can be my ears?"

"Happily," David said, smiling. "What can I do?"

Farmani said deliberately so that David would not miss a word of it, "There is an opera singer by the name of Eva Klein who performs at that Opéra Garnier quite often. She lives near there. Her companion is a Jewish girl, Miriam. Perhaps somebody in your circles already knows her. In either case, I want you to follow her movements closely and report to me. She seems to be in some trouble with a German officer. I want you to confirm the truth of this. Bring me anything else that you may find of interest. If possible, she will be the next person that we have to move safely out of the city."

David repeated the names, committing them to memory, and promised his aid in the matter. He said, "I will be quick and discreet. No fear. I am sure somebody will know something. I will track her movements personally and see that no harm befalls her."

Farmani said, "I rely on you and trust you. Just be really quick. The Nazis won't take long to harm their victims. I don't have to tell you; you already know."

David said, "Yes, I wish I could say otherwise, but they are as ruthless as they are swift in retribution when they feel they have been wronged. I hear you. I promise I won't disappoint you or let her down."

As David left his office, Farmani contemplated the day's events. He knew that Eva Klein and her companion were trustworthy, but he felt it was too soon to show his hand to her just now. He did not want to reveal his part in the plan to save Jews or to help them leave the country unnoticed. Not all of his plans were clear to himself either yet. Besides, he was certain that the fewer people who knew what he was up to, the better it was for himself and for them. He also wanted to verify which Nazi officer he was up against. If they got wind of the fact that he was instrumental in helping the girl, he would be their next target, and that wouldn't be the wisest move. He momentarily remembered the Nazi officer with whom he had played only a little while ago—Richter. Farmani knew that people like Richter would be like hounds on a scent if they even suspected him. He knew he had to proceed with great caution. Neither did he want to get caught, nor did he want to give up doing whatever he could to save as many lives as possible. He intended to set things in motion so that many more like Miriam would find a safe haven until they could make their way out of the country.

Chapter 7:

Operation Lifeline: 28 June-03 July 1942

As Farmani lay in bed that night in his small bachelor apartment, his mind was swirling with ideas. Dupont's words had given him some confidence. He made a list of the things that he needed for his mission. His first concern was secrecy. The Nazis' watchful eyes were everywhere, and any hint of his plan could endanger the lives of those he sought to save. Farmani knew he would have to meticulously review each step, ensuring every detail was shrouded in the utmost secrecy. From the encrypted messages to the hidden safehouses, everything had to be foolproof. Next, he grappled with the logistics. How would the Jews be safely transported out of the city if there was a need? Farmani knew that the Gestapo's checkpoints were becoming increasingly stringent, making it perilous for anyone attempting to escape. He thought of alternative routes and connections with individuals who could aid their covert escape. He knew that the Resistance could aid him in this part. The only question was how he would touch base with them.

In addition to the above concerns, the financial aspect weighed heavily on his mind. Funding the operation required resources he did not possess. He wondered if the Resistance would be able to help there. He wasn't sure if they would have the means. The other thing to consider was reaching out to wealthy benefactors who shared his passion for liberation. Their support could provide the money necessary to ensure the success of his mission. His mind flitted to thoughts of Madame Leclerc briefly. He knew she would be of great use in the days to come. He would ask her more directly if the need arose. He also thought of the old colonel, her friend. Farmani was less certain that he would help. The man did not seem to be as clear as Madame Leclerc as to where his duty and loyalties lay. Besides Madame Leclerc had a son, of whom she seemed to be proud, working on the side of the Allies. She had told him as much. What could she hope to gain by supporting the Nazis? If anything, she would want to help her son as much as possible. It seemed quite probable that she would be a willingly helpful ally. However, Farmani was not one to reveal his hand so early on. He would wait for the right time to win her over.

As he immersed himself in this complex web of thoughts, an overwhelming sense of responsibility washed over him. The freedom of these innocent souls rested on his shoulders. He knew the risks were great, but the reward of saving lives far outweighed any personal danger he confronted. Every sleepless night, every ounce of anxiety, would be worth it if he could make a difference. He was still unsure whether he had it in him to see this battle through to the end.

With a renewed sense of purpose, Farmani resolved to push forward and find the means to do what he set out to do. He knew his unwavering commitment to justice and humanity would guide him through the darkest of times. As he teetered on the precipice of this treacherous journey, he reminded himself of the few words he remembered his father once uttered. So few had been their scattered interactions that these particular words had made an impact on him. He had said, "In the face of adversity, stand tall and fight for what is right." He knew now that the "right" he had to adopt was greater than everything—himself, his country, the Shah's orders, and even his own petty interests. He would have to set aside his preferences to do what his conscience was telling him to do. What kind of man could turn away from the voice of his own conscience? Though it had been years since he had uttered any of the prayers he was taught as a child, he knew that even the highest form of worship was in doing what your conscience bid you to do. In his mind, there was no doubt that saving as many Jews as he could was the task that was assigned to him. It did not matter who or what obstacles stood in the way; he had to do what he was duty-bound to do.

And so, his thoughts finally turned from doubts to determination. He was ready to rise, prepared to defy the forces of oppression and rewrite the destiny of those persecuted. The mission to help Jews flee Paris would become his legacy, a testament to the resilience of the human spirit in the face of unimaginable horrors. He named it in his head: "Operation Lifeline"—it would be the means of providing hope and support to his countrymen and as many others who needed it as he could find.

And with that, he closed his eyes, secure in the knowledge that he would take things one at a time and sort out everything needed to set the wheels in motion.

***

As July arrived, Farmani had more work in the consul office. The Nazis had asked for a list of people who had applied to him for permission to leave the country. Farmani was sitting on the list, stalling for time. On the one hand, he wasn't sure that this list wouldn't be checked against the people leaving at the border. He did not want to take a risk and compromise his position by sending a completely fake list. On the other hand, he did not want to give away the names of the people he would be helping either. The Nazis had also asked for a list of Jews who were Iranians to be marked separately. However, Farmani knew what should be done in that regard. He decided to mark all of them as Iranians as their new passports would show and to simply neglect to mention who were Jews and who were not.

If pressed, he could show the official letters he had sent earlier about Iranian Jews being Jugutis of Aryan descent. He was fairly sure that these measures would do for the present. Even so, he was a little apprehensive every time he thought of the repercussions. He wondered if there was anything he was missing—any new avenue or loophole he could use to his advantage in securing the freedom of the Iranian Jews. As for other Jews, he knew he would try to save them too. But here, he had to be more cautious.

As he kept dwelling on all these matters, a soft knock interrupted his train of thought. He knew it was David. Only he would come into this office at this hour. Farmani wondered if he already had any news on Miriam. However, it was a different matter altogether that he had come to discuss. While meeting other Jews in the city who might need their assistance, David met a young woman. Her name was Antoinette Laurent, and she was a member of the French Resistance. He wanted Farmani to meet her urgently. David was convinced she would make a great ally in the work that lay ahead. Farmani knew better than to doubt David's instincts. In the short span that he had known him, he knew that David was a good judge of people. He promised him that he would definitely meet this young woman at the earliest.

***

David had met her purely by chance at one of the tiny cafes of the city where he was scouting for a fellow Jew and for those who were seeking to flee the city. He had hoped he could rope in this acquaintance for Farmani's plans. He had not only found the person he sought but also someone even better. His friend, who declined to become a part of the plan, put him in touch with her instead. David knew at once that she was a keeper. David, who knew only broken French, was able to converse with her fluently because she knew German, among many other languages.

Antoinette Laurent was born and raised in Paris, France. She was born to a father who was in the legal trade, from whom she had inherited a strong sense of justice. Her mother was the daughter of a tradesman. It was her mother who, with her reading of French history and legends, developed in her a deep love for her country. As the world plunged into the chaos of World War II, Toni knew exactly why she had been endowed with these two qualities—justice and patriotism. The world needed people just like her right then.

In 1940, when the Nazis first occupied Paris, Toni witnessed firsthand how many of her friends and family members were ousted and driven out of the city. She had not sat around waiting for General de Gaulle's call to action. Determined to resist the enemy, she joined the French Resistance at the first possible opportunity. It hadn't been easy to infiltrate the ranks of a mostly male bastion. However, with sheer determination and power of will, Toni had proved that she could do everything that a man could. Operating under the code name "Étoile," which meant "star," Toni was a valuable asset to the Resistance movement, and people soon took note of her.

Toni frequently carried out covert operations, gathering and disseminating vital information to her fellow fighters. A versatile linguist who had a natural flair for learning new languages, she put her fluent German to good use to intercept enemy communications, extract valuable intelligence, and relay critical messages to the Resistance leaders. She also oversaw some of the radio messages that were relayed in and out of the city. Toni's courage and resourcefulness earned her the respect and admiration of her comrades quickly, as she was given even tougher assignments. Most recently, she had gone undercover, masquerading as a nurse to gain access to German military facilities just outside the city, smuggling documents and supplies she could lay her hands on to support the Resistance effort. It had been a daring operation that had helped the

Resistance fighters locate enemy strongholds and create disruptions there.

She was twenty-three years old, though her confidence and upright bearing made her appear wiser than her years. She was slender and athletic. Her brown hair was cut short. Less than a decade later, her hairstyle would become a well-known fashion statement and immortalized as the pixie cut worn by actresses, celebrities, and even common women. However, Toni did not care for style. Her hair looked more practical than fashionable on her, though it lent a charm of its own to her elfin grace. It also helped her don the various wigs needed for her disguises with less discomfort. Toni was stronger than her slim, tall figure suggested. She was an agile sprinter and indefatigable—strengths her comrades soon realized and put to good use. She had glittering brown eyes and a mouth that was quick to smile, set in a sunburned face that most Parisian women would be ashamed to flaunt. However, she was at ease in her skin, a quality that many were quick to notice. This was also what assured even people who met her for the first time that Toni was thoroughly dependable. If she said she could do it, then it meant that she wouldn't rest without accomplishing it. She was dressed in a dark, loose, thick tunic of some sort, belted at her waist, and trousers beneath it. It was clearly meant to allow her to move through the crowds and the streets at night without attracting too much unwanted attention. Inexplicably, at close quarters, even her male attire added rather than detracted from her attractiveness.

When Farmani met her, he knew he had one of the allies he wanted for his grand plan. She was the missing link he had been searching for. The interview was held in one of the seedier taverns of the city. It was at her behest that the venue was chosen. She was under the radar of the enemy. Most Nazis already knew of Agent Étoile from intercepted communications. Yet her identity had not yet been compromised. Hopefully, the Nazis would be looking for a man. Be that as it may be, Toni did not want to draw attention to herself. This was a place where she often met with her comrades and fellow Resistance fighters. Everyone knew her here and were friends. She knew she would receive help here in case she had to make a speedy exit.

Farmani hardly noticed the dingy interiors of the place. It was dimly lit, with soft, warm lighting casting a cozy glow over the space. The walls were adorned with posters and photographs. The floors were made of worn, creaky wooden planks that added to the rustic charm of the place.

The bar counter stretched across one side of the room, showcasing an array of aged bottles and glassware. Behind the bar, shelves stacked with liquor bottles created a colorful backdrop. The only bartender, dressed in a crisp white shirt and suspenders, skillfully mixed drinks and engaged in lively conversations with people who walked in with their requests.

Small, weathered tables and chairs were scattered throughout the tavern, each adorned with a simple, checkered tablecloth. The seating area exuded an intimate and convivial atmosphere, with patrons huddled closely together, sharing stories and muted laughter echoing forth. The soft hum of conversation filled the air, accompanied by the occasional clink of glasses and laughter. A vintage jukebox sat in the corner, playing tunes that transported people back in time. The melodies added a touch of nostalgia and whimsy to the ambiance, encouraging lively dance moves and tapping feet. In the far corner of the tavern was a brick fireplace that would provide a comforting warmth during colder evenings. Toni was seated at a table for two. From David's description of her, Farmani had no trouble recognizing her.

He quickly joined her and asked, "Toni?"

She extended her hand and said, "Farmani, I presume. Cohen told me a little about you." She had a quiet but deep voice that was in stark contrast with her petite build. She spoke quickly and clearly. Everything about her seemed competent, brisk, and time-saving. Her whole manner seemed to suggest that she did not believe in idle chit-chat. It was as if she could have been out on a mission right this minute, and she was indirectly hinting at the time she was losing being here and giving you her time. Merely being in her presence made one want to apologize for using up her precious time.

Farmani assessed her as being quick-witted and efficient. He knew that this was a woman he could rely on. But he had questions for her first. "Do you think you could help me with moving people quickly out of the city?"

"Yes, we have been working on this for a while now. We have safe houses here, some in Vichy and other parts of the country. We can assist them into the hands of others like me. There is a network of sorts, though we are scattered and resources are scarce," she said.

"I can supply the documentation. There are a few whose identity I would like to be kept buried. Some may need assistance going abroad. Does your reach go that far?" Farmani asked.

"We can assist, but we will need the means. We don't get donations. It is hard, and the Nazis are hiking up the prices of everything. If they can pay, we can make arrangements. It is not a hundred percent foolproof, but we have managed to get quite a few across to Spain and Portugal," Toni said. She was fiddling with the sleeve of her tunic that reached her elbow. Though she was trying hard not to show it, it seemed like she was impatient, ready to charge ahead on a mission.

Farmani asked again, "How much notice do you want before a target has to be moved?"

She looked at him and smiled a little. "You're one with a lot of questions, aren't you? We need a week or so at least. We can work faster, but the chances of mistakes are higher when there is little to no preparation. You understand that, don't you?"

"Quite," Farmani said before continuing, "These people rely on me, and I gave them my word of honor. I wouldn't want to let them down. Yes, we will provide the means. I understand you won't be able to sustain the project without funds. Have you heard of the roundups?"

"Yes. We have heard of it. It doesn't seem long before it will happen. In fact, there are reports that it might even happen before August—more like mid-July, though that's not officially confirmed," she said.

"Oh!" Farmani had not heard this, and he hoped fervently that he would have enough time. He collected himself and asked, "How many of you are there in your team?"

"I think that would be best left unanswered. Just as I don't expect you to tell me how many work on your side. If there is a breach in the operations, I feel it would be safer for everyone involved not to know too many details. I will be your point of contact, just as David or you will be mine. For now, I think this is best," Toni said, weighing her words carefully.

"You are the expert. But how can I contact you?" Farmani asked again.

"Just send word through any of the bartenders here. They know where to find me," she said. She was still fidgety. Farmani thought of a little dog on the scent of a bone, being restricted on a leash. Toni Laurent's restlessness was contagious. Even he was feeling that she ought to be set loose on her mission.

"Okay," he said. "Do you have any questions you would like to ask me?" he asked her.

"I think we should devise codes. It would be faster to carry to each other, and even if the couriers were caught, there would be no leakage of the message because they wouldn't know what they were carrying," she said this fast. Farmani did not even notice when she pushed a tiny booklet into his hand.

He deftly conveyed the booklet into his coat pocket. "But what about..."

She did not let him complete the question as she said, "I have different codes with different people. Yours is a new pattern. You don't have to worry that the messages will be decoded or passed on by somebody on my side. Your booklet will tell you how to code your messages to me. I will use the same code to answer you or send you new messages."

Farmani couldn't help but marvel at her intelligence. She was simply great at her job. She could even answer his unasked questions.

"Are there more questions for me?" Her eyebrows were arched, and a humorous smile was playing around the corners of Toni's lips.

Farmani couldn't help but smile at her in turn. "Why are you here, Toni? What's in this for you?" He was curious. Why a young woman should throw herself heart and soul into a deadly mission such as this confounded him. It wasn't that there weren't women like her, but they were few in number and scattered. He wondered what had inspired her to become a Resistance fighter.

She shrugged, and suddenly, the friendly smile had vanished. She stared at him stonily as she said, "Same as you, I guess? I just want to serve my country. There is no tragic story of a lost husband or lover, I assure you. I want to do what I think will help France. I can't stand it being soiled by Nazi pigs. I assume there is nothing forcing you to help Jews either, right?"

"Only wanting to see justice prevail, I suppose," Farmani agreed.

"Well then. That's that. You and I, we are just kindred souls," she said. She took up the glass of cheap liquor that was in front of her and said, "Santé" before gulping its contents.

"Santé," Farmani said cheerfully as he raised his glass to his lips. As she was getting up to leave, he said, "One more thing. I could use a few extra hands. If there are some of your friends who would want to help out, I would be very grateful."

She nodded once and said, "I think I can find at least a few who would want to teach the Nazis a lesson. I'll see if they are amenable. I will send word if I find candidates up for it."

She drained the last of her drink and then quickly got up and moved—or rather slid gracefully into the cover of darkness. Farmani sat a while contemplating the stroke of good luck that had put him in touch with people like David and Toni Laurent. But for the war, he might never have met them in this life, he mused.

***

Things started moving pretty quickly with Toni Laurent and David Cohen by his side. Farmani, with Cohen's aid, identified Jews who needed to cross over to Iran or neighboring regions. Farmani then supplied them with the papers that were needed. Without too many questions asked, the staff of the Iranian embassy supplied him with the relevant papers, exactly as per his directives. He passed it on to the people waiting to leave the country either directly or via Toni Laurent.

Things started gathering further momentum when non-Iranians started approaching him. Initially, Farmani had focused on helping the Jews of his country. However, very soon, there were others—non-Iranians who were relatives or spouses of Iranian Jews who came to him. People wanting help had heard of the Iranian consul. They suggested him to others who wanted the same help. As more people flocked to his office, he found it hard to refuse them aid merely because they weren't of his nationality. He decided that he would just close his eyes, hope for the best, and hand them over the documents.

He justified his actions by asking himself what difference there would be between the Nazis and himself if he differentiated people based on whether they belonged to his country or not. To him, even entertaining thoughts of such prejudice seemed bigoted, especially when he considered that such a small favor on his part could make the difference between saving their lives and handing them over into the extermination camps.

Operation Lifeline, as it was aptly named, began thus in the last week of June and gathered speed by July. Its main task, at this stage, was mainly only to issue papers for the people who wanted to leave the country but were held prisoner by their Jewish status. By July, Farmani had already issued sixty or more papers allowing whole families to flee France.

He understood the risks involved but continued issuing passports anyway.

Chapter 8:

On the Radar: 05 July 1942

Captain Klaus Richter was in his office. His hat was placed beside him on his desk. Like his person, his cabin and desk were the epitome of neatness. There were only a few files stacked tidily upon it. If you opened the desk drawer, you would find the bare necessary writing tools and stationery organized from what he would be most likely to use to the one he would hardly use.

Richter's office was part of a once stately home that had belonged to a French citizen who had fled and left the country. The entrance to the house was via an ornate wrought iron gate now guarded by two men in German uniforms. A short driveway led to the front porch, where a few chairs were placed for visitors. It was plain that these chairs were a Nazi addition. Though utilitarian, they matched neither the beauty nor the taste with which the rest of the rooms of the house were furnished. A spacious living room was now converted into a foyer where more important guests could wait. The furniture was merely rearranged for more space, not dismantled or removed. Richter's office was located in one of the top bedrooms. Here, of course, the bed and other large furniture had been removed so that small-partitioned workstations could be accommodated. Richter's desk was right beside a window that offered a view of the city square, and the other desks were removed from his as if to provide him space and privacy. It was by far the best workstation a man of his ranking could hope for.

He was the embodiment of discipline. He believed that being organized in little things translated into being meticulous about bigger plans in life too. If there was one word that Klaus Richter would have liked to describe himself, it would have been *ambitious*. He knew that he had a lot to accomplish and give to his fatherland.

Once long ago, Richter had harbored hopes of becoming a teacher. While he was at school, he had the intelligence and love for scholarship that might have made him an excellent teacher. But fate had other plans for him. Perhaps it was not so much fate but more his father's worldview and contacts that shaped who he had become.

General Richter, Captain Richter's father, was a decorated soldier who served his country in the Great War. The tough old man had wanted his only son to become a "real man" in all senses of the term. Teaching, according to the old man, was for weaklings—men who could not use their strength and intelligence to fight for their country and serve it more fully. A true German man's duty was to his family and country. Klaus Richter was a dutiful son. He joined one of the best academies in Berlin when he was not yet out of his teen years. The academy shaped him into the man he became.

It was no mean feat. Klaus Richter faced the violence behind the academy's walls in the name of *shaping boys into men* "manfully," indeed. He never once cried when he was punched, made to run naked on the grounds, or beaten up by a group of his seniors. Of course, one mustn't think that Richter was singled out to be abused in this manner. Every new inmate went through the same passage of rites as he did. Some refused to stay and ran away before the third month was up, while others, like Richter, steeled themselves to stay back no matter what the cost. It was at the academy, during one of the more brutal "training sessions," that Richter inherited his scar as well. In a bayonet fighting drill, one of his classmates—a senior and much bigger boy had been aggressive and attacked him before he was ready. Their trainer never chastised the boy. Instead, the boys were only given a long lecture about how to "expect the unexpected during the war," as Richter kept bleeding. After the class, another student was instructed to "stitch him up." Without any anesthetic to dull the pain, Richter stood without moving a muscle as the other boy cleaned and stitched up the gash on his cheek.

As a young man, his ideals about German manhood metamorphosed as he became more drawn to Hitler's oratory on Aryanism. He was thrilled that Adolf Hitler also seemed to understand the importance of crafting tough men who would not let down the country in another war, should it come. He enlisted in the Hitler Youth program without any hesitation, hoping to provide his services anywhere the higher-ups thought fit. He was disappointed at its temporary disbanding in 1923 when Hitler was arrested for what Richter considered a noble attempt of duty to the German state. However, at 16, Richter did not want to take a chance on his own future. He kept his head down and completed his education.

By the time Richter reached his final years at the academy, he was no longer one among the tormented. The tables had turned, and he got to exercise the same rituals exercised on him on some poor fresher. All the juniors who had undergone "ragging" from Klaus Richter and his gang remembered his pitiless eyes that brooked no mercy. They knew better than to beg or plead with him. Klaus Richter, like other patriots around him, was convinced by then that the ideal of manhood lay in the suffering one could take. Since this was the standard he held himself to, he expected nothing less from the men around him. He was only as exacting on others as he was on himself.

After completing his studies, Richter rejoined the wings of the Nazi youth movement when it was reinstated in 1926. He followed the rise of the Nazi party closely. He was convinced that only good could ensue for the country via Nazism. He was elated when Hitler took up the mantle of power in 1933. It meant that the citizens of Germany also believed that change could happen only via strategic aggression. Klaus Richter believed that the time was finally ripe for him to become more active in his service to his country. He had been waiting patiently for the right time.

During the years just before the war, he went on to enlist and serve in the paramilitary corps and might have made it into the higher ranks of the army eventually. But a chance encounter with a senior SS officer who had been impressed with Richter's ambition and drive had led to his induction into the elite secret service force of the Nazi government. He had taken it up enthusiastically because he knew he could serve Germany better in office than on the battlefields. He had taken up a junior role willingly, setting sights on the greatness that was sure to come his way as he rose through the SS. As the Nazi government strengthened its hold over the nation, he worked in several SS offices across the country until the glorious day that France fell into Nazi hands. He had then been stationed in Paris to report to the government in Berlin periodically, a duty he took very seriously indeed.

Klaus Richter had no real human vices to speak of. This was also a testament to his towering patriotic sentiment. He was a virtual teetotaler, except when social etiquette demanded it. He never smoked. He valued his health and fitness. He believed they were his gifts to his country and knew that he needed to preserve himself if he truly sought to serve Germany. He would have served his health on a platter to his country in combat if it was required, but he wouldn't whittle it away by smoking and drinking. He wasn't corrupt, either. He wasn't in the war to make personal profit from it. He believed in the purpose of the war. He wanted to be one of the instruments whereby Germany would win back its glory and honor. It was the same with women for him. Like all men, he had had brief affairs with women over the years. However, he always chose them with utmost care. He would only narrow down on those already married or who did not care to form any attachment. He wanted to be unencumbered in his dedication to his country. Besides, he loved his single lifestyle and bachelor life too much to complicate it with the presence of a woman. He abhorred children and did not miss fathering them either. It would seem that military life was the ideal one for Klaus Richter, after all. He was also a man who actively cultivated reading and intellectualism. He had read Friedrich Nietzsche's works and agreed with every syllable of Hitler's *Mein Kampf* when it was published. He had kept abreast of Henry Ford's tirade against Jews in the *Dearborn Independent,* which was reprinted and circulated in German as well. He loved to think of himself as the perfect combination of brawn and brain.

Today, he was visited with a strange puzzle. With only a few days to go before the imminent roundups that his government was planning, Richter found that Jews were "missing" by the hundreds. He had issued directives to embassies and local administrators to give him the numbers of Jews and non-Jews leaving the country. He added up these numbers, and something did not make sense. Apparently, there were only several Jews leaving the country, and yet, the number of them in their settlement areas was dwindling. This latter report was from the Parisian police force tasked with keeping tabs on the Jewish population.

This could only mean one thing. The Jews were leaving. This did not shock him greatly. One did not expect rats to stay where they detected a threat to themselves. He was, however, perplexed as to why the border security was letting them pass when they had been instructed to scrutinize the papers more carefully and to detain Jews.

At first, he was worried that the Nazis were being bribed to let these fugitives escape. Being a man of honor and ever loyal to his fatherland, this conjecture angered Richter. He had often noted with contemptuous amusement how the French were turning on themselves, collaborating with the Germans, and even giving each other away. On the other hand, the same notion about a German galled him. He believed there could be no greater sin than turning against your own country. He was determined that if there was even one corrupt Nazi allowing Jews to pass through the net in exchange for baubles, he would personally tackle the man.

However, it would seem that Richter had been too harsh and rash in judging the character of his fellow Nazis. The border security, in turn, reported that among the people leaving, there seemed to be an unprecedented number of Iranians. More than half the people wanting to leave could produce seemingly valid Iranian passports. Interestingly, these passports had no mention of the religion of the person, which was why the security forces were finding it hard to detain them. He looked at the names of the people who had been let through and frowned. He couldn't understand why passports did not carry the religion of the holder. Every ID paper issued by the Reich had a mention of the ethnicity of the person. It seemed natural that occupied lands should also have this same requirement on their identification papers. Iranians in France ought to have their religious affiliation on their passports.

He made some discreet calls and found out the name of the Iranian consul. At first, Richter could not place the name, though it did seem vaguely familiar. Finally, he remembered the man with whom he had played cards. His whole attention was arrested by the memory of that man who had filled him with unmentionable loathing. To him, there was not much difference between a Persian and a Jew. For all he knew, this Farmani himself could have been a Jew masquerading as a Muslim and playing everyone false. He could tell that Farmani was a libertarian who loved music, wine, and women. He remembered how Dubois kept supplying the young man with drinks and how they chatted through the party. This intensified his disgust for the man. That such a hedonist should be in a position to decide the fate of his people was telling about the Iranian state itself, according to Richter. *A decadent employee of a decadent state*, Richter thought.

Next, he called some of the bigwigs and asked what exactly was happening with Iran and what the German stance on Iranians was. After several calls to officials, it was confirmed to him that all Iranians, including Iranian Jews, were exempted from the Nuremberg Laws. What was more, all Iranians were, by default, considered Aryans by blood! Richter realized this conspiracy went higher than a mere consul stationed in Paris.

"Letters have been doing the rounds in Berlin about how Iranian Jews are Jugutis and Aryan by birth," said a contact over the phone.

"And what the hell are Jugutis?" Richter asked incredulously.

"Well, it seems historically speaking, these Jugutis were Persian Jews who were assimilated into their culture by marriage. They have been given the Aryan status too," the voice confirmed.

"So they are Jews, aren't they?" Richter was now thoroughly confused.

A sigh at the other end was followed by, "I guess so. But at present, they aren't subject to the Nuremberg Laws."

Richter wasn't one to give up so easily. He persisted, "These letters. Do you know the source of them?"

"Well, I don't know the name of the author, but word has it that it is from the Iranian consul to Paris," the other person said.

"I see," Richter said. He had an ugly smile as he fingered the scar that ran across his cheek. The numerous phone calls, long wait times, and holds had not been a total waste. He might not have a legal way yet to detain these Jews slipping through, but a plan was forming in his devious mind.

The exemption made no sense to him. *Why should a few Jews be spared when the whole lot of them were nothing but an impediment to the wheels of German progress?* It seemed that he should write to somebody in authority urging them to reconsider this silly clause. It seemed to him that a mere technicality was preventing the Nazis from using the final solution more effectively. He was also bothered about how unscrupulous elements such as this meddling consul might use the loophole to save Jews other than Iranian ones.

It should be said here that Klaus Richter saw himself as a man of "justice." It seemed to him only fair that laws should be uniform in their application. Either they should apply to all or none (of the Jews). His upbringing on the Nazi-Aryan staple did not, for a moment, make him question the humanity of the Jews. He was convinced they deserved the treatment being meted out to them. He was irritated at the suspicion that some pseudo-scholarship and a former alliance with the Shah of Iran was blinding the Führer and keeping confirmed rogues safe from the desserts they richly deserved. Richter reasoned that now that Iran was a Soviet-British ally, Germany ought to scrap the exemption granted to the Iranians. He wondered how to get ahead of this problem. He wanted the maximum number of Jews to be rounded up in Paris when the time came.

Wondering about the lack of a "religion" column in the passport again, Richter was struck with a thought. *What if these papers were not being issued by the government of Iran?* He thought back to Farmani. Suddenly, he wondered if it was that man's doing. He did not put it past a rat like Farmani to fish in troubled waters. The ongoing war, general mayhem, and lack of a uniform code would make it perfect for an anarchist like Farmani to help get the Jews off the hook. The more he thought about it, the more it all made sense. It was like the pieces of a puzzle falling into place. The fact that the escaped Jews were thought to be carrying Iranian passports and the German official tally of Jewish residents in the city did not match the lists sent from the consular offices, which declared a much smaller number—everything seemed to add up now. Where were all these missing Jews? What if they were not missing but masquerading in plain sight as *Aryans*? The mere thought made him boil with rage.

Interestingly, Richter had no doubts that Farmani was behind the issuance of these scam papers. He had known instinctively that the man was not to be trusted, even on that day when they were playing cards. There had been something so slick about the chap that the German hated. He had hated the guts of the man preaching to him that Iranians were immune to the Nazi laws. How dare Farmani attempt to teach him the laws of his own country! He thought with smug satisfaction about how he had forced him to intone "Heil Hitler."

However, he also knew enough about life to know that a man like Farmani would have several tricks up his sleeve. His contempt for the Persian did not for a moment detract from the natural caution he knew he ought to exercise against him. For Richter assessed correctly that though Farmani may be a careless sensualist in his personal pursuits, he was capable of being loyal to a cause. He also recognized that Farmani could be an intelligent and courageous opponent—one hard to exterminate if he himself did not proceed with caution. So Klaus Richter decided to do exactly that. He decided he would find a way to catch the slippery Persian right in the middle of his bluff. The idea came to him in a flash. In fact, he was so pleased by the simple, even unoriginal, solution that presented itself that he allowed himself the luxury of a smile.

He summoned Lieutenant Heinrich Müller and told him everything. Müller was only too willing to please and do the bidding of the older man.

Müller scratched his head and asked, "What do you think we can do? It seems we need to keep an eye on him."

Richter smiled and said, "Precisely. We need to know the people working with him and then catch the man right in the middle of his game."

"How so?" Müller asked. He was always a little slow to catch on, and Richter loved this sidekick to whom he could explain things in detail. An egoist, Richter loved to demonstrate his intelligence at work. It also happened that, at times while speaking to Müller, he could refine his ideas and think of new lines of working based on the younger man's questions.

"We get someone on the inside to spill the beans on him," Richter was now smiling widely. The other man watched on in fascination. It was rarely that one got to see Richter in such a happy frame of mind.

"A mole?" Müller asked a tad belatedly.

"Yes. That's what we should aim for. He must have a team that knows at least a part of the plan. We get to them," Richter said.

Müller asked persistently, "We bribe them?"

"Either that, or we need to find recruits who would be willing to infiltrate their network. Of course, if they are discovered, then they would be a liability to us. But that is a risk that we will have to take. Let us see what we can do," Richter said.

Müller nodded in silence.

After Müller left, Richter was still thoughtful. Surely, there was more he could do even without confronting Farmani directly. He thought again about the letters that were being circulated as proof of the fact that Iranians were "full-blooded Aryans." The official he had spoken to had confirmed that they had been written by the Iranian consul to Paris. Richter had no doubt that Farmani could be eloquently persuasive when the situation demanded it. These letters, until refuted by the Reich, would be used by the man to continue his clandestine operations. Unless the Nazi government issued a counter-law revoking the status given to the Iranians, there was not anything that he or other officers could do about the Jews who were fleeing and who claimed they were Iranians. He had to do something fast to ensure a dialogue was opened about this issue in Berlin. From experience, he knew that orders that came from there could not be refuted or rejected.

He took up a pen and paper and started writing down a few points for a letter. This would be only an initial draft. He had to ensure that he got the facts and tone of the letter right. He did not want to sound like a vindictive man who was trying to get another official into trouble. He did not want to get credit as a whistleblower. Instead, he would only raise some concerns about the status of Iranian nationals and ask for clarifications. He knew he would need to be extremely cautious because he did not know anybody in Berlin so far high up in the ranks. He did not, at all costs, want to sound like an upstart and unnecessary troublemaker. The aim here was not to draw attention to himself.

Two can play this game, he thought as he continued writing to one of the leading officers of the SS in Berlin. If anyone should hear of the bogus nature of these claims, it should be none other than one of the chief architects of the final solution itself, Richter thought smugly. As a member of the SS himself, it would also look natural for Richter to be addressing one of his superiors about a doubt he had regarding the nature of the claims being circulated about these so-called Jugutis. Richter hoped that Otto Adolf Eichmann, who, if rumors were to be believed, had the ears of the Führer himself, would not be so busy as to completely disregard the letter he was penning to him. He hoped that just as Farmani's letters were creating a notion about the Iranians, this letter of his would pose enough questions to plant the seeds of doubt in the minds of the racial ideologists in Berlin to question and hopefully thwart the "Juguti" claim.

Chapter 9:

Unlikely Allies: 05-07 July 1942

It was Toni Laurent who introduced Hans Gauthier to the team. Hans used to be a locksmith before the war started. He had a slight limp owing to a hunting accident when he was younger. He had thankfully not been recruited by the Nazis to the warfront. He was excellent at forging documents. You could give him any paper, and he would reproduce it with just the details you wanted. Toni knew him from her line of work with the Resistance and thought he would be a good addition to the team Farmani was building. Farmani was greatly appreciative of Toni's dynamism and verve to help him out. He couldn't thank David enough for looping her in.

Toni had sent a coded message via a young boy who hand-delivered it to Farmani at the office. The note cryptically said: *Have a person of interest for you. 7 O'clock at L'Auberge du Chat Noir in Rue de la Fosse. He will use my code name. -Toni.*

Farmani knew the venue. It was a homely and discreet establishment tucked away in the heart of the city, frequented by locals and travelers alike. The inn's ambiance and charm made it a popular spot for those seeking refuge or a quiet retreat. Almost as soon as he entered the establishment, a man who seemed to be going past bumped into him. He said, "Thank the lord the stars are bright tonight it is pitch black outside."

Farmani followed the tall man. The man had said "stars," but it was close enough to what Toni had mentioned in the note. They turned a corner, and Gauthier waved Farmani to a small

107

park that was still open. They took a bench beneath a tall tree. There were a few couples and lone walkers. The starlit sky offered some light. Otherwise, the park was lit by a single lamp post at its center.

Gauthier was a tall, taciturn man in his early forties with a lean build, standing at around 6 feet 2 inches. He had a strong and wiry frame, suggesting both physical strength and agility. His chiseled jawline and piercing blue eyes seemed to reflect his unwavering attention to detail. His hair, a deep shade of auburn, was neatly trimmed and styled away from his face. It would seem his meticulousness was reflected in his appearance as well. He dressed impeccably in a tailored suit. Its dark color accentuated his sophisticated and mysterious persona.

His main skill was in the fact that he could replicate flawlessly various types of documents, from identification papers to travel visas, helping members of the Resistance navigate through the increasingly restrictive checkpoints. Preferring to work behind the scenes, Gauthier was a master of deception and subterfuge. From their conversation, Farmani gathered that Hans was also good with disguises and an excellent spy when the situation demanded. His tendency to listen without talking too much almost always got his subjects to talk freely.

Farmani wanted to be as direct as possible with Gauthier. "So, will you be able to provide the necessary papers? How long will it take?"

Gauthier, who was smoking, said in between great puffs, "It will take me a day or two. You have to give me a clear picture of what exactly you want."

Farmani said, "Of course." He couldn't contain his curiosity as he asked, "Do you have others working with you?"

Gauthier barely looked at Farmani as he said, "Yes. The officials have left us alone because everyone thinks we are artists working out of our studio. Some of us are painters, and we keep up the farce. Every time there is an inspection, we show them our work."

Farmani asked, "I have another question. Can you alter official papers too? Take out stamps and imprints made on it?

Gauthier said with a chuckle, "Sure can. Learned it from a friend who was in the dry cleaners. Lactic acid can erase ink without leaving much of a trace. It is a neat little trick, is it not?"

Farmani was delighted that Gauthier would help in providing documents that the people they were helping could use at the borders and check posts. Some of these papers could be prepared at the embassy too, but he did not want too many questions or comments going up to his seniors in Iran. With Gauthier, there was no such threat. He could work as a free agent irrespective of what his government demanded of him and issue the papers here in his official capacity. Nobody in this country or at his home would be the wiser. It was the most perfect arrangement possible under the circumstances.

***

Karl Gagnon, the second ally that Farmani would come across, came to him, so to say. He was an ex-policeman who had a grudge against the Nazis. He had lost his girlfriend, who had been a Jew. She had converted and was on the verge of marrying him, but the authorities did not seem to care. She had vanished a couple of months ago, and all attempts to trace her had failed. In a last-ditch attempt, Gagnon had walked into the Iranian embassy to check if anyone matching her description had recently claimed papers from Farmani's office. Farmani looked at the papers carefully, scrutinized her photo, and asked Gagnon for his. Everything looked legitimate. He had to tell

Gagnon that nobody by that name or description had come to him. He was beginning to feel a little sorry for the man.

Gagnon held his head in his hands, "They have taken Rachel. I am sure of it. Those swine! I wanted her to flee from here when the chance presented itself, but she wouldn't. She thought my influence would be enough to save her. That's what I thought too. They told me all I would have to do was get her the right papers, and she would be okay." The man was in great distress as he said this.

Farmani felt bad, but he had to ask, "I am so sorry. Why did you think you would find her here? Was she Iranian?"

The man was distraught. "To be honest, I don't quite know. I was at wit's end, trying to see how she could escape this hell hole. They told me Iranian and Argentinian Jews were being let off. I heard it via the official network. I was desperate to believe it and I had told her I would try to get her the papers. But even before I could work out a plan, she disappeared. She's nowhere to be seen. The other Jews in the city haven't seen or heard from her."

Much as Farmani wanted to help this man, he also wanted to be certain of him. He asked him, "Where did you hear that Iranian and Argentinian Jews were being spared?"

"I work as a cop, remember? I heard it from my friends who were pals with German officers. I was still working for them at the time. I never really paid much attention. I thought I could get her the double immunity of the Iranian embassy if it came to that—if she had any difficulties with her papers. As it stood, she was classified as a French Jew," Gagnon said.

Karl Gagnon possessed a strong build, with broad shoulders and a determined posture. His thick, dark brown hair was neatly combed back, revealing a high forehead. His grey eyes seemed to reflect intelligence and anguish. His face was marked by worry lines etched across his forehead and deep-set furrows between his eyebrows. His strong jawline was lost in a stubbled chin. He was wearing a worn-out brown leather jacket, under which was a simple white button-down shirt, neatly tucked into dark trousers, paired with scuffed leather shoes that had seen better days.

"And then?" Farmani pressed. He wanted to know as much as possible about Gagnon.

"After she vanished, I searched everywhere, but there was no trace of her. It was as if she had never existed at all," he said. He continued after a pause, "It was only because I had taken her papers to get them approved by my superiors that I still have them with me. But for them, even I might have suspected that I was going mad and that I had imagined her into existence," he said. He ran a hand over his chin, which could definitely use a shave.

"How long did you know her?" Farmani asked.

"We met just before the occupation started. She was studying to be a teacher at the time." He suppressed a big sob that seemed to take even him by surprise. His eyes frowned in an attempt to blink back tears. There was a tic at the corner of his lips that threatened to give away his emotional turmoil any minute now.

Farmani felt sorry for this young man who could have been only a little younger than him at most. To lose a partner you loved dearly in this manner was difficult. Even death was better, in a sense. It gave you better closure than when a loved one went missing. You desperately kept hoping they would return, and yet, you wonder if it were not better for them to die rather than suffer somewhere where you could not reach them.

"After she disappeared, did you not try to use your connections?" Farmani asked. He wondered how a policeman could not have seen this coming. The French collaborators usually knew the German plans a little ahead of time. But then again, it all depended on how high up or deep your reach went. If senior Nazis knew you in person, there was a lot you could accomplish, and rules could be bent to accommodate you.

"Of course I did," Gagnon thundered, momentarily angered that someone should suggest that he had slacked on his duty to his woman. "I asked everywhere I could and literally ran from pillar to post, enquiring about her. But nobody seemed to know. Or those who knew wouldn't tell me." He looked at Farmani apologetically and then said, "I'm sorry to have raised my voice, but you can't imagine how I feel. She was my—everything. She had even converted for my sake and had ostracized herself from her folks, who fled back to Israel without her. I feel so guilty about not having taken better care of her. You must think me the worst kind of man to have for a fiancé."

Farmani was reminded of Eva when Gagnon said these words, and he was suddenly filled with pity for this big man. Eva's family, too, had left her behind, and suddenly, Farmani could understand Gagnon's plight. He knew it must be terribly hard to feel like you have let down a person who depended on you for support and help. He wondered how he would feel if Eva was punished for his actions. He suppressed the terrible thought even as it rose to his mind.

He added, "I can understand your plight. Please do not beat yourself up over this. It is unfortunate, but you could not have known or prepared for every eventuality."

Gagnon hardly seemed to have heard his words as he continued, "I have not gone back to the force, and they have dropped me from their list of collaborators. Neither did I want to continue working for them. I went in the first place only because I wanted to protect her. Now, I have no motive to work with the murderers who stole my love. I wish I knew what to do. I will continue searching for her, but God knows that I would teach them a lesson if I knew how."

Fists clenched and breathing hard through his nostrils, Gagnon reminded Farmani of a raging bull on a rampage. He thought that he wouldn't want to be the Nazi Gagnon was hunting down. Farmani had a quick vision of what an ally a man such as Gagnon would make for his team. Yet, there was something holding him back from asking him the question or telling him more about himself. It was self-preservation for the most part. He wondered if it was prudent to show one's hand so soon. There were German and French spies working for the Nazis.

Gagnon wasn't German, Farmani was sure. However, he couldn't entirely be sure if all this story about a missing Jewish girl was a ruse to lure Farmani into indiscretion. On the other hand, time was of the essence too. He had to pick his team fast and start chalking out a plan of action as soon as possible. There was no telling when the Germans would start rounding up the Jews in the city. Besides, who could tell if any of his other allies were who they claimed to be? What was to prevent some of them from working for the Germans later? Stranger things had happened during wartime. Out of necessity, coercion, or compulsion, people could always turn around and join the other team.

Well, Farmani mused he himself wasn't being entirely honest with his country. The Shah certainly did not want government representatives to actively work against Germany, which was still an Iranian trading partner. Yet, here he was helping Jews against the Nazis. A few years ago, Farmani would never have dreamed of going against the Shah's directives. But things were different. How could anyone look away and follow orders when that action (or was it inaction?) killed innocent people?

Farmani was torn between taking on this stranger who did not have the credentials of the French Resistance to recommend him and yet, letting him go his way also seemed a colossal waste when he knew he needed more hands on the team.

Finally, he told Gagnon, "Just let me know where you stay, and I will send you word if I meet her or she happens to come here. Just give me some time."

Gagnon rose to leave and said, "Thank you. I appreciate your gesture. I know there is little hope, and it seems impossible that there should be news of her after so much time. Let me know what I can do if there is anything to help you. You have been one of the rare kind voices who did not turn me away at once. For that, I am grateful, if not anything else."

Farmani told him, "I only did my duty. I will let you know if there's any development."

The two men shook hands before Gagnon left. Farmani spent some time going over the story the man had narrated and tried to recall any inconsistencies that he may have heard. One couldn't be too sure in matters like these. He finally thought to himself that he was being paranoid. He decided he would ask David and Toni's opinion and then go ahead and adopt Gagnon into the operation, should they agree to it. But instinctively, Farmani also knew that Karl Gagnon would not be a man to let such an opportunity pass through his hands without grabbing at it. Gagnon seemed like a man who would enjoy teaching the Nazis a lesson.

***

Gagnon's fiancé wasn't the only missing person that Farmani would hear about that day. David Cohen soon reported back to him about Miriam. He narrated Miriam's story or as much of it as he could piece together from his observations and talking to people who knew her. Eva's Jewish companion had lost a brother not very long ago. He had vanished just like several other Jews seemed to be disappearing overnight in German-occupied lands. David, true to his word, had followed Miriam and enquired about her. Apparently, a German officer by the name of Von Falken had been pursuing her relentlessly. Most of the Jews in the area whom David spoke to were sure that Von Falken had something to do with Aaron's disappearance. Of course, there was no proof except for the fact that the two men had had a falling out not so long ago, with Aaron having shouted at the Nazi that he would "kill him if he ever approached his sister again." It was just after this that he had disappeared under mysterious circumstances. Miriam had, of course, tried to search for him, but she had no allies to help her, and she knew that Von Falken might have had a hand in it. Times were such that there was only so much help that Jewish subjects could expect from the state.

As far as her relationship with her employer was concerned, Miriam was devoted to Eva Klein and had stayed back even with the occupation just so that she could be of assistance to her. The two were inseparable, and recently, Miriam had been staying more with Eva, possibly because of Von Falken's unwelcome advances. The man had been heard jokingly telling whoever would listen to him that "Miriam was his." He had seen her at the opera and claimed to be "in love" with her. He wanted to set her up as his mistress in the city. She had declined several times, and yet the man only seemed to pursue her with renewed vigor. Everyone who knew Miriam knew that the man terrified her and filled her with disgust. However, she knew she was helpless against him and could not report him to the French or German authorities. As a Jew, she had no rights as a citizen. David also told Farmani that the only reason the two women had not asked for help so far was because they no longer knew who was a collaborator and who was working with the Resistance groups. They were quite confused about who to turn to help for. Both of them had very few reliable contacts in the city since the occupation.

David felt that moving Miriam from the city to one of the safe houses would be the wisest thing to do if they wanted to save her. But it was also a dangerous mission, especially because she was already in the gaze of the German officer. Von Falken was a lunatic, and someone who knew him closely told David that the Nazi had a penchant for torturing people in general. With Jews, his cruelty would leap to unbridled proportions. He derived a sadistic pleasure from making people suffer. Miriam could not keep rebuffing his advances for long. He would soon lose his temper and do something nasty to her or to people she loved to teach her a lesson.

Farmani's blood ran cold when he heard the last statement. He knew that even Eva could be at risk as long as Miriam was constantly seen with her. To save Eva, he would have to save Miriam too. He would have to do something sooner rather than later to ensure that Miriam was conveyed somewhere safe until the German officer found another target and lost interest in her. It would be risky to move her, but there was no way around it if they wanted to save her. German men now acted more entitled than the citizens of France.

There was no telling when Von Falken would do something more drastic than just asking Miriam to be his mistress. Though they were prohibited by their own laws from pursuing sexual relationships with Jews, Farmani knew of several Nazis who exploited Jewish women for sport. It was a dangerous situation and one that had to be averted at all costs.

Farmani thought for a while and then quickly took out his notepad. He scribbled a few lines. To a common reader, the note contained instructions about delivering a certain kind of French cuisine for a celebration to be hosted at the embassy. The message also contained a line saying how important the cuisine was to the success of the party. He asked David to hand over the note in person to Toni Laurent. He was to wait for her reply and bring it back to Farmani at the earliest.

Once David departed, Farmani sat back in his chair, deep in thought. He wondered if Toni would take on the assignment. He would have to tell her the risks in more detail, of course. She needed to know that the target was already being monitored by the Nazis and that, therefore, the operation would have to move under utmost discretion and at lightning speed. He hoped Toni would be part of the mission in person. He felt confident in her abilities to take necessary action. He did not know the other operatives and was apprehensive that somebody less experienced might make a mistake that would give away the game for everybody.

His anxiety was soon answered by a return note from Toni. It was delivered not by David but by the young boy she often used to run her errands. The note was a simple one confirming the delivery of the cuisine by a certain time the next day. It affirmed the delivery of the dish by none less than the baker himself. Farmani sank back into his chair, breathing a sigh of relief. It was great to have an ally with such zeal.

Chapter 10:

Love Amidst Shadows: 10 July 1942

It was a trying day for Farmani at the consular office. It was not just the weather, which was hot, but also his distractedness. He had just rolled up his sleeves to the elbow and had decided to tackle the many files that faced him when the telephone in his office rang. It was the routine call from Tehran asking how things were going.

After giving them his updates on the situation in Paris, he tried to ask about the progress of his letter and whether the Shah would speak to the Führer soon about a renewal of the promise given to the Iranians, but his superior had no knowledge of what was happening on that front. He had dutifully handed over the letter to the Shah's personal secretary, and that is where his power ceased.

The man advised him, "You need to be patient, young man. The Shah will take up the matter if he feels it is of importance."

Farmani said, "But a renewal of the promise would mean diplomatic immunity for all our countrymen and women. The Nazis are rounding up Jews faster now, and without a clear consensus on how Persians are to be treated, many of our citizens could end up being transported to the dreaded camps."

His superior only said, "Well, diplomacy takes time. You know how it is with the Shah being caught between the Soviets, the British, and the Germans. He can't openly lobby for an Aryan label for his people. It wouldn't go down well with the Allied forces."

Farmani was bitterly disappointed that his country was not taking a more proactive role in seeing to it that its citizens were safe. But looking at it practically, he also knew that things like these could not be rushed. He would simply have to wait and watch how the story unfolded.

Just as the call ended, he thought he heard a soft knock on his door. He was surprised because he had been pretty sure that David Cohen was out meeting with some more people who had asked for their assistance in leaving the country. He could not think who else would come to meet him at this hour unless there were others who had come to him directly to ask for the same favor.

It would be untrue to say that Farmani was not beginning to feel intensely tensed each time he issued a new passport. Every single document with his signature was also one that his seniors in Vichy or Iran were unaware of. If word got around about what he was doing, he could be held for treason for issuing government-authorized papers without permission from the higher officials. While he used the embassy staff to prepare documents for people—mostly those who posed no real problems—he relied heavily on Gauthier and his team to do the rest of the work for others who might struggle to get permits. The last couple of documents that had gone through his hands were not even for Iranian nationals. Those were for Jews who were married to Iranian Jews. Technically, he should have taken permission before issuing those papers, but by now, Farmani's only motive was to save as many as he could. To him, whether they were Iranians or not did not matter. They were people, and they deserved just as much of a right to live as anybody else.

Gauthier had proven to be a worthy ally who rose to the occasion and crafted documents that would have beaten the originals in their seeming authenticity. He was as swift as he was discreet, and Farmani never once doubted his loyalty. Soon, he was also planning to rope in Gagnon for help regarding the logistics. Who would know the city better than an ex-policeman who must have access to information on people and areas within the city? He could still have friends on the force who might tip him off about locations where more safe houses could be established. However, as Operation Lifeline was getting stronger, Farmani was also uneasy that he might attract the suspicion of the more eagle-eyed Nazis. He also had confirmation from a few reliable French sources working in an administrative capacity that the Nazi roundups were about to happen around the 16th or 17th of July. The dates, though still unconfirmed, gave him a week in which to plan the escape of a few Jews who had contacted either David or Toni for help a little earlier.

This was why Farmani was startled when the knock came. For a minute, he wondered if it was a random Nazi checking. With what they were planning for the Jews, it wouldn't be so bizarre. With a beating heart, he quickly covered the distance to the door and opened it.

His surprise soon turned to puzzlement and delight when he saw before him Eva Klein standing at his doorstep. She was dressed in a summer dress of pale yellow with puff sleeves that stopped just above her elbows. She donned a matching bonnet and gloves. Even her pretty ballerina shoes with small heels were the same shade of yellow. The sudden presence of color in an otherwise drab office made it seem as if spring had just stepped into his room, and, for a moment, Farmani, usually a man of many words, was left speechless. He had a vague idea why she had come, but he couldn't be sure.

Eva said softly, "I came to thank you. I had to." She was smiling, but her eyes were slightly watery as if she was in some danger of weeping if she did not hold herself in check.

Farmani felt confused but composed himself to reply, "Eva! What a surprise. I do not understand why you are thanking me. But please come in all the same. I am glad to see you."

Eva came in and made herself comfortable in the chair across his table and said, "Please do not pretend ignorance. I know what you did for Miriam. I will remain indebted to you forever for helping her."

Farmani had by then guessed that Eva might have been referring to Miriam earlier, but he still couldn't understand how she knew of his connection in it. He said, "I am glad too that Miriam is safe. But I do not understand why you give thanks when it is not due. I know nothing about what became of her. Why don't you tell me?" This last was a partial truth. Toni had sent him one of her coded messages telling him that Miriam had been removed to safety last night. He wanted to confirm what exactly had happened. He wanted to hear the story from Eva's perspective.

Eva said, shrugging her graceful shoulders, "Very well, if you want to play it that way. A tall young woman with short hair came for Miriam early evening yesterday. She said that it was within her power to save her from the clutches of the German officer I was telling you about. We were apprehensive, of course, and did not readily trust her. For all we knew, she could have been sent by the Nazis to kidnap her. But the young woman assured us that she was part of the Resistance. She seemed to know all about Miriam. She told us that her operatives had confirmed Aaron's—Eva' brother's—

disappearance had been orchestrated by the same Nazi, Von Falken. The initial clandestine roundups had caught the Resistance fighters unawares too. The woman told us they had been unprepared to save the Jews but had kept track of them. Miriam had presumed he was dead, but the young woman—she wouldn't reveal her name—told us that they had word from Aaron. He is being held in one of the Polish camps, but they are working to free him. Miriam still had her doubts, but the woman told her something in Yiddish—a message from her brother, and she was convinced that it was indeed a message from Aaron. The young woman promised me that she would send me word when Miriam reached one of the safe houses. She only asked me to tune into a German station by 3.00 AM this morning, which I dutifully did. At first, I was worried when I heard nothing. But at a quarter past three, I heard Miriam's voice talking to me over the radio—the Resistance has their ways of interrupting Nazi broadcasts looks like. She assured me that she was among friends, safe and sound. She couldn't reveal her identity or where she was, but I recognized her voice at once. I am assuming she must be headed for the south, from where they will transport her out of the country. Only the last line of the message seemed confusing. It was also a bit that had a lot of static, possibly the Germans trying to jam the radio signals. She signed off with, *I owe my life to the Persian prince.*"

Farmani blinked a little, and his confusion was apparent as he said, "I am sorry? Did you hear it wrong, perhaps?"

Eva blushed a little at this and said, "Miriam was convinced that you were a suitor, and she often referred to you by that nickname. At first, I thought she was merely teasing me. But I am almost sure I heard her words right. She said she *owed her life to you*. I did not mishear it, nor can I have constructed a sentence like that out of the blue. It can only mean that you helped save her, though I have no clue how Miriam came by this information. Perhaps the Resistance fighter told her, I do not know. I only know that I am grateful to you. Miriam has

123

been my only source of comfort here, and to have lost her would have been unthinkable."

Farmani remained quiet, but in his head, he was thinking things through. He realized that it was perhaps time Eva knew more about him. He tried not to be distracted pleasantly by the thought that he was a topic of discussion between Eva and her most trusted confidant. He realized that if he and Eva were to even contemplate a future together, she couldn't be kept out of so vital an aspect of him. It was only fair to her and their budding relationship. He said, "There is nothing to thank me for. I merely played a cog in the wheels of justice delivered. I am glad that you approached me and notified me in time so that the Resistance fighters could be of some assistance."

Eva said, "So she was right. I thought a lot about whether I should just keep quiet as you never told me that you were working for such a noble cause. If—"

Farmani hushed her as he said with his jovial crooked smile she had come to love so much, "Shhh. Even the walls have ears here in Paris now, madame. We have talked enough here. Let's move to the cafe outside, where we met the other day. The general din there will make it hard for any eavesdropper to make sense of what we say."

Since it was nearly lunchtime, they strolled over to Cafe Heritage where a few days ago they had sat with Miriam. Farmani could sense that Eva was sad about Miriam's going, even if she was relieved about being out of danger. Though she wanted what was best for her friend, Eva suddenly realized that she was now very alone in this great city occupied by enemies. Farmani gently patted her arm that she had linked through his. She looked up gratefully at him but said nothing. He left her to her thoughts for the moment.

Cafe Heritage was a quaint little place that had more space outside than within. Delicate wrought iron chairs and tables were set on the pavement beside the cobblestone street. Ornate facades and towering buildings around and overlooking it gave the cafe an almost nest-like feeling. Even with the rationing of food, no matter at what time of the day you walked into it, the smell of freshly brewed coffee and pastries wafted through the entire area. The open area of the cafe was a hub of lively conversations and a frequent gathering place for intellectuals, artists, and locals alike. For Farmani, this was the best place for a heart-to-heart conversation because while a spy could watch them, they would find it hard to hear anything being said owing to the general hubbub of the cafe.

Once they were seated comfortably, Farmani ordered pâtés and coffee. The food that was available now was never like it was before the war. The pâtés, for instance, were meatless and mostly made of flour alone, and coffee was more chicory and water with hardly any sugar in it. It was maddening to think that the produce of the country was being channeled for the Nazi army. Eva decided to order a salad. As they ate their meals, occasionally thinking back to times when food and wine always flowed freely in the city, Farmani and Eva felt grateful for each other's company during times such as these. On his part, he felt a weight lift off his chest as he felt he had found at least one other person with whom he could be completely honest.

She finally broke the silence and said, "I wonder when this will end. Sometimes it seems like we will be stuck in it forever."

He looked at her and asked, "The war, you mean?"

She smiled wanly and said, "I suppose it is an unoriginal thought. But I can't help feeling tired of living in the shadows like this."

Farmani said, "It may be unoriginal, but it is true. Nobody is gaining anything by keeping this war going on for so long. However, imagine if you should feel like you are living in the shadows what about the men, women, and children being transported to the camps of Europe? Somebody ought to fight for their sake."

Eva said, "You are right. We have much to be thankful for. At least we aren't being hunted down like animals. And yes, I agree, no matter the hardships on us, nobody deserves the fate being meted out to Jews." She paused for a while as another train of thought struck her, "Miriam's words over the transmission surprised me. I did not think—You did not strike me as—"

He said, "That I would be the selfless kind to put others ahead of me?" He smiled so that the question would not come across as rude to her. "Until the war, I wouldn't have pegged myself down for this role either, I'll admit. I came to this city to enjoy myself, and that has been the center of my life so far. I love good food, wine, and music. But even a hedonist like me cannot turn a blind eye to what is happening. Besides these people—they were once our friends and almost like family. I do not understand how we can see them any differently now. It is like in the blink of an eye, the world has gone mad." He wasn't smiling anymore.

She took some time to frame her next sentence well so that he wouldn't be offended. She finally said, "Kameron Farmani, when I met you for the first time, I assumed you were a self-seeking dandy out to serve your own interests. I wouldn't have blamed you; the war has done that to most people. When I look at people here turning against one another—Well, I am pleased to note that I was mistaken about you. What you are doing is brave. Risky and foolish, some may say, but I am happy there are people like you willing to stick out their necks for justice's sake. It reinforces one's belief in human goodness." She looked at him steadily.

He laughed out loud once and, with a mock bow, said, "I am grateful to have risen in your esteem. But again, you have given me more credit than I deserve. I am only a link between people who need help and the people doing all the work. I can't say there is anything very courageous about what I am doing."

She insisted, "But perhaps that is the need of the hour. How else would all these people find the right people? Miriam's greatest fear in approaching anybody for help was that they might turn around and deliver her right into the hands of that odious man. And now, hopefully, she will leave this hellish nightmare and will have the chance to start afresh somewhere. Isn't that something worth calling one's legacy?"

Farmani looked into her eyes and read rightly that she was still apprehensive about Miriam's fate. He said, "She will be safe. The young woman you met is one of the best operatives in this area. You can rely on her. As for my legacy, I don't know. I am just going to keep doing whatever I can for however long I can. It is possible that my country might call back its employees now that Iran is being occupied by the Soviets and the English. I honestly don't know how long I can keep this up."

Eva closed her eyes for a minute. Perhaps she was trying her best not to think of his absence and then finally said, "I want to be a part of what you have undertaken. I don't know what exactly I can do; I am a singer. But count on me to be your ears or eyes or courier. Just allow me to support the cause. I feel so restless sitting about and just not doing anything. With Miriam gone, too, now, life feels emptier than ever. Tell me what I can do, and I promise you won't be disappointed in me."

Farmani looked at the beautiful, courageous woman sitting across from him and was overcome by emotion. He gently held one of her hands and squeezed it. He said, "Eva, it is a complex game of lies and deceit. I don't know whether it would be wise for you to be involved in it. I never told you about my plans all this time, simply because I did not want to put you in any danger. Besides—"

She interrupted him and, gently disengaging her hand from his, held it up in front of her face, just in front of his lips, to stop his next words. He looked at her, startled, and knew he had made a mistake.

She said flatly, "I have known my share of burdens, Monsieur. When I offer my help, I know what I am signing up for. You don't have to protect me. You forget that the Opera House is a place where a lot of people, including Germans, gather. As a performer, nobody will notice me, and my presence there will be taken for granted. You have nothing to lose by making me your ally."

But you do not know what I begin to feel for you. You do not know what I stand to lose if something were to happen to you, he silently thought. He knew that now wasn't the time to discuss his feelings for her. A time would come for that. Resignedly, he knew that it would be impossible to dissuade Eva from a course of action she had decided on. If she worked with him, at least he would have the satisfaction of being near her and being able to keep an eye on her. It was pointless to argue with her—besides, what she was saying made sense—as an artist, she would be able to keep in touch with people and hear things that probably others wouldn't.

Another idea suddenly struck him. He asked, "How much of the Opera House do you know? Do you have a clear idea of the passages and rooms that are usually not used by the public?"

Eva Klein tossed her head up and said, "I know the entire building like the back of my palm. The only region that I haven't explored is the cistern beneath the theater. It is so rarely cleaned, and the water so dirty that nobody but the caretakers would venture there. However, I know the attics, the labyrinths, and all the rooms leading in and out of the building."

Farmani then said to her, "Remember I told you about the roundups? They say now that it could be as soon as the middle of this month. Do you think we can hide people there until the frenzy dies down? I haven't discussed this with the rest of the team, but since you have a better idea of the building, if you should think it safe, then perhaps we can work out a plan. I can get you an estimate of the numbers we are looking at after discussing it with others."

Eva said, "They may not search the Opera House very thoroughly. I think it could work. I could give you a detailed layout of the entire building, and perhaps you can then decide whether to use it as a safe house for them. In my estimation, it would be best to split everyone into smaller groups of four to five and then use several hiding spots or rooms within the building. It might make detection less easier than if you were to put everyone in a single location."

Farmani combed his hand through his hair, "Yes, that makes sense. I will have to work out the logistics with others on the team." He fell quiet for a while after that. She looked at him, hoping he would say more, but he remained lost in his thoughts.

Chapter 11:

The Unraveling: 10 July 1942

Klaus Richter was pacing up and down the length of a room next to the cabins where others like him were busy at work. This room was one where meetings for the SS members were convened when necessary. The room was bare except for a large, oval wooden desk right in the middle of it. A bunch of wooden chairs were stacked toward one corner of the room to be pulled up to the desk when the need arose. The curtains were drawn, and a single bulb lit up the room. The only adornment was a large Swastika flag mounted on one of the walls.

To say that Klaus Richter was angry was an understatement. He was a towering pinnacle of pure, unadulterated rage. He had been to the library these last few days. He had checked out every book he could lay his hands on about the history of the Persians. He had also consulted a few historians in the city. Under the pressure he put on them, they had no choice but to double-check the facts and confirm his suspicions. He had not come across a term such as the "Jugutis" anywhere, even once. None of the historians he had contacted had heard of the term either. Admittedly, none of them were experts on Iranian history, but it seemed remarkable that there were no written records for this Iranian sect of people, who seemed to be rising in numbers day by day. He was convinced that the term and the argument were a fabrication by the Iranian swindler—an elaborate lie to help the Jews escape.

There was another matter about which he was extremely upset. Thorough investigations by his men and the intelligence department stationed in Paris had led to his suspicion that Farmani may have aided non-Iranian Jews to leave the country too. This, above everything else, put him in a distemper. *How dare that man hoodwink the fatherland. Who did he think he was?* The guts of the man simply angered Richter more than ever.

He still needed concrete proof, without which it would only be his word against Farmani's. If the fact that Farmani had helped Jewish people flee could be proven, Farmani would become a traitor to his own country and to Germany as well. He had to establish enough evidence to confirm his strong hunch. This was what he was after. But he wasn't sure how he would collect it.

There was some hopeful news, however. He had sent a few telegrams to various officials in Berlin, and there had been responses, not from everyone, but from a few in the higher echelons, promising to look into the Iranian exemption from the Nuremberg Laws. It was too early to predict an outcome, but he was satisfied. At least, somebody would look into it and hopefully convey the matter to the right authorities where detailed research could be undertaken. More than anything, people would start talking about it and question the reports Farmani would send them in the future. It wasn't enough, but it was a start.

As he was deciding what his next course of action ought to be, Müller came into the room ostensibly in search of him. After the customary exchanges, he said, "I have some news."

Seated on his chair, Richter's ears pricked up. Steepling his fingers before him and leaving a little forward, he asked, "Is it about the Iranian? Has there been some progress?"

Müller said, "Yes. We have somebody on the inside now. They seem to be moving faster as the roundups arrive."

Richter asked, "Is it certain? Will he serve us? Is he sure that they will use him?"

The other man replied, "Yes. He has received his instructions and done a little ferreting work for them. He reports to me for the present. Should I ask him to call on you instead? Perhaps he can give you more details of what he has seen and heard."

Richter ran his finger along the thin scar that marked his cheek and said thoughtfully, "No, let him report to me only if there is something really urgent or important that we should know about. We don't want to give away his identity. We don't know if they are keeping a watch on the movements of their members either. I am sure that they will not trust everyone readily in view of the fact that every Resistance group is discovering Nazi sympathizers within its ranks. Let him not mingle with us strictly more than is necessary. Without him, we will find gathering evidence an almost impossible task. How does he keep us informed now?"

Müller said, "For now, he sends us messages via one of the street boys willing to make a fast buck. They deliver it here at the office. The notes are in codes, of course."

Richter said, "Excellent. Let the system continue. Next time, send the courier with a reply asking the agent to report in person only in case of any important development that he thinks we should be apprised of immediately. Meanwhile, was he able to tell anything more about where the documents are being issued from?"

The younger man seemed hesitant to say this but finally admitted, "He is too new. Plus, they have saddled him with only a certain part of their operations. He hardly knows the other agents. Even while working with them, he only knows them by their agent names. Agent Étoile was the only name he could give us, but then we already knew of this particular agent, who has been taking bigger and bigger risks. They say Von Falken lost his girl owing to this agent. Our mole hasn't met any of the others in person. Farmani seems to be deliberately keeping them separate for the most part and giving them only small roles that they can work on independently. I think they have foreseen how their network could be infiltrated and are taking precautions to ensure that in case of capture, they won't be able to tell on one another."

Richter said, "Von Falken's girl? The Jewish girl, you mean? He was always a fool! If he wanted to have a fling, nobody would have stopped him, of course. But why did he have to make a spectacle of himself in that fashion? Wanting to set her up as a mistress when the law clearly prohibits us from pursuing those filthy women! He was always an impulsive and rash imbecile. So you say the girl has fled? Perhaps with the active help of the Resistance?"

Müller nodded in the affirmative as Richter seemed to be turning things over. He did not care for Von Falken's loss, of course, but it did worry him that Farmani may have links with the Resistance groups in the city. It was bad enough that the Nazis were working overtime in stamping out these presumptuous foolhardy citizens who thought they could topple an empire with their petty disruptive acts. However, two enemies ganging up against you was never any good. It would also mean more resources and organization in Farmani's activities. This did not bode well for him or the Nazis at all. He had to try to alienate Farmani from the Resistance and single him out for capture.

Richter then asked, "What about the singer? Hasn't she been spotted more than once with him?"

The other man said, "They are always sighted in public spaces. It does not seem anything more than a harmless attachment on both sides. We don't think she plays a part in any of this."

Richter said, "But the girl who fled was her maid, is it not?"

Müller replied, "Yes, but again, it doesn't seem like she got help from her employer. It seems more probable that her brother, who we had pegged as already a part of the Resistance, must have been instrumental in planning it. There seem to be reasonable grounds to believe that he would have asked his friends to help her since he knew she was being targeted by Von Falken. In fact, Von Falken and he had a falling out not long before his disappearance."

Richter said, "Well, just don't rule out any possibility prematurely. Keep an eye on the singer. She could be more than a mere *harmless attachment,* as you put it. Harmless attachments are rarely ever just that." He paused for a while as he went over Farmani's possible connection to Resistance groups.

Richter continued after a while, "Well, the Resistance always had its ways of functioning. Farmani may be a meddler, but he is a man of some intelligence. I had my contacts in Berlin convey parts of the letter he wrote to the Racial Policy Office. He has gone to considerable lengths to present historical facts to prove what he is saying. Most of it looks legitimate, though he must have distorted facts in places. For instance, he says that the Persian Emperor Cyrus freed Jewish exiles in Babylon in the 6th century BC but that a small number of the Persians themselves started finding the teachings of Moses attractive. These people, he claims, took up the Jewish faith even though they were no different from the Aryan Persian race. He calls them "Jugutis," and yet I can find the term referenced nowhere else. I am sure that he has not fabricated it entirely. The fact that Emperor Cyrus freed the Jews is correct, but for the rest, how is anyone to verify it? It will take some effort to disprove it. I am not even sure whether Berlin will be able to spare the resources or men to look into it all."

Müller nodded, wondering what Richter was driving at. The historical facts that seemed to excite the older man went over his head. All Lieutenant Müller wanted to determine was how he was to direct his men in dealing with the dissidents. Whether the claims made by Farmani were true or not did not interest him in the least. He wondered why Richter was spending so much time and effort over it and not just allowing the racial experts in Berlin to do their job of researching it.

Loyal as he was, Müller was at times a little irritated by his superior's pomposity. As far as he was concerned, life was much simpler if you read and analyzed less but took clear and decisive action where it was needed. He was all for doing and did not care much for idle chit-chat. But he was smart enough to keep these thoughts to himself. There was something about Richter he knew was ruthless, and Müller did not want to be the man who rubbed the other man the wrong way. He always strived to be in the good books of Richter because, instinctively, he knew that the latter was not a man who would take repudiation in his stride.

Just before dismissing him, Richter asked finally, "What about the preparations for next week? Have you double-checked that everything is in order? Do the teams know their points of contact?"

Müller said, "Yes, the men know which areas which teams are in charge of. The trains are ready and equipped to take 30,000 at the least. The rest can be held as prisoners until the trains come back for them. Our teams will be helped by the Gestapo and the local forces as well. We have communicated our needs to them, and they have assured us of their help in terms of men and logistics. We have also kept the higher authorities in the loop so that the European camps can be made ready to accommodate the new additions at the earliest."

Richter said, "Very well, then. Sieg Heil," with his right arm extended.

Müller reiterated the chant for victory just as earnestly, "Sieg Heil."

***

On the evening of the same day, Richter had his driver take him to a certain tavern in one of the darkest and gloomiest parts of the city. It was a dimly lit establishment on the outskirts of the city, away from the prying eyes of the general public and the Resistance bands. The small shack had heavy drapes covering every window. Within the building, the wooden chairs and tables, scarred from numerous secret meetings, were lost in a smoky haze. Even the customers spoke in hushed whispers as women solicited men, and shady deals for everything from unregistered ammunition to drugs were sealed with furtive glances thrown over shoulders from time to time. A less experienced man than Richter would have instantly turned away if he had mistakenly stepped into this place. It was a tavern where sin, vice, and evil roamed free.

Richter chose a seat away from the single bulb that illuminated the entire room. He knew that the person who wanted to meet him would find him. He lit his cigar slowly, taking in the scene before him. He asked the grizzly bartender for a malt whisky and waited patiently for his man to arrive. That the latter may not come did not perturb the Germans in the least. So sure was he of himself and his men. The fact was that it was in his contact's interest to meet him more than it was his own. He knew that if the latter did not show up, it was only because he might have been held up by an emergency.

Richter was not a man to be easily fazed by changes in plans. As his colleagues and people who knew him well would tell you, he was always cool as a cucumber, even when things hit

137

rock bottom. He did occasionally get angry, but that anger always fueled better ideas than the ones his rational mind suggested. His rage always gave way to greater clarity of thought and did not impede his actions. He was also one of those rare men who did not fear a personal threat to safety. He welcomed adversities as an opportunity to demonstrate his grit and determination to serve his country.

Possibly, the only thing that Richter was afraid of was being double-crossed from within his own ranks. The fact that it had only taken a couple of days to find an informant willing to infiltrate the enemy network spoke a lot of the times he was in. It would be just as easy for the Resistance to plant their spies in his network and among his men. This was the only thing that worried Richter endlessly. He was a vigilant man, and his caution bordered on paranoia when it came to testing the loyalty of his men. Despite what he had told Müller, he was about to meet the person who had been planted in Farmani's team to ensure that they would not betray him in the end. Without Müller's knowledge, he had found a way to contact the double agent and sent him word to meet him at this place. He did not know the identity of the person yet but was confident that the latter would recognize him.

Richter had made inquiries about the preparations for the Jews to be transported to the final solution as senior SS officials referred to the arrangements made. He was satisfied to see that everything was in accordance with what Müller had said. It was now less than a week before things would start happening, and Richter could not wait. If they could fill up those trains, Berlin would be happy, and finally, he, Richter, would get the recognition and adulation he deserved as one of the key players in ensuring that everything went smoothly. He filled his head with pleasurable thoughts about being called and honored in Berlin in the near future and bagging that promotion he knew he was due for. His pleasant reveries were prematurely cut short when a hooded person swathed in a shawl sat in front of him. At first, Richter was annoyed. In the gloomy light, he thought that one of the working girls of the tavern had come to proposition him. He was about to shoo her away when he saw that the hand placed on the table before him was not that of a woman but that of a man. He knew that his agent had found him.

The man before him was tall and well-built. Though his face was partially masked by the hood of his jacket and the shawl he had draped around himself, Richter noted a heavy jowl and a pugnacious countenance. For a minute, the German wondered how he could have mistaken this man for a woman.

The agent said in a raspy voice, "Heil Hitler! I got the note asking me to report to you. I expected to find Lieutenant Müller. That is why it took me more time to locate you."

Richter smiled and said, "Lieutenant Müller reports to me, and though he assured me you were a worthy man, I wanted to make sure and meet you in person once."

The other man only nodded once and then looked askance at Richter as if he was awaiting further instructions or questions.

Richter leaned forward and asked, "So, what have you learned so far? I know it has not been very long for you on the team, but is there something that you would like to tell me?"

The man kept his voice low and said, "As I told Müller, they are planning to hide some Jews in the city when the roundups are due. They have made some arrangements for the transport, but it would be better to find them before they are removed from the locations."

"And these locations are?" Richter knew the agent was deliberately holding out the most important information for the end. It was an old trick of the trade.

"Well, that would depend. What exactly are my rewards to be for revealing them to you?" The man asked slyly, still ensuring that a deep shadow kept most of his face hidden.

Richter said, "Have you cause to mistrust us? If you do what is expected of you, everything you have asked for can be worked out. The Reich never reneges on promises made in good faith."

"Well, what is this good faith though? I work my butt off in a role when I never know who will make me the scapegoat. To me, it sounds like a vague term. What is the guarantee that you won't bump me off and use the next person when your use for me is over?" The man asked.

"Well, the need is just as much yours as it is ours to ensure your safety. You know that we can't replace you in a hurry. If they discover you, they will be extra cautious with the next bunch of recruits. To worm one of us into their circle of trust will take more effort and time. Speaking of which, are you sure that you are not being watched by them?" said Richter.

"As far as I am able to infer, the Iranian is working with a small team. I don't think he would have the means to keep an eye on all his operatives. He has a few Resistance connections for sure, who then take on the operations from there. The papers are his brainchild. I am not part of the activities that deal with the issuance of papers and passports. I have no clue where they get or, rather, make the papers for the fugitives. But I have reason to believe that he is not using his embassy for the work," the man said.

"Why would you say that?" Richter wanted the man to keep talking so that he could draw his own conclusions about him and what he was saying.

"Well, because logically, I don't think the Iranian embassy would supply hundreds of papers without some permission from their government. I don't think the government is involved in the process at all. I believe the consul is playing a lone game," the man said.

"You don't *think*? Don't you *think* you should stick more to what you have proof for?" Leaning forward, Richter asked contemptuously, though, personally, he was quite sure what the man was saying was true. Despite having been arm-twisted to formally declare war on Germany by the Soviets and British, the newly appointed Shah was trying to appease Germany more than anything by referring to Iranian neutrality. Richter did not see him permitting his consuls to deliberately go against the Reich's mission.

"At this stage, I can only tell you my surmises. I have met the man only once. Even my recruitment was confirmed to me by another Jew working for him, who I only know as the Agent Monk. They basically want my services in telling them the safest parts of the city to harbor Jews and which parts will remain most unchecked during the next week. I had to reach out to some of my police pals to give them this information. And mind you, if at least a few of them aren't allowed to escape, then my game is going to be up sooner than you think," the man replied.

Richter looked at him and said, "Yes, we understand that your position has to be preserved. But again, your position is replaceable unless you provide the vital details we are looking for. I ask you, what is the location?"

The other man sighed and answered, "I was asked to check out the safety of The Opera House for the 16th early morning."

Richter sat back again, rubbing his thin hands in satisfaction. A sardonic smile lit up his otherwise ascetic face.

Chapter 12:

The Opera House: 15-16 July 1942

When Adolf Hitler arrived in Paris after it fell to the Nazis in 1940, one of his first destinations in his tour of the city had been the Palais Garnier. It was curious that the Germans, who generally destroyed local art, architecture, and history wherever they went, were willing to integrate themselves into the French operatic scene rather than dismantle it entirely. This was perhaps because the Führer had an appreciation for art and architecture that was superior. This was also perhaps why he had asked one of his chief architects, commissioned with the building of Germania, a new and improved capital instead of the present Berlin, to include a monument along the lines of the Paris Opera House in the completed city.

The Paris Opera House was being managed by a director whose hands were tied. A benevolent man, Jacques Rouché, who wanted to desperately retire at the age of 78, was held back in his position by the pleas of his employees because they could not bear to see the directorship taken over by a Nazi. Though he tried to focus on putting up traditional French classical shows, he had to placate the Germans by occasionally allowing Wagnerian and the Berlin Philharmonic performances in between. There were rumors that Rouché, who had fought to retain his Jewish employees, now banned from working anywhere, let alone the Opera House, was paying their salaries out of his own pocket.

Farmani had approached Rouché via Eva, and the old director ratified their plan to house the Jews for a couple of days within the vast walls of the Opera House. He couldn't help them financially or provide them with any resources, of course. Doing that would come to bite him later on if the plan failed and the Nazis caught wind of the scheme. In that eventuality, he could lose his position and probably even be tried for treason. All he could do was ask the caretakers to leave the rooms open. There would be good reason for such a request as well because a certain German drama troupe was performing at the Opera House around the same dates as when the Jews were to be given refuge. It would only be natural to leave several of the rooms open for the dress rehearsal and other needs of the German artists. The plan was that along with the rooms needed for the actors, some of the other passages and wings would also be left unlocked, which could later be explained, if needed, as a lapse of memory or judgment on the part of the caretakers.

In the early morning hours of the 15th of July, lay people outside the Opera House would have witnessed a cleaning crew especially tasked with sprucing up the building in view of the German troupe about to perform there over the next couple of days. What the spectators would have missed a couple of hours later when the crew finished their work and left would be that the number of cleaners who had arrived was many more than those who left.

There was a lone stranger who had stood by a little away across the street, patiently watching the crew arriving and leaving. His tall hat and coat, despite the warmth of the day, threw a long shadow over his face. Nobody really took any notice of people like them. Since the war, there had been several vagrants like him all over, milling about, searching for odd jobs or the odd meal that came their way. He calmly stood there, smoking, as the cleaning crew arrived, finished their job, and left. A little while after the last of them left, he threw away the cigarette remnants and lumbered away, slowly mingling with the city throng that moved along the streets daily.

***

It had been a busy couple of days for the members of Operation Lifeline. They had arrived at an almost foolproof plan of gathering and giving instructions to the Jews they had promised to aid. There were some thirty-odd of them who had to be hidden from the Nazis during the roundups and then transported to a safehouse within the city immediately. Later on, another team was tasked with moving these people to the south in Bordeaux, which was also part of occupied France. From thence, they were to be shifted to the cities of Marseille, Toulon, or Lyon in the Free Zone, where they would be transported out of the country. They were to be taken out in batches, with women and children prioritized. However, since they had to be gathered together at first, the Opera House was the safest bet. Rouché had assured the team that the Palais Garnier had rarely been searched, especially because of Serge Lifar, the ballet director who had been an open collaborationist and German ally ever since France's occupation.

It was with great effort and tact that all the Jews were inducted into the large rooms and dark passageways of the grand building. In order not to raise suspicion, they were dressed up as cleaning crew members in overalls and jackets. They could carry little else on them apart from a small ration of bread and the papers they would need later to leave the country. They were separated and installed in rooms, chambers, the hollow of staircases, and other places where the regular staff of the building, the performers, or the audience of the German drama would not notice them. They were to remain in hiding until they got the designated signal from one of the Resistance members who would come to move them out.

A lot of planning and hard work had gone into the scheme, and everyone could only hope with bated breaths for the best outcome. There was no guarantee that the local Parisian police force or the Gestapo would not check the building. This was the best that the team could devise under such short notice for so many people. They knew that the Germans would waste no pity on Jews who were discovered. Everyone, inside and outside, who was part of this plan waited, hoped, and prayed that things would go according to plan.

***

Just before the afternoon on the 16th of July, an urgent message came to Farmani from the director of the Opera House. It was a hurriedly scribbled missive that said that the French police had requested a search of the building and that he could not prevent them from doing it. He had bought the team some time by asking the police to wait an hour till his staff could finish their lunch, help them unlock the large doors, and assist the men as he himself was old and rather enfeebled. The police had agreed to wait. It was in this interval that the old man had written the note and had one of the boys deliver it to the Iranian consul's office.

As soon as Farmani got the message, he quickly wrote a couple of messages. The first one was for Gagnon, the second for David Cohen, and the third one for Toni Laurent. He did not know which of them were free. Each of them had been assigned duties at various venues in assisting with the movement of Jews at various safe houses. He wasn't even sure where in the city they could be found. He asked the errand boy to be as fast as he could, told them about the usual places the three people could be found, and to use his wits to ensure that the notes got to at least one of them if not all three of them.

Farmani then debated what he should do next. It would look odd for an Iranian consul to go and meddle with a search warrant for the Opera House in Paris. There was no reason for him to be present at such an incident or venue. His presence in an official capacity would only raise Nazi suspicions further. It was best to stay put in his office so that one of the three he had written to could find him.

***

Toni Laurent and David Cohen got the messages almost at the same time. The courier, using his street smartness and talents, searched for them and found them. As for Gagnon, nobody could trace him, and finally, the lad had to give up because it would only have been a waste of precious time.

Toni hurried to the Opera House as fast as she could, hoping that she could move the Jews before the police started searching. She quickly sent word back to Farmani before she set out on her own toward the Opera House.

When she got there, she saw that the police were just entering the building. She quickly used one of the side entrances she knew would be open to get access to the west wing of the building. From here, she kept moving into the vast interiors of the building using a series of internal passages she knew would take longer for the police to figure out. She was able to reach one of the rooms furthest from the main entrance in this manner. She used her knuckles to rap against the wooden paneling of the room: one long and two short taps. Within seconds, she could see shadows detaching from various objects in the room.

She whispered hoarsely into the darkness in Yiddish, "Danger. Come with me now."

She counted five or six people who came out of this room. It had been one of the other agents who had checked the list and hid them here. She was not even sure in which wings and passages everyone was. But she had seen the maps of the building and knew the layout. Remembering the plan and moving like a lithe jungle cat who could smell danger, she quickly covered whatever sections of the building she could, hoping the police would start at the entrance and search from there. She could not approach the north or east wings from where she knew the police would be starting their checking.

As she and her group kept pushing forward through the labyrinthine passages, she felt on edge. The lives of so many now hung on just her presence of mind and ability to remember the map correctly. She wasn't much of a praying woman but felt the hushed mystery of the Opera House suited for sending up a silent prayer. She hoped that she could make it to all the chambers before the Nazis got there.

In half an hour, she could hear echoes of screams through the passages. With a sunken heart, she realized that the Jews hidden in some rooms and wings closest to the Eastern wing were discovered. There was no time to halt or to go back for them. She knew that there was no way she would be able to surprise or fight against well-armed Germans with the half-starved, unarmed army of people behind her. At this point, the only sane thing to do was to keep moving and save the remaining people. She hissed at the people who were with her that they needed to hurry because the police would arrive and methodically comb the passages and corridors that they were in no time. They moved in a single file. Some instinctive, protective urge had led them, even without instructions, to have the ladies and children right at the front, just behind Toni, while the boys and men made up the flank and rear of the group.

The corridors and passages led them through a series of twists and turns, reminding her of an eerie dark maze, sections of which were briefly but dimly lit up by the light from the auditorium, where it seemed that the play was either being staged or rehearsed. As they turned corners, they could hear snatches of music too. For the most part, these hapless men, women, and children crept and followed each other in almost pitch dark in single file or in twos where space allowed, not daring to breathe too loudly lest they were heard.

At the head of a subterranean flight of stairs, she whirled around, holding her thin hands in front of her tall frame. The people, she quickly counted, some 21 of them, paused and eyed her uneasily. She showed them through a mixture of gestures and mime that they would be taking this set of stairs going beneath the building. It was a narrow tunnel between the cistern and the Opera House floor. They would have to crawl through it one at a time. This would lead them to another short landing, from where an upward flight of stairs ought to take them outside the building. She did not know why this secret passageway had been built. But it was the only way that they could go out now. This tunnel was not marked in the maps of the building. Its location had been conveyed to them by Rouché and was a last resort because the door at the other end led to an alleyway of sorts. Toni had no way of telling whether there would be guards stationed there.

Quietly but swiftly, the 21 people whose lives dangled by a thread now crawled through the tunnel, one behind the other. Children and women went behind Toni, who knew the direction, while the men came behind last. The entire journey took only half an hour but seemed excruciatingly slower because, behind them, they could hear the faraway screams of men, women, and children—people who were to have seen freedom with them. So they hauled themselves forward, keeping mum even when stray stones poked into their flesh or when a cobweb brushed against their faces. To make the slightest sound would be to give away all of them. Remarkably, even the children, who seemed to sense the importance of their passage, were deathly quiet. When the people in the middle of the passage bumped into the ones in front, they knew that Toni and the women right behind her would have reached the narrow passage.

Toni quickly scaled up what was more of a ladder than the staircase that she had anticipated. These passages were just as new to her as they were to the people she led. Her only advantage was a knowledge of the layout of the building from the map that Farmani had obtained from Rouché and passed on to her. When she reached the door, which was in front of her, she was sure that her heartbeat would be heard right through the door if there was a man stationed outside. Cautiously, she pushed the door and was momentarily relieved that it was open. When she peeked around, it did not seem like there were too many people about

The group made its way into a busy street—these men and women who had been in hiding and hoping for a mass exodus. They had to make their way to a certain spot by the next day. And now they would have to do it on their own—each one for themselves. They had been warned of this eventuality. They who had been hoping to remain together had to separate and find their own way to the designated place from where they would be transported to the next location. It was Plan B in action—but it was certainly better than sticking to Plan A and being caught.

What was wonderful about the times they lived in was the fact that it made everybody more adventurous and enterprising. These were the only two qualities that ensured that one survived and lived to tell the tale. Nobody objected anymore to changes in plans because they were necessary for survival. The 21 people who did make it out of the Opera House that day were not unhappy. Yes, they were extremely scared. But they were relieved that they weren't part of the nine who had no choice in not making it out of the building. Wars changed people's perceptions thus.

***

It was late in the evening when Farmani received more news from his comrades. Toni had sent word that 21 had escaped from the Opera House. The note did not say much more, but he was no fool. He immediately understood what might have become of the remaining nine. He took a deep breath because it would take some while before he got to know who the people who did not make it were. In fact, he knew that even Toni couldn't be expected to know the details of who escaped and who did not. For now, he had to take heart from the fact that more than two-thirds of them had made it safely.

He felt frustrated that what they had considered a good plan had gone awry, but he was, at heart, an optimist. While his heart went out to those who were captured, he also knew that his team had done the best possible for them. There was no use in beating up himself or his teammates over it because the possibility of checks at the Opera House had been very real, even if it hadn't been enforced over the last couple of years. He knew that the Nazis were bloodthirsty and desperate to round up the maximum number of people they could. Their government had gone to elaborate lengths to establish a system to transport Jews to the camps in Europe. Being able to capture less than the numbers they were prepared for would be seen as a failure. Berlin would be sure to comment on the laxity of the officials here if they were seen to be slacking off on their duty. It was no surprise that the administrators here were leaving no stone unturned to catch every single person more than they could. Anger still burned through him when he thought of these ruthless men who were killing innocent people. However, in a part of his mind he had not acknowledged to himself, he had expected nothing less than what had happened. It wouldn't do to focus on the men, women, and children they had lost. Instead, they needed now to focus on what could be done.

There was something else that puzzled Farmani, nevertheless. He had heard back from both Toni and Cohen. Toni directed Cohen to keep a watch on the Opera House and to report to Farmani in case she could not make it with the team. He was now aiding her in collecting and directing the escaped people toward their next point of contact, where Resistance members were waiting to help them. Cohen was accounted for, and so was Toni. Farmani quickly sent back the courier with a message to tell David to continue the mission and to follow Toni's instructions.

He had heard nothing from Gagnon. This was surprising. As far as he could remember, Gagnon's only tasks thus far had been to ensure providing a detailed map of the city with special attention to areas that would be checked more by the police, SS, and Gestapo. He was asked to get in touch with his ex-colleagues and provide as much information as he could about impromptu raids and arrests. He had been quick and seemingly thorough in his job. Farmani could not really complain that Gagnon did not catch on to or warn them about the checks enforced at the Opera House. Perhaps his reach did not go up that far, or perhaps it had been a last-minute order from the higher-ups. One had to give Gagnon the benefit of the doubt. In these times, nobody really knew what was happening. However, it was strange that the man had not responded to the message even after so many hours. *What was he doing right now that kept him so busy on a day he knew the roundups would happen?* Farmani wondered.

Farmani thought back to Gagnon and his story. Toni Laurent had done a preliminary check for Karl Gagnon using her contacts, and they had confirmed his story. There was indeed such a man who had a missing Jewish girlfriend on the police force. She had found out that Gagnon had been doing the rounds at offices and trying to track down his missing fiancée. His version of the story seemed to be convincing in the light of the facts she could find.

However, a faint suspicion started forming in Farmani's head. He couldn't shake off the feeling that there was something a little off about his story and the fact that he had so easily come to him exactly at a time when Farmani had been searching for recruits for his team. The Iranian was not a strong believer in fate and chance occurrences. At the time, he may have simply seen it as a stroke of good luck. Now, though, he wasn't as sure.

He also wondered how search warrants for the Opera House had been issued when even the director had assured them that precedents of this had been rare in the past. Suddenly, Farmani felt a cold, dreadful sense of foreboding. He mentally ticked off each member of the team that he worked with personally. He knew that of all of them, Gauthier was vouched for by Toni Laurent. He also knew that David Cohen was above reproach. The more he worked with Cohen, the more he came to rely on the latter's resourcefulness and courage. The other operatives only acted on Toni's commands and were not really part of the planning process. They would not even know that a person like Farmani was in on the details. Toni would make sure of that.

It seemed likely that there was a chink in the armor, and Farmani had a suspicion of who it was most likely to be. He knew he would have to exercise more caution in the coming days to ensure that his part in the rescue missions was more low-key because if those were traced back to him, they would definitely try him for treason. If France or Germany did not, then Iran would not spare him. He would be suspended, at the very least. This would mean that he wouldn't be able to issue the life-saving papers that he was able to do now. He also understood how imperative it was for him to separate the two parts of the operation—the forging and issuance of the documents and the actual movement of the Jews out of the city. He knew that for now, all the rescue missions would only be linked to Agent Etoile. He also knew that the Germans already knew of this agent, though they had not yet managed to unmask her identity. Farmani smiled inwardly at the thought of their discomfiture if they realized that the person they considered one of their toughest opponents was a gangly young woman. Nobody, other than Toni and David, knew what he was using Gauthier for. As long as these shreds of information and evidence remained disparate, his operation would remain safe.

The only other problem he could foresee was Eva Klein. Not for a moment did he suspect her of betrayal. Eva's evident love for Miriam made her being a German ally an impossibility. He knew her innocence, and it was more than just instinct and the feelings he had for her. He was sure enough of her to know that Eva would not help the Germans against him. The problem that he saw was completely different.

Even the most unthorough examinations would reveal to the German spies that Eva Klein was his weak spot. They must have caught sight of her with him several times now. He knew that sooner rather than later, they would make the connection between the Jews at the Opera House and her. Even if there was no concrete evidence against her, just the suspicion would be enough to haul her up for questioning. The thought made him shudder involuntarily. Nazi questioning always involved torture. She would not be spared despite being a woman. It was horrible even contemplating it. Through her, they could get to him. If something happened to her, he would never be able to forgive himself. Now that she was working for the cause, it was only going to get more dangerous for him and her. Pursuing a relationship would make things even more complicated.

He had known that it would come to this. For some time now, he had struggled with what he had to do. He had procrastinated, hoping there would be a way forward without him having to do the inevitable. But the time had come. Though she was his light and hope, he knew it was time to get her out of this. The thought made him anxious, and he knew that she would stubbornly push back against his arguments. Nevertheless, he had to do what he had to do for the greater good of everyone involved.

Chapter 13:

The Conversion: 02 August 1942

The roundups officially ceased on the 17th of July. The Germans had not had the victory they had so presumptuously prepared for. While they had arranged transportation for 30,000 Jews, a much more meager number of 13,000 were actually captured and transported via trains. If not exactly a win for the Allied cause, it was satisfactory to note that the Nazis had miscalculated their success—and by such a huge margin at that. Hopefully, everyone thought, the Nazis would keep making similar errors of judgment and would be beaten sooner than people had hoped for. This was the unsaid general sentiment of the average person in France. The citizens had already lost too much in the course of the three years for which the war had been raging. Everybody wanted to see German defeat as early as possible without more casualties. It was dawning on everybody that the massacre and the people killed in the fighting, blitzkrieg, and bombing were probably not worth the outcome that they would get anyway. If the Great War had taught them anything, the real work would start only after the war ended—when cities, lives, and livelihoods would have to be rebuilt. Everybody was already so tired that reconstruction seemed a distant dream indeed.

As far as Farmani was concerned, the Resistance had managed to get a total of 1000 Jews to Vichy, France, including 15, who eventually made it safely from the Opera House. While exact numbers were impossible to get, a good number of them, perhaps more than half of these 1,000, were already on their way to Palestine or other neutral countries away from all the madness happening in occupied Europe. That he had been instrumental in saving even so many lives made Farmani happy. He vowed to be more careful in the future so there wouldn't be last-minute problems such as the one that happened at the Opera House. Meanwhile, he cultivated a greater awareness of how the French and Germans were conducting the roundups so that his team could take lessons from what happened this time and would be better equipped to handle things the next time around.

The Préfecture de Police rounded up the Jews and held them captive at the indoor sports arena of Vélodrome d'Hiver, called Vel d'Hiv in short. This sports arena had been originally constructed as a cycling track, not far from the Eiffel Tower, when the one at Salle des Machines was listed for demolition by the city council in the early 1900s because it supposedly ruined the view of the Eiffel Tower. Vel d'Hiv was used for several other sports apart from cycling, such as boxing, wrestling, ice hockey, and roller skating, to name just a few. The 1924 Summer Olympics had been hosted here as well. Before the war, its grounds were often used to host circuses that visited the city. It was reported that the Jews were held at Vel d'Hiv for a week or more without adequate food, water, and sanitation facilities before being transported to internment camps such as Drancy. It was from here that they were borne away in cattle cars to Auschwitz and other death camps.

Farmani did not know what use such information could give him, but he stored it all away because he wanted to be sure that he missed no detail about Nazi plans for Jews. He hoped that after these roundups, there would be a lull in the activities of the French and German authorities, which would give his team some valuable time to quietly get more hidden people to nearby safe houses in the city. Though reading the news, which was getting more surreal and bizarre by the day, was disquieting, Farmani kept at it because he believed there was no point in shielding himself from any of it. It would be like the proverbial ostrich, faced with danger, burying its head in the sand. He knew that he was living in historical times and that, hopefully, future generations would learn from the madness happening now and not repeat it.

Additionally, he also kept closer tabs on all his team members, especially on Gagnon. His note had finally been answered the day after the Opera House mission. Gagnon claimed that he had been kept busy with Jews who had to be helped in a different part of the city, though he had not provided any details of with whom he worked. Farmani was not entirely convinced of his tale but also could find no reason to suspect him yet, either. It was possible that Gagnon was aiding other Resistance groups in the city, just as he had given them his help. Everything was possible during wartime, and the best you could do was to look out for the safety of everyone working with you. Farmani intended to do just that.

He knew he had to have a serious discussion with Eva Klein soon and urge her to leave as soon as she could. However, he was equally certain that the strong-willed woman would not budge so easily. He procrastinated speaking to her. He resolved not to involve her too closely in the day-to-day operations of his team for now. He felt a pang of remorse at this, but he also knew that some things were just so. With a shrug and his characteristic optimism, he remembered a Persian proverb he had heard long ago as a child, "If fate does not adjust itself to you, then you adjust yourself to fate."

***

Farmani was surprised when he was summoned to Madame Leclerc's in mid-August for evening tea. He had not forgotten the staunch old lady and had been meaning to ask her for support himself. Most of the Jews who had some money in their possession had already left, and the remaining needed financial assistance if they were to make good their escape. Farmani was surprised about this call that seemed out of the blue, and he could not help but wonder if it was more than a mere social call.

Located in the heart of Paris, Madame Leclerc's vast mansion exuded opulence and grandeur. The sprawling gardens, which must have been meticulously manicured once, were adorned with marble sculptures, which had not lost their beauty, even if they looked a little deteriorated from the lack of daily care. The ornate façade of the mansion was an awe-inspiring sight. Inside, the spacious interior boasted intricately designed ceilings, gilded furniture, and priceless artworks. The grand ballroom, with its sparkling chandeliers and parquet flooring, was the epitome of luxury and reminded one of the extravagant gatherings it must have hosted for Parisian high society. The mansion stood as a beacon of sophistication, even if a little worse for the wear and tear of the war years.

Farmani was prepared to sound Madame Leclerc on the subject of finances for the Jewish cause. But he wasn't prepared for Madame Leclerc herself to introduce the subject. It seemed that there was a lot of news that he had missed during the last couple of weeks.

Madame Leclerc looked a lot older than the last time he had seen her at the fête. Seeing the widow in all black, Farmani suddenly realized what was different about her. He had a shadowy suspicion why she may have called to see him. And yet, he was also curious as to why she had chosen him.

She invited Farmani warmly into her spacious parlor saying, "Thank you for answering my invitation and agreeing to meet me here. I hope I did not inconvenience you a lot."

"Not at all," Farmani said, bowing his head respectfully.

She said without preamble, "You might have not heard as yet. I got the news two days ago that my son died in North Africa a week ago."

Farmani, who had guessed as much from her somber attire, said, "Sorry to hear that, madame. His name will go down in history as one of the brave who fought for justice. May his soul rest in peace."

Madame Leclerc bowed her head acknowledging his words. She only touched her handkerchief to her eyes once. It was clear to Farmani that she hadn't called him home merely to discuss her son. There was something more that she wanted to ask of him.

She opened the subject with direct forthrightness as if there was nothing more for her to lose by speaking her mind, "I know what you have been doing for the country. Yours and mine too. I meant to ask you a long time ago. I think you know what I must have called you for. Do not fear that I know. I am your ally."

Farmani wasn't scared of her in the least. In certain cases, your heart is a better judge of people than your brain. It was so with Madame Leclerc. He knew that she was not a threat or that she would betray him to the authorities. Considering the matter logically, she had no use for money or wealth. Her only son was killed in a foreign land owing to this futile war waged by the Nazis. She, of all people, had no motive to work with them. However, he knew he had to tread carefully around the people who were in contact with her. There was no telling who would use a vulnerable person like Madame Leclerc right now to find more information about him. She might assume they were offering her help but inadvertently betray information to an enemy wanting to pry. He instinctively thought about the furtive Colonel Dubois.

He asked simply, "How did you know?"

She smiled a little and said, "I heard a little of Miriam, Eva Klein's companion, from within my social circles—about that odious Nazi and how she disappeared soon after. I went to Eva and pressed her for details. I did not hold back about why I wanted the information. She was hesitant to reveal your name at first. But I told her about Eric's demise, and she trusted me enough to tell me about you. I hope you don't hold it against her. She waxed lyrically about your bravery. I admit I was a little surprised that it was you behind the saving of so many lives. I wanted to reach out to the Resistance, but I am an old woman. I did not know whom to approach. When she told me about you, I felt so much at ease. You are a known person, and from the beginning, I have felt your presence a comfort to me. You remind me of Eric." She paused here, and her eyes looked moist. There was a faraway gleam in her face. It was as if she was looking at Farmani but also through him—beyond him.

She continued with an effort, "I want to know how I can be of service. Please feel free to tell me your needs, and I give you my word that I will have it arranged for your team. I used to be more cautious, for Eric's sake. Now, I have nothing to lose. I lost my husband in the Great War, and now my only son in this war. I am at liberty to do what I think is right. No rules or laws can hold me back anymore. As for my life, there is no value in it if I cannot be of service to anybody around me. More than anything, I want to see justice prevail. If I were a man, I would bloody my hands with their lives to exact my revenge. But my sex does not even have the comfort of engaging in a duel. Besides, what good would it do to kill a few Nazi soldiers? They would be replaced in a blink by others younger, stronger, and more bloodthirsty. I have realized that soldiers are only pawns in the game—whether they are ours or theirs—ultimately, their lives don't count. They are just figures that add up to the toll of the dead or wounded. I need to have a purpose in my life. I am not interested in taking any more lives. But I do want to save lives if there is a way." She suddenly seemed to come to herself. Her eyes snapped back sharply, almost angrily glaring at Farmani.

Farmani knew that Madame Leclerc's rage, as much of it as she would allow herself to express, was not directed at him. He nodded and said gently, "Thank you for trusting me and for offering your help. For a long time now, I have been contemplating approaching you. Most of the people who want to leave the country have had their possessions and property confiscated by the government. They have no means to leave, and if they stay, well—I don't have to tell you what will become of them. They have nothing to eat, nowhere to go, and most of all, there is the constant fear for their lives. With a benefactor like you, we can help them get the required papers and establish safe houses with adequate food and water for them to stay out of sight until the coast is clear for them to leave. It would be a great service. We don't know how many of them we can save, but we intend to do whatever we can. Even if we make no impact on the numbers that get across safely, at least it will make a difference to the people who do make it. That is all now that matters."

Madame Leclerc smiled at him. Farmani was elated that he had gained one more ally. But his joy was short-lived when she said words that chilled his heart, "There is one more person who would like to help us. I discussed it with him first, before calling you here. He is running a little late. But I think you must have a fair idea who I refer to."

Farmani had a good idea of who it would be. There was only one person he had seen Madame Leclerc hobnobbing with on most occasions. He hoped, for both their sakes, that this was a wise move on her part. He prayed that her emotional sentiments had not clouded her intelligence. Farmani thought that as Madame Leclerc's friendship with Dubois went way back, she probably knew more about the man than he did. As it

163

stood, he could not bring himself to trust Pierre Dubois the way Madame Leclerc seemed to. He knew that Pierre Dubois wasn't all bad and that, left to himself, he may even have some redeeming traits. Yet, the times were such that he could not risk his operations or the lives of his team on a mere chance. He had to be sure. So he waited for the old colonel to make his appearance. For now, he couldn't be sure whether he had just walked into a booby trap or not.

As these thoughts ran through Farmani's mind, Pierre Dubois stepped into the room and asked the butler to serve him a drink. A strange change had come about in the once-ruddy, genial old man. It wasn't so much his appearance as his demeanor. He still wore the dull grey uniform. His hair was slicked in a middle parting, and his triangular chin beard was groomed to perfection. But the old man showed signs of deflation and dejection. It was as if another man was merely playing the part of Pierre Dubois—an actor who only knew how the real Dubois looked.

"Bloody hell! May those Nazis rot in the deepest darkest hell. Nay! The hell is too little for those swine. I wish they would all die a death worse than what they mete out to the people in the concentration camps," he said, sipping on the drink he held in his hand. With his free hand, he was rubbing his pate where he was going bald.

It was the first time that Farmani had heard the man swear. It startled him. It was as if a violent and wicked monster had eaten up the jovial and likable old man that he knew.

Madame Leclerc sat beside his chair and lightly took his hand and cradled it in hers. Farmani looked from one to the other for an explanation. He could not understand what had made Pierre Dubois change in the two fortnights that they hadn't met and why that should be tied up to him or the cause. He waited patiently until the lady could soothe the distressed old man.

Madame Leclerc spoke on Dubois' behalf, "Pierre is in shock. A person whom he loved was caught and taken away during the roundups. I don't know how much of his story you already know. He lost his family in the German bombing during the Great War. His wife and infant boy were both killed. He wished to keep their memories alive and never remarried or considered having a family of his own ever again. About six years ago, when we first started hearing rumors of a war with Germany, somebody abandoned a baby just outside his door. He cared for the little child who was hardly a couple of months old as his own. It was the closest that he had come to having a family after he had lost his own so many years ago. This girl, whom he named Phoebe, lived with him. When the Germans invaded us two years ago, he let it be known that he had sent away Phoebe to family members he claimed he had in Austria. He did not want to forge papers in her name because he was afraid that somebody might leak this information to the Nazis. The fact was that he could not part with her, and yet he was horribly afraid that digging into her past might reveal that she was a Jew. He thought that she would be safer with him than with anyone else. The girl was hardly seven and of unknown parentage. Except for her safety, he never cared about her descent. She was the child he had never been able to raise with his wife. He kept her hidden away in his home. An old caretaker alone shared his secret and helped him in helping with raising the girl. Nobody else knew of her presence." Madame Leclerc paused to say something to Dubois who had tears in his eyes.

She said wearily, "Long story short. The girl was found. Since she had no papers was too late to have them made. The Nazis were just desperate to meet the numbers they had prepared for. They carried her away, and since then, he has been distraught. The Germans have not pressed charges against him because nobody knows for sure whether this girl is Jewish or not. From his sources on the Parisian police force, we believe that she was taken to Drancy. We can't trace any whereabouts of her further than this."

Farmani had tears in his eyes. Imagine losing a family all over again to the Germans. He suddenly understood why Pierre Dubois had turned turtle and collaborated with the German forces for so long. It was not for himself. It had been for his little girl. He had known that her only chance, if discovered, was to have people who would vouch for him among the higher-ups. But he had miscalculated. The help he had relied on never came.

Farmani asked, "Did you not seek somebody's help?"

Pierre Dubois groaned, "Curses upon him! May bloody murder visit him, and I will spit upon his grave. I applied to Richter for help because he knew me, or so I thought. He listened to my story and said, *The girl is an orphan, and it was good of you to care for her so long. Now, we shall take it from here to decide whether she will clear the race test. If she is proven to be of the Aryan race, then she has nothing to fear.*" The old colonel broke down here.

Farmani remembered the man. It was hard for anybody who met Richter to forget his pitiless gaze and the scar that seemed to stand for the darkness of his heart.

With some effort, the old colonel said, "She was only a little child. How can they be so merciless? She was my daughter, my light, my little Phoebe. She was God's gift to me after Marthe and Albert were taken away. I failed to protect her. I should have just sent her away before they invaded. I thought my influence would be enough. That man is pure evil. I hope he—"

Farmani said softly, "You must keep your heart. I know of some people, and we will try to find her. Meanwhile, if you could try to tell us more about Nazi plans, we can save more like her. We have been working on it since June. The

Resistance has been fighting longer. With the support of people like you, we can do more. Come on, Colonel Dubois, will you let the Nazis beat us? Will you let what happened to your daughter happen to other children like her?"

Dubois said, "But I am not sure that they will discuss things with me anymore. Since she was found at my home, they will have suspicions about where my sympathies lie. I do not know how I can be of assistance to you, much as I would like to."

Farmani said, "Well, Pierre Dubois. If there is something I know about you from our frequent partnerships at contract bridge, it is that you are not one to be taken down easily. I am sure you can convince them. Come up with an argument as to why she was at your house and why you felt indebted to shelter her. Regain their trust and be our eyes and ears. At least they did not arrest you when they found her. That is a good sign. It shows that they are willing to give you the benefit of the doubt and consider you a valuable ally. You don't have to rush over the process. Take your time in winning them over. I promise you that you will get a chance to get even with them. They will reap what they sow, and God willing, you will be there to see it. But do not give in to despair, please, I beg of you."

Dubois looked up at Farmani, and there was some of the old fire in his eyes. He held the younger man by his shoulders and said, "By Jove! You are right. I will not give up. I will fight for her. For justice!"

With the old man's voice still ringing in his ears, Farmani stepped out of the mansion. His work was only getting started. With allies like Madame Leclerc and Colonel Dubois, he felt more confident of what his team could achieve. He only hoped that Dubois would be able to become their ears and eyes as they continued their mission.

Chapter 14:

A Battle of Wits: 07-15 August 1942

It was more than a month from when he wrote it that Farmani heard from the Office of Racial Policy in Berlin. He was nervous as he slit open the envelope. He was afraid the letter would signal a revocation of the Aryan status for Persians. He worried that they may have seen through the ruse and that he would be summoned for disciplinary action for trying to circulate fake terminology or distorted historical facts. His hands were shaking as he held the letter up to his eyes. But after having read through it twice, he decided that though it contained no confirmation of his theory, it was not a rejection either. The letter was, in fact, not addressed to him at all. It was what experts who had been consulted on the matter had written back to Berlin. The Berlin Racial Policy Office had merely forwarded a copy of the same letter to him.

To Whomsoever It May Concern

The claim made with regard to the Aryan/Juguti status of the Persian Jews has been researched as best as possible from our end with the limited means at our disposal. We have found certain accounts mentioned in the letter consistent with historical personages and facts. However, in order to verify the full extent of the claim, we would require more time and funding from the government. Insofar as we can tell, initial investigations suggest the veracity of the claims. However, we recommend a fuller study of the subject before a final consensus can be reached.

Sincerely etc.

Farmani breathed a sigh of relief. He noted with satisfaction the line that said that initial investigations seemed to suggest the truth of his claims. Until a fuller report was issued from Berlin, he could use this letter to continue issuing documents for Iranian Jews. He meant to educate everyone willing to listen about Jugutis and disseminate this theory by word of mouth to as many as he could. He knew that his letters and replies to them would only reach a select committee in every German-occupied land. He needed to have local allies who would also know that Iranians were to be spared.

Farmani decided that the time had come to take action. He decided to organize a bridge party on behalf of the Iranian consulate. He sent out gilded invites on the official letterhead of the Iranian consulate to everyone of note within Parisian circles and even select SS officers who had a say in the control and administration of the city. He focused on his contacts and their acquaintances. This was easy because, as a regular player, he knew the bridge players by now.

He booked a hall for the 15th of August at Hotel Napoléon, a luxury hotel near the Arc de Triomphe. Originally opened in 1928, The Napoleon was termed then a boutique hotel because it catered exclusively to the upper classes of Parisian society. Later on, it gained the rank of a luxury hotel and petit palace. Hotel Napoleon had its in-house love story as well. Shortly after it opened, an eccentric, rich Russian businessman, Alexandre Pavlovitch Kliaguine, bought it for his fiancé, who was an art student. He wanted his young bride to hone her skills and complete her course ensconced within the luxury that the hotel could offer. The couple still had their quarters at this hotel, where they stayed whenever they were in the city. It was also the frequent haunt of literary giants like Ernest Hemingway and John Steinbeck. Crowds, however, were more thrilled whenever Ella Fitzgerald, the celebrated American jazz singer, or Errol Flynn, the Australian actor who had dubbed Napoleon "the place," visited the city and stayed at the hotel.

Farmani had decided to invite Klaus Richter, not just because he was a good player but also because he wanted him to be present when he would be discussing his theories. It was more than just a need to rub the man's face in the news from Berlin. He wanted to be sure that men like him knew of the exemption and that there would be no further trouble from any quarters in issuing documents or presenting them at the borders for people to move through easily. He knew it was a dangerous game because the man, being an antisemite, was sure to get furious. But some things had to be done when they had to be.

***

When the day dawned, Farmani dressed up with care in his best three-piece suit and hat. He knew that a man's character was assessed by his position first and then by his grooming. He was always one to take care of his appearance, but more so today because he was the host. He did not want to seem either sloppy or overdone. He was an Iranian at heart, but his long absence from home had made him more of a European in his habits. He knew that the more a man could seem at home in French society, the more he would be accepted. The more he was accepted, the more people would be willing to listen to him and take his words seriously. Now that he had the official letter from Berlin, he knew that he needed to apprise as many people as he could about its contents and the power it granted to Iranian Jews. The word ought to get around that there were at least some Jews who were free of state persecution. Of course, he did not mean to restrict the issuance of papers to Iranian Jews alone. However, this was the theory he was going to float.

He thought back to some of the stories that he used to hear from the many servants and caretakers his family had back in Tehran. He had forgotten most of these tales. They belonged to a part of him that he had rarely unlocked since he was sent to boarding school in England at the age of eight. But for some reason, he was suddenly reminded of one of those stories. It pertained to the great Persian holy warrior, Prince Rostam. He had grown up hearing tales of brave Rostam and his trusted stallion, Rakhsh. There was one story of how they defeated an evil dragon. Rostam knew that as strong and able as he was, he would not be able to slay the beast on his own. So, he created a diversion. He asked Raksh to bite the dragon on its belly. Rakhsh readily complied, and when the dragon was busy trying to ward off the annoying horse, Rostam took the opportunity and decapitated it.

The story made him smile because it reminded him of one of his favorite nannies who used to put her heart and soul into narrating each chapter of Rostam's life. At the time, young Farmani used to worship Rostam as his hero. After he went to school in England, these stories grew fainter until he had all but forgotten them, until today. He realized how important teamwork was for beating enemies. The stronger the enemy was, the more sense it made to have strong allies attacking it from every side.

He listed out the number of people whom he had met and whose aid he had taken to establish Operation Lifeline. Starting with David Cohen, Toni Laurent, Hans Gauthier, and other Resistance workers who were only known to him by their agent names, to Marc Dupont, Madame Leclerc, and Pierre Dubois. He thought briefly of Eva Klein too. There were so many people whom he had met and interacted with. He had learned so much in the space of these two years than he had ever before. It was as if, in the short span of the occupation, he had grown up to become a more mature person.

It was true that he still had a fondness for good wine, music, food, and all other pleasures of life. However, if he had seen the pursuit of them as an end in itself earlier, he knew that life had more to offer. He had found a sense of peace emanating from a real purpose in his life. What would Rostam have been without the tasks that were set before him? What would Kameron Farmani have been without having found his true purpose here in Paris? He lingered over that question for a while as he straightened his tie in the mirror for the umpteenth time.

He had often thought back with longing to a time before the war had started. He had been free as a bird. All he had to do was to clock in his eight hours at the embassy as a junior attaché. His work rarely ever went past the official working hours. He attended so many functions and parties as part of the Iranian diplomatic troupe that he had lost count of them. Once in a while, he would have to compose letters for the consul—tasks that a man of his intelligence and caliber found very easy but still used to grumble about. Farmani realized how fickle people were—that even when they lived in relative comfort and ease, they would still find something to complain about.

What a contrast that life had been to the one he was living right now, where he had to work day and night, and still, there was only more to be done. There was no guarantee of a salary, and he did not even know how long the Iranian government would retain him on their payroll. His life was fraught with uncertainty, not just in terms of his job. There was also the risk of being discovered as a "traitor" who had gone against the dictates of the country—both his own and the one he was residing in now.

Even so, he felt that he had lived a fuller life after the start of the war. A dirty business as it was, the war and the Nazi invasion of France had woken up a part of himself that he hadn't even known existed. For that, Kameron Farmani was eternally grateful. He was still not sure whether it had made him a religious man. But it had surely woken up his dormant spirituality. Everything he saw, touched, tasted, heard, and experienced now seemed to be colored in hues of that same spirituality.

His father had once told him that when he stood in the divine paradise of God, Jannat, it would not be the worldly things he had accumulated that would matter. God would ask him only for a tally of his righteous deeds on earth. A young Farmani had never paid much attention to his father's words—particularly when they related to religious teachings from the Quran. At the time, religion and spirituality had meant nothing to him. To him, the ultimate bliss in life had always centered around having luxury at one's bidding.

He knew that if he were to return to Tehran, he could live in relative comfort. He had a big mansion, servants, and every comfort that money could command. Yet, he knew that to return now would be a grave mistake. He would have all the bodily comforts he could want but not the mental serenity he now possessed despite the hard life here. He momentarily chastised himself for even thinking that his life was hard now. He thought of the numerous Jews who were being carted off in cattle traps across Europe and corrected his inner voice. He paused to reflect—*I am so lucky to be alive, young, and healthy in these times. I am so lucky not to be persecuted and to be continually fearing for my life or for those of my family. I am so humbled that fate has seen me fit to be an instrument to render service to people who need it.*

With those thoughts echoing in his mind, Farmani finished the last rites of his toilette. It was time now to face everyone and complete this last act. He thought a little anxiously about Richter. He predicted that he may have some trouble with the stubborn German. He steeled himself for whatever was coming.

***

Farmani welcomed each of his guests with a pleasant smile. There were less than fifty people in all, and by mid-evening, the hall of the Napoleon that he had booked exuded a warm, quiet gaiety, with the smell of delicious refreshments wafting about. There were twelve square tables laid out in the room, with four chairs around each. Farmani had organized it so that the initial matches could be played simultaneously with no time being wasted. He had made no lists for pairing individuals as a team. But then, most of the people here had already played together and had regular partners. People just naturally seemed to fall into partnerships and groups of four, and in no time, the entire room fell silent, except for the subdued chatter at each table as the players focused on their game.

Without having to say anything, Farmani found himself opposite Colonel Dubois and flanked by Captain Klaus Richter and another German. He wondered briefly what had happened to Heinrich Müller, assuming he remembered the young man's name right, who had played with them the last time. He wondered if he should ask Richter about him but was momentarily struck by how the Nazi was glaring at him. There seemed no question that the German was shooting him a gaze of pure venom. When he saw that Farmani had caught his stare, he slowly withdrew his gaze back to the cards on the table. Farmani wondered what it meant and why Richter seemed so hostile.

The two teams took their positions at the bridge table, the game ready to unfold in an atmosphere of intense focus and anticipation. Farmani, who was by now known for his strategic brilliance and unflagging determination, faced off against Richter, who was a formidable opponent with a reputation for cunning and calculated maneuvers.

On Farmani's side, Dubois, with his keen eye for detail, carefully reviewed the cards, while Richter's partner studied the hand with a glance as sharp as a sword. Farmani, exuding quiet confidence, assessed the unfolding game with a blend of sharp intuition and tactical prowess, ready to outsmart their opponents at every turn that presented itself.

As the cards were dealt and the bidding began, both teams engaged in a silent battle of skill and strategy, each move akin to a masterstroke in a complex game of wits and cunning. Farmani and Dubois navigated the bidding process with a mix of precision and calculated risk-taking, while Richter and his partner responded with astute bids and shrewd counterplays.

The young man who was playing with them, Farmani learned, was a German banker by the name of Georg Schneider. He was a man of average height and had black hair oiled back against his temples. As one would expect of a banker, Schneider was cautious and yet took calculated risks in the game. He was not a brilliant player, but his strengths amounted to the fact that he could make accurate analyses where needed and had oodles of patience in holding on till the time was right. It struck Farmani that perhaps Richter had brought a partner with whom he thought he had better chances of winning.

The game progressed with an air of silent tension; the only sounds in the room were the soft shuffle of cards and the focused murmurs of discussion between partners. Each play and counterplay unfolded with the grace and precision of a carefully choreographed dance as both teams sought to gain the upper hand in this high-stakes battle of wits. Though it was a close match, Farmani and Dubois were leading. As before, Richter was not taking his losses graciously. His muttering was getting louder so that players at the other tables were looking at them.

At one point, when Dubois played his hand, Richter said sneeringly, "As sneaky as a Jew, aren't you? But just as the ones in the Opera House, we shall see who has the last laugh."

Both Dubois and Farmani stiffened at the unfounded and unjust prejudice. Farmani said nothing because he did not want to give away his knowledge of what happened at the Opera House. For all intents and purposes, nobody knew that he was a part of that mission. But looking at the smug expression on Richter's face, Farmani had a shrewd suspicion that somehow the Nazi knew of his involvement. It made him shudder inwardly, but he continued to play coolly. As for Dubois, the associations of the roundups must have brought back memories of his daughter. His face was set firm, almost stern, but he said nothing. There were people whose games had been interrupted by Richter's words. Some of them were staring angrily at him.

As the game reached its climax, Farmani's final hand played out with an almost palpable sense of anticipation, the outcome hanging in the balance as both teams maneuvered to secure victory in this pivotal showdown of bridge supremacy. Onlookers would have described it as a thrilling display of skill and strategic finesse. Eventually, Farmani and Dubois emerged triumphant once again—their victory a testament to their unparalleled expertise at the game and perhaps, more than a slight dislike for their adversary.

***

After the last game was wound up, delicious nibbles were served, and people lounged about chatting and having their drinks. If there was one man, in particular, who was in a foul mood, it was Richter. He could not let Farmani leave without one last showdown.

He sidled up to him and said loudly, "You win again, consul. My congratulations."

Farmani, who had been discussing the Nuremberg Laws and its implications for Iranians, in general, stopped short and said, "Thank you, Captain Richter. It was a pleasure playing against a gifted adversary like you."

Richter looked at him and said, "Well. It seems that you have been playing your cards well here and elsewhere. I couldn't help overhearing *your twist* on the Nuremberg Laws. But I suppose you haven't mentioned to anybody here that *you* wrote to Berlin to reinforce that immunity. Quite a neat little trick, I must add. Blindsided the rest of us."

Farmani looked at him squarely in the eyes and said, "There was no trickery involved. I wrote to Berlin because the Führer himself had bestowed the Aryan status on all Persians—I was just explaining this to these good folks here. In my letter, I only reiterated that the Jugutis of our lands be given the same privileges as the rest of the Persians."

Everyone in the room looked at this tense verbal duel that was now unfolding. Though, internally, Farmani felt uneasy, he also knew that Richter was playing into his plan. Everyone gathered here would now hear of "Jugutis" and their Aryan status. The German was helping him disseminate his theory faster and with greater ease than if he were to approach each person in the room and talk to them.

Richter scoffed, "I personally checked every historical record possible. I have yet to come across a term such as the *Jugutis*. I wonder if you could provide me with the name of a text or study that references the word. Otherwise, I can only say that this is another Jewish camouflage, a common trick to save their hides and that you, Monsieur Consul, are, for reasons best known to yourself, aiding them against France and the Reich's better judgment."

Farmani drew himself up to his full height in outrage. He knew he had to express, "You are now insulting a government official of the Iranian state. Please choose your words with more care, captain. I have aided only my fellow countrymen, as permitted by the Reich and France. In fact, I have a letter here that backs my claims insofar as Berlin has been able to study them. Until a day comes when there is a revocation of the exemption granted to Iranian Jews, I do not see why I should not be permitted to do or talk about what is only my duty." He took out the letter that he had received a few days ago.

Richter glared at him for a while. It was clear that he was thrown by the letter which he read stony-faced. He carefully placed his hat on his head. His face was unreadable as he mumbled, "Well then. We shall await that day." He then walked out of the room. He must have been disturbed because he forgot his customary salutation of "Heil Hitler" this time.

After his exit, the tension in the room dissipated, and normal conversation started flowing freely once again. Farmani was satisfied. That day, an observer would have remarked that the Iranian consul looked positively exuberant about something. He had, after all, played and won the actual cards dealt and the metaphorical cards too.

***

Now that one part of his scheme had gone better than expected, Farmani knew there was something he ought to tackle before it got out of hand. He made his way in deliberate steps to Rue Halévy. Ever since his conversation with Eva about Miriam at the cafe, he had known of her residence. Though they had spent time together between their work schedules, he had never suggested meeting her at her home. He had thought it imprudent. But the time had come to have a serious conversation with her. He needed to get some things off his chest.

It wasn't hard to find her house because David had kept an eye on Miriam; he had also told Farmani about which building it was. It was a small apartment complex, and Eva's flat was on the first floor. He quickly mounted the stairs and, with a beating heart, stood before her door.

She opened on the third knock. She was cautious. She first opened her door just a crack and inspected her visitor through the chink, before unlatching and opening the door. She was wearing a lavender dressing gown, and her hair was damp. The floral fragrance of some soap hung in the air. It was clear that Eva was fresh out of a shower.

Her shock turned surprise at seeing him at her doorstep quickly turned to a teasingly wicked smile as she said, "So the consul has found his way to my humble abode, it seems. Please do come inside."

Her apartment was a cozy and eclectic space, indicative of her artistic nature. The walls were adorned with colorful paintings and photographs, showcasing her love for art and culture. The furniture was a mix of vintage and modern pieces, creating an interesting juxtaposition. The color palette was vibrant, with splashes of deep reds, blues, and greens. He could tell that in the mornings, the rooms would be filled with natural light, streaming in through large windows, illuminating the space and giving it a warm and inviting feel. A small corner of the apartment was dedicated to her collection of sheet music and opera memorabilia, reminding visitors of her passion for her craft.

Farmani said, "This is a nice space you have created for yourself."

Eva said proudly, "I know. I furnished it myself—piece by piece. Would you like anything to drink?"

Farmani said, "Just some water. I had dinner on the way. I wanted to see you about something."

She got him what he asked for and sat across him in the living room, "Shoot away then. What's troubling you?"

He said, swallowing hard, "I have changed my mind. I don't think you should be a part of all this, Eva. I am almost convinced we have a mole in our midst. I also have a shrewd suspicion about who he is working for. It simply won't do Eva. I can't sacrifice you."

Eva said nothing for a while and then asked, "Do you know who he is? This double agent working in our midst?"

Farmani said, "I don't. That is also why I don't want you to run errands anymore. The more people you come in contact with, the more dangerous it is for you. Especially since the Opera House mission."

She looked crestfallen and said, "But you don't know that there is a mole for certain, then. I could still—"

He said firmly, holding up his hands, "No, Eva, you don't understand." He paused for breath and then said what he had been meaning to say for some time now, "I care about you—no, no—I'm falling in love with you. There. I have said it. I assure you this is not some infantile infatuation. I have been around women before, but from the moment I met you, I knew. I can't bear to see something happen to you. Please. You need to stay out of this."

She looked at him. Her cheeks and neck were on fire, and her eyes sparkled. She said, "And what about me? Will you not even ask how I feel about you?"

Farmani had to hold himself back from the strong urge he felt to envelop her in his arms. But he said, "What good will that do, Eva? I am asking you to stay away from me. If you feel the same, that would be torture. If you do not, that too would be torture." She was mesmerized by the intensity of feelings his eyes held.

She smiled once. She got up and stood in front of him. She touched his cheek softly with her fingers as she whispered, "Kameron." She then leaned forward, planting the gentlest of kisses on his lips. Then, standing back a little, she said simply, "I will not stand between you and your work. After all, it is your mission. You decide who stays on the team."

He was surprised that there was no further debate or arguments. He had prepared himself for long, drawn-out discussions. He got up and looked at her. Suddenly, something came over him as he closed the gap between them, took her in his arms, and kissed her firmly this time.

***

Much later, as he walked back to his apartment and tried to catch some sleep, the floral scent of her soap refused to leave his nostrils.

Chapter 15:

Betrayal: 03-06 September 1942

It was now September and an important day for the members working for Operation Lifeline. The Jews who were hiding in safe houses across the city were to be transported in batches to parts of Vichy, France, and, from there, out of the country. Gauthier had exhausted his men working overtime to provide papers for all the Jews in hiding, who seemed to be multiplying rapidly. In some cases, there was no way to create entirely new documents. They focused on removing the stamp reading "Juif" or "Jewish" on the actual papers issued by the French authorities.

Many safe houses had elaborate radio equipment whereby Resistance members were able to pass on messages to their teammates stationed outside Paris and sometimes even outside the country. This communication became stronger as the months went by. Most messages were in coded language, and the volume of communication was so great that the Germans found it increasingly harder to decipher them. Instead, they focused their energy on trying to jam the signals so that the French found it hard to use radio waves. However, their need to fight back against their oppressors was so fierce that they found alternative frequencies to get their messages across.

These were exciting times for everyone fighting to free the Jews and Mother France. The fact that Hitler's speeches were becoming more rhetorical and that he continued talking for two hours or more without conveying any real information to his people seemed to suggest that even the Germans were under a lot of pressure in this interminable war. If nothing else, that spurred on the Resistance groups and others working against the Nazis even more.

Unfortunately, the vigor of the Resistance groups was met with equally repressive repercussions. In the city and elsewhere, Nazis were cracking down on dissenters more harshly than ever. Instances of police brutality and arrests were now so common as not to even raise eyebrows. The common man had problems of his own even when not engaged in antiwar activities. Most of them were engaged in the daily task of trying to keep themselves alive with the 200g of food ration allotted to them. As winter was fast approaching, there was the intense cold to be borne as well. With fuel prices skyrocketing, heating was now a luxury that most homes could not afford. People managed as best as they could by wearing tattered old clothes, one on top of the other, and with layers of blankets. This was for the case of people who actually had clothes and blankets to call their own. The others would have to hope for the best as they froze and starved all through the coming cold months.

***

David Cohen came with another packet. This was how Madame Leclerc arranged funds to reach the Resistance groups. Her trusted servants bundled up the notes, sealed them in envelopes, and dropped them in designated public mailboxes from where Resistance group members collected them before the residents of those houses happened to check the mailboxes for letters. It had to be done quickly and covertly before residents noticed or reported the suspicious movements of the people collecting the parcels to the police.

Despite the added danger of receiving these funds, operations had become smoother overall. There was more money for one thing. For another, the team members had now worked together enough to know what their jobs were and to whom they had to relay important information. The use of agent names ensured that the identities of the operatives remained anonymous and, at most times, even among themselves. Each agent only knew one or two others with whom they coordinated things. This ensured that in case of capture and possible torture, they could only betray that many others.

Farmani had recently helped with the logistics and had even personally been present during the moving of people from certain safe houses within the city. His official supply of passports from the government was almost over now, and he did not have to be present in office as much as before. He had, therefore, decided to play a more active role in the other areas of the operation. However, being a government official, he still had to be careful. His identity had to be protected. He often resorted to hats, masks, and scarves that concealed his face from other agents and even the people he was saving.

Serving as a masked vigilante often helped him take his mind off thoughts of Eva Klein. Though he had known her only a couple of months, the self-imposed break that he had wanted between them affected him almost with physical withdrawal symptoms. There were nights he couldn't sleep because he couldn't distract himself from her scent and the feel of her slim body. He had never experienced feelings this strong for any other woman. If he hadn't known any better, he might have said that it was almost akin to the grief of loss.

Cohen was about to leave when he said, "I was checking the messages being relayed today. Has there been a change in plans for tomorrow? I thought they were to be sent to Villa Air-Bel. But the message seems to suggest a location closer to Montpellier now?"

Farmani's head snapped up in attention. He had known nothing about this change of plan. He frowned and said, "Are you sure you heard it right?"

Cohen replied, "Yes. I cross-checked with another agent who was with me, listening to the same message. He too heard Montpellier. How is this possible?"

Suddenly, Farmani remembered something. He knew that the last one to send and receive messages had been Gagnon. A ghastly thought struck him. He said, "We need to urgently speak to Laurent and change the location. It can't be Air-Bel. Let us see how best it can be arranged."

After much back-and-forth messaging between Toni and them and meeting her in person, it was finally arranged that the Jews would be taken by road to a safe house in Grenoble, which had been more recently set up.

***

When the day arrived, both Cohen and Farmani helped Toni lead the Jews hidden away in a dilapidated house in Paris to parked trucks that would transport them to Grenoble. These special trucks had also been an indirect gift from Madame Leclerc. With her generous grants, they had been able to build a secret chamber of sorts into the base of the truck where about fifteen adults could stay crouching. On the top were regular cattle tethers, where the drivers would gather cattle from a farmhouse just outside the city. If officers of the Reich stopped the truck to check, all they would find would be two tired drivers transporting cattle to a farmhouse in Toulouse. Or at least, that is what their documents would say.

Interestingly, Gagnon was nowhere to be found. He had been informed via a written message that he was to be replaced on the mission with Cohen. He must have done his own digging but did not write back to ask about whether the venue was being changed or why he was being replaced. The last they heard of Gagnon was that he had been seen skulking around in one of the city's railway stations. There was no further word from him. It seemed that the man had just disappeared without a trace.

It seemed clear as daylight that the man was playing a double game. Farmani was convinced that he was working for Richter. Though he wasn't sure why, Richter's attitude to him at the bridge party had suggested something more than mere animosity toward a diplomat working for another country. It only seemed natural that Richter would hire a spy to keep an eye on the movements of the Iranian embassy, especially if he suspected that Jews other than Iranians were also being provided papers.

Farmani thanked his lucky stars that he had the foresight not to involve Gagnon in any operation that dealt with documentation and papers being provided to the Jews. He was also happy that Gagnon did not seem to have any idea about Gauthier's involvement. The vital links of the operation were safe and secure, as far as he could tell. The fact that no checking or inspection had come so long after the Opera House mission said that the man still had no concrete evidence against the team.

However, Farmani was still worried. He wondered what Gagnon may have unearthed and what he might be able to relay to the Nazis. He also wondered what his motive was. Gagnon had been trying to trace his fiancé. Had the girl been found? Had the Germans twisted his arm with her safety in exchange for the information that he gave them? There were so many unanswered questions and loose ends that he would have wanted to investigate if he had the time. But there wasn't any time, and their resources were stretched to their limit as it was. He had to work faster, under the assumption that they may all be discovered at a moment's notice now. This was the only way to beat them at their game.

***

It would be another two days before they heard anything about Karl Gagnon. In fact, the turn of events was so surprising that Toni Laurent asked for a personal meeting with Farmani and Cohen together at the same old den where he had met her first.

The cafe looked seedier than before, with the flooring and walls looking even more worn out and black with soot. However, that did not seem to deter the regular customers in the least. It was as crowded as ever, and people were laughing and chatting loudly. Farmani felt the heat emanating from the closed space very claustrophobic.

They had no problem in locating Toni. She was seated toward the back of the room in the dark. As usual, she was wearing a dark-colored tunic over her well-worn pants. She had a dark blue beret placed angularly on her brown hair, which had grown longer than the last time he had seen her. The liveliness of her eyes and malleable mouth persisted, and Farmani took a moment to marvel that a slip of a girl like her had not just survived but flourished here in the city, engaged in the deadly missions that she was. Surely, he was only seeing the shell of someone with uncommon grit and strength.

In her deep voice, she said at once without any preamble, "Karl Gaganon is our man. He has been working with Captain Richter for a couple of months now. We are to presume that he was the one who betrayed the Opera House mission. When you told us of your suspicions, we tailed him, but he gave our agents the slip once or twice. It was only after the recent fiasco that we were able to catch him sending a boy off with a message. This boy went straight to the Nazi office. They don't know this yet, but we have one of ours planted there as a sweeper now. He saw the note going to Richter, who looked as smug as a pig in mud. But of course, this was before the plans were changed. The truck reached Toulouse yesterday. So that's all well. Thank God you picked up on the Montpellier confusion in time. We would have lost Jews and our agents too otherwise."

Farmani knew that his question may not be answered, but he asked anyway, "And what became of him? Why have we not heard of him at all?"

Toni was fidgeting a little by now, "He won't disturb our work anymore. The man you knew as Karl Gagnon is dead."

David Cohen asked sharply, "Dead? Are you sure? But how?"

Toni said, "Well, not our doing, I promise. He was killed by the Parisian police force. They mistook him for a dodger, and when they found those papers on him, he was a goner anyway."

Farmani quipped, "What papers?"

Toni chuckled a little as she said, "This man who claimed he was Karl Gagnon was somebody else. The real Karl Gagnon died about three months ago. He had been searching for his girlfriend, and nobody knows this for sure, but he was probably shot down by the Gestapo for digging into things they did not think were of his concern. This man possessed Karl Gagnon's papers. And since we know that he was working for Richter, we assume that the Nazis simply arranged for a lookalike to take on Gagnon's identity and come to you with his heart-wrenching story. We had done a background check on Gagnon but never dreamed to check that the man was indeed Gagnon."

Farmani quietly reflected on how convincing Gagnon had been in his narration of his missing fiancée and of his genuine anger at the officials. He wondered if the real Gagnon had been replaced with the fake one after he had come to him. But that part would remain a mystery. He, however, asked, "How did you realize that this man was not Gagnon?"

Toni shrugged, "Oh, we have our men in the police force. They were the ones who had confirmed reports of Gagnon for us initially when you came to us for a background check. The police found the real Gagnon three days ago. He was tied up and seemingly left to die in a dilapidated house destroyed by bombing just on the outskirts of the city. They couldn't at first identify him because he did not have any papers on him. But his right arm bore a tattoo that one of the officers remembered as belonging to Gagnon. When they caught the traitor a couple of days later claiming to be Gagnon, he never had the tattoo."

Farmani could not remember a tattoo on the arm of the Karl Gagnon who came to see him. But then again, the man had been wearing a coat and his arm was out of plain sight.

Toni said, "We think that he tried to establish his links with Richter. But since his identity was busted, I don't think Richter would have protected him anyway. After all, he was only useful as long as he remained "Karl Gagnon." The police and Gestapo, who couldn't establish whether he was one of theirs or ours, simply shot him to end the confusion."

Wryly, Farmani mused that that was all a life was worth these days. If you could not establish who you were and what information you carried, then you were shot down like a rabid dog. Sadly, he wondered how things had come to the point where people acted so mercilessly. It wasn't that he felt any pity for this Nazi who was merely play-acting Gagnon's part, but he suddenly felt old and worn. He felt tired of all the bloodshed that he would be a witness to for as long as he was a part of this mission.

He finally asked, "Anything more?"

Toni's face took on a more serious aspect, "Unfortunately, there is more. And you will not find this pretty. Probably, the Germans killing him weren't thorough enough. They left his keys on him. We got those keys and decided it would be worth a shot going through his things. It took us a while to hunt down where he was staying. I will spare you details of all those bits. It was a small room in the poorer quarters of the city. He did not seem to have many possessions. All we could find was a spare gun and a diary. He hasn't been able to gather much evidence against the members of the Resistance. However, he seems to have some written communication from an unidentified Nazi. This letter talks of a letter Eva Klein wrote to somebody in the Opera House asking for a floor map of the building. How he got his filthy hands on this letter, we can't say and as much as we searched for this letter, we never found it at his place. The fact that this letter is from her, that she is a singer there, and the fact that Miriam escaped the clutches of Von Falken could raise suspicions about Klein's sympathies. This letter could be used as evidence against her to denounce her as a traitor or a Resistance fighter, especially given the Opera House events in July. I don't think she should stay back to check whether Gagnon delivered this letter to Richter or not. We have the time and resources on our hands to get her out now."

Farmani's heart sank. This is exactly what he had been so scared of. Because of him, she was now entangled in a web of lies, deceit, and evil that may lead her to further trouble. Eva had gotten copies of the maps to acquaint them with the layout of the building when she felt that she could explain the locations better with a floor map than one drawn from her knowledge and memory of it. He knew that Eva Klein would not last long in the horrific prisons. They would prolong her trial and make it a public spectacle to make an example of her to other citizens planning to help the Resistance. He shuddered at what other kinds of punishment they would concoct for her. Torture was the modus operandi via which the SS and Gestapo extracted information and buried dissenting voices. Farmani could no longer bear the thought.

He said, "You are right, Laurent. I will talk to her. She needs to leave. Her safety and our safety too, perhaps depends on it. She is not a stupid person. She will see the reason behind it."

David Cohen was watching him sympathetically. Though they hadn't discussed it, he had guessed that Farmani and Eva were more than just colleagues working to deliver justice to the Jews.

Farmani nodded at Toni Laurent. There did not seem to be more to discuss on either side. As was her way, she gently walked away into the night after she had given them all that was important.

Farmani had his hands on his forehead now. He was internally questioning his worth as a leader. He had allowed a spy into their midst, and now the girl he loved would probably bear the brunt of his stupidity.

Cohen laid his hand on the other man's shoulder gently as he said, "It is not your fault, you know. Nothing you did could have changed the outcome."

Farmani looked up at him, "But I should have had someone tail him. We could have discovered his game before this. If we had exposed him, perhaps we could have saved more at the Opera House. How could I have been so remiss? And Eva—" He stopped short.

Cohen said logically, "You know somebody else could have stumbled upon the brainwave of checking the Opera House that day. It is a public building, after all, and the Nazis were desperate to outdo each other by capturing as many Jews as possible. There is no guarantee that they would have been safe even if we had caught wind of Gagnon's plans in time. As for Eva, let us be thankful that we have realized she is in danger now before it is too late. Let us not waste more time beating ourselves up over ifs and buts."

Farmani said, "You are right. We need to act fast now. Since the letter she wrote was not found in her possession, there is a high chance that Richter or one of the others may have it in their position. The best bet now is to ensure she is out of the way. Richter will use her in exchange for information from us. They will neither spare her nor us. We must speak to her at once. Meanwhile, we need to speed up the other work for the remaining people who have to leave. Richter will use this opportunity to crack down on them."

The two men got up, intending to make their way toward Rue Halévy. They had a lot of work on their hands now, but they were resolved to see this business through to its end. Farmani knew now that the stakes were high and that they had to play smart in order to clinch the game.

Chapter 16:

High Stakes: 16-19 September 1942

Klaus Richter was elated and furious. Granted that these were two contradictory emotions, but they consumed him to such an extent that he did not know how to contain them both within him or which of them he felt more. Since he was not a man who gave in to feelings generally when he did experience them, it tended to throw him off kilter.

On the one hand, he had a reply from Berlin. On the other, he had just learned of Karl Gagnon's—or rather Max Weber's—death. The following was a letter that he had received from no less than Adolf Eichmann. Even if the man's secretary had crafted the letter, Eichmann signed it himself. For a few minutes, Richter couldn't take his eyes off the signature that other Nazis in Germany would have loved to frame as an autograph on their walls. When he could finally focus on the contents of the letter, this is what it said—

> *Hauptsturmführer Richter,*
>
> *Heil Hitler! and greetings from Berlin. I thank you for your initiative in writing to me and explaining in a detailed manner the issue of the so-called Jugutis. As you suggest, it looks to me like a Jewish conspiracy—a mere attempt to disguise them and help them flee the just desserts of their actions.*

I shall on my authority ensure that your concerns are investigated by the best experts in the field, and be sure to let you know of the outcome.

Meanwhile, I implore you to exercise caution and to keep an eye on whoever is issuing these papers in Paris in support of the Jewish people.

Let us hope to capture traitors who work against the interests of the fatherland sooner than later.

Sincerely

Adolf Eichmann

Richter was excited to be holding a letter penned by one of the highest-ranking SS officers of the Reich. He had not really expected a reply when he crafted the draft he sent to Eichmann. He had only hoped that the letter would reach Eichmann and that the senior officer should be apprised of the situation here. The fact that he had written back personally to a low-ranking officer like himself filled him with a sense of purpose and importance. He was confident that if the issue warranted the notice of a man like Eichmann, matters would proceed rapidly and with adequate consideration for the delicacy of the situation. He was also pleased that it had been him who had notified Eichmann about this situation before anybody else could reach him. Hopefully, Eichmann would remember him and favor him for promotions and other positions of honor within the Nazi ranks. Richter was not interested in promotions for the hike in salary it would offer him. It was power and fame that were his personal elixirs, not money. That, and the fact that a traitor like Farmani would soon be brought to heel.

Just as he was getting high on this scenario of future glory that would be his, he got a message. It was not signed by anybody and soon his preoccupation with who wrote it turned to the contents of the letter. It mentioned two things that nearly gave him an apoplectic fit. The first was the fact that the real Karl Gagnon had been discovered and identified owing to the presence of a tattoo, which they had failed to notice. The second was that of the capture and murder of the pseudo-Karl Gagnon by the French police, who could not determine who he was. The deaths of either of the men were no great loss to him. However, the information that Weber relayed had been really useful to him. He mourned the loss of the steady stream of information on the enemy that would now no longer flow to him.

Richter was no fool. He understood the implications of what had happened. He knew that just as he was notified of Weber's death, very soon, the same information would reach Farmani and his team. He also knew that they would have quite a good idea of who Weber, the pseudo-Gagnon, was working for. It angered him that he would no longer have access to their moves but that they should know of his involvement in their schemes. Introducing a new spy instead of Weber would not only take time but would be harder now that the entire team would be extra-cautious of any new joiners at this time.

He still had no real proof against Farmani's involvement in the Resistance. However, he had a plan. He had in his possession a letter from the singer to one of the officials of the Opera House asking for detailed floor maps of the building. This letter was dated just before the roundups. He had not missed the timing of the letter. Though not conclusive, he could still cause the woman no end of trouble, using it as proof of her betrayal. But he wanted more. He did not care for the woman unless she was used as a pawn to capture the real prize he was after—Farmani's head.

A shadowy plan was taking shape in his devious mind. The more he thought of it, the more he fell in love with it. He knew that Farmani would not be able to resist playing the hero. What better opportunity to lure him into a trap? This was probably the only chance that he would have to catch that oily traitor right in his game. His affection for the fair maiden would undoubtedly work against him.

He knew that he would have to act fast. There was no point in overthinking the potential outcomes. The more Richter thought of it, the more he was convinced of the road he saw ahead.

***

Though Farmani and Cohen had intended to talk to Eva that very night, urgent matters came in the way of their actually reaching her. They thought that matters could be discussed and arranged for at once in the morning. With the mounting pressure on them to move fast, they did not really think that a few hours would make a difference in Eva's situation.

Farmani helped Cohen in devising alternative routes for the Jewish people to escape from the city. Together, they also came up with new ideas for transporting Jews out. The cattle transportation was a good ruse, but they couldn't have multiple such trucks working on the same pretext. It would eventually seem fishy that suddenly, so many cattle sales were happening. It took them some time, but they finally narrowed down to a couple more ways in which the transits could be disguised as something more innocuous.

Unfortunately, Cohen and Farmani were wrong about Eva. Their delay in contacting Eva did change things. When they reached Eva's apartment in the morning they found it to be locked from the outside. This did not perturb them greatly. Eva could have been rehearsing or performing at the Opera House. It had been a while since Farmani had corresponded with her, and so he did not know of her exact schedule. They decided to leave a message with a neighbor who knew her well.

The whole day, Farmani devoted himself to pushing Gauthier about the paperwork and giving instructions to Laurent about when and where they should start with the transfer of the Jews. There were so many details to be decided on that he was kept on his toes.

When evening came with still no news of Eva, Farmani was concerned. This was strange. She was always one to send back word as soon as possible, and it did not seem likely that she was at rehearsals for so long.

When he went back to her apartment and enquired with the neighbor, his concern grew to alarm.

The neighbor, an elderly white-whiskered gentleman whose name was Mssr. Claudel said, "I don't think anybody has come to the apartment the whole day. I met Eva yesterday afternoon. For a while now, she has been more or less here. She told me that she would not be taking on work. It seemed to me like she was taking a break from her singing. Now this is only my personal opinion—and if I am not greatly mistaken—I think that young woman was suffering from some sadness. First, her maid left her and then—well, I don't exactly how to put this—but there was something that was eating her up. In the last couple of weeks, she had shrunk in size, and her eyes had lost that mischievous sparkle that people so loved. I felt that she wasn't taking care of herself, not eating or sleeping well, perhaps. Though, when I asked her about it she only smiled and said that she was in good health. Whatever was bothering her, poor soul, she kept it to herself. I have never seen Eva Klein so lost and desolate."

Farmani had a good idea of why Eva Klein should feel lost and disconsolate. When alone, he felt the same, most of the time. There was only one word that could describe the change in her—heartbreak. He could tell this with certainty because it was what had pushed him to work harder and not to think about himself these past couple of weeks. Eva, perhaps, chose to deal with the same emotions in a different manner. He felt guilty that he had contributed to her sadness at a time when she had no other friends to call her own. It wrenched his heart that even her neighbor should see the change in her while he had not bothered to check in on her.

He also knew for a fact that Eva loved the sanctuary of her home after work. Even assuming she had decided to practice her voice more, it was not like herself to keep away from home for so long. Claudel also confirmed that it was unusual for Eva to be away from her flat for so long without leaving word about where she was off to.

Taking everything into consideration, Farmani was now sweating and feeling extremely queasy. It wasn't that he felt that she would do something drastic. Eva Klein was not a coward, and neither was she of a dramatic temperament. However, he could not help feeling that something had happened to her. He remembered the letter that Gagnon had found and most likely handed over to Richter. He was now sorry that they hadn't gone to her place immediately after meeting Toni. He cursed himself for the precious time that he had wasted.

For his peace, more than anything else, he quickly hurried to the Opera House and asked everyone he met if they had seen her over the last two days. Nobody seemed to remember having seen her. Her cabin was locked and the caretakers confirmed that nobody had asked for them to clean out her rooms. She always had them cleaned before she used them.

Like a madman now, Farmani hurried back to his office, and sure enough, there was a cryptic note waiting for him. It had been delivered only about an hour earlier, and the sender who had it delivered via an errand boy left no name or return address. Farmani's foreboding grew. His hands trembled as he slit open it open.

Suddenly, he realized that he had unnecessarily feared the worst. He had forgotten the simplest explanation. It was a letter from Toni Laurent, coded as usual. It said that she had personally gone to Eva and convinced her to come away with her. Eva was now lodged in one of the many safe houses of the city where the Jews were hidden.

Farmani marveled at Toni's insight. She must have located Eva right after their conversation the night before and had taken it upon herself to convince the singer to flee. The matter of the letter Eva wrote to the Opera House must have convinced Eva of Toni's words. He realized that it was much better as it had happened. Where Eva might resist his help stubbornly, she would listen to Toni. His involvement would have necessarily prolonged matters.

He read the brief note and realized again why Toni Laurent was such a valuable asset to them. She used the word "heart" in the letter so many times that Farmani was sure that it must be a subtle hint as to her location. He would have time to ponder over that later. He was relieved that Eva Klein was in safe hands.

He knew that now he had a small matter to clear up. He immediately sent word to Cohen with a few brief instructions for the next couple of days. He had complete faith in the latter's ability to pick up vital news.

***

David Cohen was covertly keeping tabs on all the places where Eva Klein usually hung around. A whole day went by, and he had nothing much to report to Farmani. However, in the early hours of the 17th of September, he noticed a troop of German soldiers marching toward Eva's house. David quickly ducked into an alleyway from where he had a clear view of the building but remained unseen himself.

He watched as a tall, fair German marched ahead of the five men who followed them. They stormed into the little apartment complex, stopping in front of Eva's apartment. They shouted in German and then in French for her to come out. When there seemed to be no response, the man moved ahead, rapped the door with a short baton he carried, and then realized that the door was padlocked from the outside. For a few moments, he inspected the door wordlessly. He looked perplexed as he rattled the lock a bit and then, without warning, drew his pistol and shot twice at it. Sure enough, the lock fell apart, and the door flew open. David watched on as the men charged inside. After what seemed like three-quarters of an hour, the men came out. The tall German seemed to be beside himself with fury.

Looking around for a while, the German pounded on the door of a neighbor. Cohen thought to himself, *They mean to interrogate Mssr. Claudel, no doubt.*

As soon as the old man opened up, the tall Nazi shouted, "We are here for one Eva Klein. Have you any idea where we might find her?"

Claudel took his own time to respond, "Sorry gentlemen," he said in the most unclear accent he could muster, "I am a little hard of hearing. Who are you here for, you say?" For effect, Claudel cupped his hands around his right ear.

The German had now turned himself in David's direction. David noticed the insignia of a Hauptsturmführer on his khaki uniform. He smiled. He had a good idea who this was, though he had never met the man in person before. He was rewarded when the furious German turned his side profile into David's view. He caught a glimpse of the tell-tale ugly scar that ran across the man's cheek. *Bingo,* David thought, *There you are—a little late to the scene, but nevertheless. Watching this unfold will be fun.*

Richter roared his reply this time as a few lights in the neighboring apartments were switched on. People peeked through the curtains to check what the commotion was all about.

"I said I am here for Eva Klein, who is wanted for questioning. Where can I find her? Speak up, old man!"

Claudel replied, "Oh, Eva Klein, eh? Let me see now. To be honest, I haven't seen her around for a couple of days now. You could perhaps ask at the Opera House? That's where she works."

Richter seemed to be controlling his fury as he said contemptuously, "We know where she works, thank you. We have enquired there. But she hasn't reported to work for a while now. So I ask you again, when did you see her last? Did she tell you that she was going somewhere?"

Claudel seemed to scratch his head and blinked as if trying hard to think and then finally said, "It was two days ago, perhaps? I don't remember now, sir. I am old, as you can see. I don't go out all that much these days. She was at home the day before yesterday—at least during the daytime, after which I haven't seen her. No, she usually keeps to herself. I have no idea where she could be. We weren't as close as all that for her to confide such things to me."

"So you never saw this woman going anywhere?" Richter asked impatiently as the old man paused, shook his head, and took a long time to consider and answer each question.

Claudel said, "I can't be sure. I get muddled up sometimes, you see. My eyesight and brain aren't what they used to be. I often saw her going to work. From my window, I can see the gate of our apartment. But no, I don't remember her having left the premises these last couple of days."

Richter still looked angry as he asked, "Eva Klein was a traitor working for the Resistance. If we realize that you have been helping her by keeping vital information from us, we will make your last days on earth the very worst. Do you understand that old man?"

Claudel looked a little scared as he nodded a couple of times, though he said nothing. After a pause to check that his message had really sunk in, Richter said, "Has anybody else come here asking about her? Have you noticed anybody hanging about this house recently or just before you realized that she was missing?"

Claudel seemed to hesitate and then finally shook his head as he said, "No. I don't remember anybody."

David Cohen breathed a sigh of relief and inwardly thanked the old man for his intuition and good sense in not mentioning Farmani's visit the day before. Though Richter would know that Farmani could be behind it, there would still be no proof.

Richter was staring at the old man, who was now cowering beneath his piercing gaze. Finally, Richter said, "Remember. The death of a dog for you if you are playing us false or caught lying. If you remember anything about the girl later you think may help us, you can reach out to me." He handed over a card to the old man.

The old man took it with trembling hands as Richter and his team took a last look around the area and marched off.

As David was about to leave, after he was sure the Germans had left, he saw Claudel still standing on the porch of his apartment with the card clutched in his hand. Finally, the old man seemed to collect himself and stood up straighter. He crumpled up the card in his hand, and though David couldn't hear what he said, the old man's lips seemed to curl upward in a sneer as they made the words, "Nazi pigs!" He spat at the ground where Richter had stood not moments ago.

***

Klaus Richter sat late that gloomy evening in his cabin, mulling things over. He was irritated and angry. Yet, he had to answer his superiors. In his extreme confidence, he had made big promises to haul in the girl who could give them answers about Farmani's role in the operation to save the Jews. And just as he thought that he had the perfect solution to bring in the girl for questioning, she had given them the slip. He wondered how Eva Klein had disappeared exactly when they were searching for her. He tried to trace back events in their logical sequence. Then he remembered about Weber. Of course, the Resistance would find evidence of him having been in correspondence with Richter and about Eva's letter being in his possession. They would have rightly guessed that if the letter wasn't in Weber's apartment and on his person, he must have handed it over to the official to whom he reported.

First, Richter's informant had been eliminated. It wasn't even the work of the Resistance but that of the foolish Parisian police force who could not recognize friend from foe. With Weber gone, he did not know who else would supply him with information on Farmani's movements. For a while, he considered Lieutenant Müller but just as quickly rejected the idea. To go to him with outstretched arms seemed humiliating, and after this night, Richter would be marked out for special contempt and disdain as the man who failed in his mission. It was not just a game between Farmani and himself anymore. His own credibility was on the line now.

He sat in his office, ashamed of how he had been swayed by his ego. Why had he promised them information when he had not yet captured the girl? He should have just waited until she was in his care before he told his superiors anything. At least that way, they may not have come to know of this fiasco. Now they would see the disappearance of the girl as his fault—either that he hadn't acted in time or that he had inadvertently given the Resistance information about what he would do next. In his defense, he had acted as fast as possible, and yet, those Resistance meddlers had been faster. His anger was mounting with every second. When he thought of having to meet Farmani socially again with his pompous smile in place, Richter had to clench his fists not to lash out physically at the desk in front of him.

When he calmed down a little, he thought of how he would face the Sturmbannführer. General Schäfer, the man he reported to, had personally involved himself in assigning him the men and resources for this "important task." He held his forehead in his hands. It was a mess. If they could not capture the girl, she would not sing. This left him where he already was—without a shred of evidence against Farmani and his activities. There was neither documentary nor physical proof of Farmani's involvement in the Resistance. All they still knew was that he issued papers to Iranians to leave the country, which for now wasn't illegal. As long as Berlin did not denounce Iranians as enemies of the Reich, they could continue to leave the French and German territories. He needed proof of Farmani's involvement in the transportation of Jews from where they were hidden. Despite all his plans to pursue and track Farmani, nobody had been able to give him any information about where in the city the rats were being hidden, who was supplying them with the necessities to survive, or where they were being moved to. He was as much in the dark about the operations of the Resistance as he was when he started his mission. Neither had they unmasked a single agent.

He could put out a notice for the Klein girl or even issue an arrest warrant in her name. But he knew how that would play out. When Nazis offered rewards for wanted people, the half-starved French people would bring him anybody who vaguely fit Eva Klein's description. By the time they questioned the woman and realized she was not the one, the informant would have fled with the reward. People would report so many women who fit the wanted person's description all over the city—so desperate would be the common person's need to claim the reward or to crawl into the good books of the Nazis. So poor, hungry, and cold were the general public that they would even be willing to conjure up such a woman into existence. There would be too many potential matches to go through that weeding out the real Eva would become a nightmare.

He was intelligent enough to know that Eva Klein would now be in disguise and hidden in a remote or unthought-of location in the city which perhaps even Farmani would be unaware of. From experience, he knew that the Resistance was thorough in all their activities. And well, if they could hide hordes of Jews, how much easier it would be to hide one woman!

His superiors weren't going to let him have another task force in a hurry. They would view it as a futile waste expense of men, money, time, and energy in what they would see as searching for a needle in a haystack. They would no longer trust him either. After all, he had let her slip from his hands once.

As his anger turned to blinding rage against himself for having been a fool, Farmani for simply existing, and the Resistance for their audacity, Richter could bear it no more. He banged his fist onto the table right in front of him. The resounding thud that followed made some officers within and outside his room peek in to see what had happened. When they saw Richter silently fuming in his stew of thoughts, they quietly walked away or got busy with their work. Most of them had heard what had happened to Captain Richter. The news of failure has a way of spreading like wildfire. Though nobody dared mock him to his face, Richter was not wholly insensible to the quiet whispers and stifled laughter behind his back. That he had never had any real friends among his colleagues had never bothered him formerly. In fact, he had always thought of himself as a cut above the rest of them. Though he did not care for anybody's good opinion of him generally, this time, their silent jeering and smug smiles stung him.

But Richter was not a person to go down without a fight. He was the sort who, if once had decided something for himself, would see it through to completion. If he were to go down in the process, he was resolved to take down his enemies with him. He was determined not to give up. He would teach that interfering Iranian a lesson even if it meant annihilation for himself and his career.

Chapter 17:

Exodus: 26 September-10 October 1942

The team now worked faster than ever on the evacuation of the Jews. Farmani had to issue documents post-haste to all the Iranian Jews. As winter approached, there were reports that Tehran would soon cut all contact with Germany, expel all Axis citizens—Germans, Italians, Japanese, and those from occupied and pro-German lands—from its soil, and declare war on Germany. Though Farmani rejoiced at the news, he also realized how perilous his own position was becoming. He knew that Iran's pro-Allied stance would soon mean a shutting down of all embassies and consular offices in Germany and German-occupied lands, including in France.

Therefore, he did not spare himself for a minute. He was in his office every day at the crack of dawn and did not leave until late at night after having wrapped up whatever documentation process he could. By now, he had stopped looking at individuals as Persian or non-Persian. Almost recklessly, one could say he issued every man, woman, and child who came to him seeking help, papers, and passports that established their Iranian- Persian and, by extension, Aryan nationality. As before, the passports failed to mention these people's ethnicity or religious affiliations. To a large extent, his efforts helped several thousand Jews flee the persecution in France. However, most of them had long and arduous journeys they had to undertake before they could reach a place they could call safe or home.

The Resistance groups focused on two separate routes via which Jews were transported to Tehran or Israel. They had to be either taken via Spain to Morocco and then via the North And West African countries to eventually Jordan, Iraq, or Iran. The other route was via Switzerland and the underground channels that operated in Pro-Axis or Axis-occupied countries to neutral Turkey and finally to Tehran in Iran. There were several countries like Italy, which, though on the Axis side, refused to participate in the pogroms against the Jews. Whichever route the Jewish refugees took, it posed threats to them. In every country, they were asked for documentation and papers that proved their identity and purpose of travel. The documents they carried were falsified or forged to erase their Jewish status. While neutral and Pro-Allied countries turned a blind eye to the possibility of their Jewish heritage, at other halts, especially those predominantly controlled by the Reich, they were scrutinized more critically, and people suspected to be Jews were even turned over to the Nazi authorities at times.

The German-controlled death camps in Eastern Europe were only multiplying by the day. There were reports of people being gassed in closed rooms and killed en masse. Farmani watched on in growing incredulity at the cruelty of the Nazis, which only seemed to be getting worse by the day. Their antics seemed to confirm suspicions that the Nazis themselves had started believing that they wouldn't win the war. Desperate men did desperate things, and Farmani couldn't help thinking of Hitler's concentration camps as the fake bravado of a leader who knew he was sinking slowly but surely.

Meanwhile, as the pogroms intensified, there were also groups that were actively dissociating themselves from Nazi allegiance. For instance, the Catholic Church of France, which had initially glorified Petain and the Vichy government, even closing its eyes to the early persecution and exclusion of Jews, was now turning around and helping Jews to get away. Several Jesuit networks were aiding, hiding, saving, and transporting Jewish children to safe locations or into the care of foster families. There were priests that Toni Laurent knew who were using the hallowed portals of church publishing houses to print and circulate anti-Nazi leaflets highlighting the atrocities of the Nazis. Others were using church resources to forge papers for Jews in hiding. For a world that seemed to be steeped in evil, these acts of charity kept alive the hope that one day, goodness would be restored.

Farmani realized, more than ever, how small a part he played in the final safety of the Jews who came to him. He could provide them with papers and put them in touch with the Resistance groups, which, with the help of Allied teams, could move them from one location to the next. However, at the end of the day, it was fortune and the attitude of the people who scrutinized their papers that determined whether they would be caught at some checkpoint or not.

It was during one of these days that Farmani received some not-so-welcome news. Reports were circulating that Adolf Eichmann had written to the German high command asking for a revocation of the immunity provided to Iranians. This was also probably in retaliation to the Iranian turnaround on the hospitality it had thus far extended to German citizens. If sources within the German ranks were to be believed, the senior SS leader had penned a severe letter stating that the claims made by a certain Iranian consul regarding the "Juguti" status of the Iranians were baseless and false and that they were only resorting to "the usual Jewish tricks and attempts at camouflage."

As of yet, there had been no reply to his letter, and it seemed like Berlin officials were dragging their feet on the matter. But Farmani felt a little shaken. If more people like Eichmann questioned the authenticity of his claims, Hitler or Himmler could have decided to reverse the racial policy on Iran even without enough evidence either way. After all, it wasn't like they had any scruples about establishing laws only after providing enough notice to the people involved. There were already precedents on how they had set up the Nuremberg Laws at a moment's notice, ripping away the rights of the Jews. There was no telling how the Nazis would decide to respond to what they may view as Iran's backtracking on its German sympathy.

Farmani's biggest fear was that the laws protecting Iranians would be reversed mid-way through their operations, leaving several of their people stranded in lands with documentation that would not help their case. Iran, as a country, was now stuck in a place that was akin to the devil and deep sea. Its association with Germany was ending but the country was now being led into a war due to Soviet and British pressures that it was not adequately prepared for.

***

It was sometime in early October that David Cohen came to Farmani to discuss some plans. It was regarding the movement of certain people from the safe houses in Paris. They were more cautious about the use of these hiding places as they still feared backlash from Richter. Farmani was rather surprised that he had not heard more from him yet.

In fact, after the failed attempt to capture Eva, it was as if the Nazi officer had completely disappeared. Farmani did not for a minute dare hope that something had happened to the evil man that would take him out of their lives forever. He knew that such happy circumstances would be rare occurrences during these times of darkness. Instead, he assumed the worst—that Richter was merely recouping and preparing to strike at them again when he had collected enough evidence. However, it had been weeks, and as of yet, Eva's letter hadn't been published and no action had been taken against Farmani and his team. In fact, except for a random act of arson against one of the safe houses that they used, it did not even seem like the locations of the other safehouse had been discovered or leaked to the Gestapo or SS. Farmani often wondered about what this ominous silence meant.

Eva had been moved into hiding, along with the Jews who had approached them for help. She had been given a disguise, a new identity, and papers so that she could move unhampered in Paris and not be recognized by the Nazis. This was certainly not a long-term solution. They hoped to keep up this ruse only until they could decide where to send her. Meanwhile, Eva, who knew that writing to her family for protection was useless and perhaps even counterintuitive, had written to an aunt in Switzerland, who she was fairly confident would take her in. She waited to hear from this old woman before making a move to leave the country. The Opera House seemed to be the only place where she was missed. Someone from there had contacted the police about their talented singer, who was now "mysteriously missing." The Parisian police force, now perhaps exhausted by the missing persons' reports that flooded them daily, had seemingly not done much. Or perhaps they had simply not considered the case important enough to make any inquiries. The other possibility was that after some investigation, they may actually have found it hard to trace her whereabouts. Whatever the reasons were, Eva seemed to be relatively safe, and the team could now focus fully on dealing with the Jews.

***

Pierre Dubois had done the groundwork for them. The old man was still nursing his wounds from the loss of Phoebe, who remained missing. The Resistance had tried very hard to trace her the last two months but could still not determine whether she had been on the train to one of the camps. For her sake and Dubois', they all hoped that she had somehow escaped from Drancy and was living somewhere in hiding or that she had been taken in by friendly people.

For his part, Dubois was a man on a mission. He could not keep still and kept needing to do something for the daughter he had lost. Once, long ago, he had made peace with the deaths of his wife and son in a German air raid. He did not want to sit idle as they snatched away his daughter too. This was the last straw as far as he was concerned.

The old man put his heart and soul into winning back his comrades and friends among the Parisian police force and the German SS. He was now frequently dining, drinking, and playing cards with them and was in on their secrets. He passed on information about the safe and unsafe zones in the city and which areas needed to be avoided. He handed over detailed maps of areas the Germans were focusing on and relayed every bit of information he considered important for the unhindered movement of the Resistance groups.

But highly motivated men were also, at times, akin to loose cannons. Without Farmani's knowledge or consent, Pierre Dubois had passed on the whereabouts of German offices and camps in the cities to more revolutionary Resistance groups that planned to attack Germans.

When Farmani learned about this, he was furious. He told Dubois, "What are you doing, Colonel Dubois? You are unnecessarily exposing yourself to risks by giving away their locations. The Nazis will come to know that the Resistance got the information from you."

The colonel stared at him defiantly as Farmani continued, "Besides, our work is to help Jews—children like your daughter—and other innocents flee unharmed. We have not taken on the task of killing Germans. After all, can't you see that many of them are merely lads acting on the fanaticism they have been fed on, while others are helplessly following orders to protect their loved ones, just as you did—not many days ago?!"

At this, the Pierre Dubois faltered. "I know in my heart that you are right. I have just lost so much that I can't seem to draw the line between what is and what I feel anymore. I am sorry; I will strive not to get carried away again."

Farmani did not want to continue an argument, and he kept the rest of his thoughts to himself. Though Pierre Dubois was a great addition to their team in terms of the information he could provide them, Farmani was beginning to sense that it was all getting too much for the old man. He was afraid that the colonel was beginning to lose his mind and that his hatred for the Germans would blind his reason and foresight. He was afraid that Pierre Dubois would, in his bursts of anger, do something irrational, costing them the mission and safety of the people they had promised to help.

He did not want to keep Pierre Dubois at bay because the old man seemed to draw energy from his work. Farmani decided to take on a more active role in the Resistance activities partly to keep an eye on Dubois' impulsivity as well as to become acquainted with the different parts of the mission.

***

Farmani and Cohen were helping a set of Jews escape from some of the safe houses in the city. They were both in disguise because they did not want to be recognized by the people who had known them by their real identities in the city. They had decided to drive it down in turns from Paris to Lyon. From there, the Jews would be taken to Collonges-sous-Salève, a small town along the French-Swiss border in the Free Zone. The idea was for them to cross over from there to Geneva.

Under normal circumstances, the drive took a person anywhere between five to six hours. However, since they would be frequently stopped along the border area between Nazi France and Nazi France, nobody could predict how long the journey would take, even if there were no other hitches on the way.

It was a large, covered truck, unmarked and rather inconspicuous. For the journey, they were Henri-Philippe and Jean-Pierre, two workers at the Galerie Nationale du Jeu de Paume, a center near the Louvre where French art and sculptures were confiscated and collected on the orders of the Gestapo. The Louvre itself had been emptied of all its masterpieces and treasures just before the Nazis arrived in Paris. However, there were empty homes that belonged to Jews and wealthy citizens with their private collections and other public collections of the smaller museums, which had not been as lucky. The German police had stripped all these buildings of their valuable art collections and were clandestinely transporting them to the homes of senior Nazi leaders. For the trip, Farmani and Cohen were transporting certain "works of art to Bruno Lohse, a German art dealer in Lyon who had bid and paid for them." They had papers cataloging the works that they were carrying that Lohse apparently wanted, as well as receipts marked to the German Gestapo. Needless to say, they were all forgeries.

They deliberately selected the smaller lanes and kept away from the larger cities and towns where troops were sure to be deployed. This was in keeping with their identities as couriers who were furtively working with the Germans in looting Paris of its art. As they drove on, they were, as expected, stopped several times as policemen checked their papers. Most of them were satisfied when they saw the catalog and receipts. A preliminary check of the truck revealed a few paintings and sculptures that, to untrained eyes, would have looked no different than the priceless ones housed in most museums.

Whenever the Gestapo stopped them, the Germans looked indifferent and made no further comments, but some of the French policemen looked unhappy and, at times, angry, but they let them pass. Understandably, many of these collaborators were forced to comply and kowtow to the Nazis. They did not relish French masterpieces in German hands. Some of the others who inspected their papers and who were more knowledgeable about the subject immediately recognized the name of Bruno Lohse, a senior SS member who worked for the Luftwaffe head Hermann Göring and for Hitler himself in supplying them with artwork for their private collections. At many halts, they were let through without further questions every time they uttered the name of Lohse.

For around three hours, nothing more remarkable than routine halts and checks happened. They had started at around ten in the morning and hoped to reach Lyon by the evening before it got too dark. If there was time, they hoped that the refugees would be able to cover the hardly two hours more to Collonges-sous-Salève the same day itself. At around one in the afternoon, as they were driving through the by-lanes, they noticed a German Kübelwagen that was following them. What was strange was that the vehicle seemed to be there no matter what route they opted for.

Sensing danger, Farmani motioned Cohen to slow down. He said, "The Kübelwagen has been behind us for the last half an hour. I think it is a Gestapo or SS vehicle. We will not be able to outpace it, and neither do we want someone there to open fire on us. Let us go slow. If they ask us to stop, do exactly that."

They kept driving for a while until they saw a man in the glass in the vehicle behind, motioning them to stop. Cohen eased up the engine and neatly parked on the side while the German vehicle went ahead of theirs and parked in front of them. Both Farmani and Cohen were sweating profusely by now.

Farmani told Cohen, "I'll do the talking."

Somebody got down from the German jeep and came up to them. It was with a shock that Farmani realized who it was. He also realized that the man was the only occupant of the jeep. But he said confidently, "Good afternoon, sir; is there any problem?"

It was Obersturmführer Müller with whom Farmani had played bridge once. He also knew that Müller worked closely with Richter and was suddenly afraid that they had been tailed on the orders of the man. However, he knew there was no point in showing their hand if the man was genuinely only doing his job.

Müller said gruffly, "I saw the truck a little while ago and wondered what you are doing out here. Care to show me your papers?"

Farmani said, "We are just transporting artwork from Jeu de Paume at the behest of one Mssr. Lohse at Lyon. We have the receipts and the catalog. You can check inside if you like to tally the catalog with what we are carrying."

Müller asked this time with some interest, "But why Lyon? I thought the chosen works were generally taken to Frankfurt, Munich, or Berlin. This seems irregular."

Farmani said, injecting a little surliness into his tone and shrugging nonchalantly, "How would I know officer? I am, but a lowly worker tasked with this mission and had to miss even my younger one's birthday to be here. You should ask your seniors about why they want it delivered to Lyon."

Internally, Farmani had been dreading this very question at every check post. However, none of the other officers had thought to ask them, and they had merely had to show the papers before they were waved through. Clearly, Richter's protege was cleverer than he had given him credit for, and Farmani felt uneasy about what would happen next.

Müller thumbed through the papers carefully. He then asked them, "You wouldn't mind if I checked inside, would you?"

Farmani said cheerfully, "Be my guest, officer. Just be careful in their handling. We don't want to face the wrath of the officer receiving them if they happen to be damaged in transit. You can imagine on whom they would pin the blame."

Farmani opened the doors at the back of the vehicle for Müller to investigate. Müller shone his flashlight over the sculptures and paintings and was almost stepping out when a muffled cough escaped the floor of the truck.

Quickly, he drew his gun and said, "What was that?" He stamped on the floor of the truck, and the hollow thud gave away the fact that there was more to the truck than met the eye.

But before Müller could say or do anything further, Farmani, who had climbed in after him, knocked him swiftly and efficiently at the back of his head. He had picked up one of the smaller sculptures and hit him squarely just above his neck. The German collapsed in a heap on the floor of the truck.

Without losing time, Cohen joined Farmani in the back, and together, they carried the unconscious Müller to his own jeep, where they left him behind the steering wheel. They boarded their vehicle and reversed the truck quickly. Choosing an alternative route, they drove at breakneck speed, knowing that they had no time to lose. They knew that there would be a search warrant for their truck and against them whenever Müller opened his eyes.

The rest of their journey was comparatively uneventful. Though they approached each checkpoint that came with beating hearts, wondering if this was the furthest they were fated to go, it seemed that word about two men supposedly carrying artwork from Paris hadn't been circulated yet.

They reached Lyon just before five in the evening. They conveyed the truck to Jean Weidner's facility, according to plan. Weidner was a wealthy textile merchant who had operations both in Lyon and Switzerland. He was also a member of the underground Dutch-Paris line, which helped Jews covertly cross over into Switzerland. He was a principal contact of Toni Laurent's.

When Farmani and Cohen rumbled into the large compound of the Lyonnaise warehouse, Weidner, an unassuming black-haired, bespectacled, pink-faced man, immediately came out to greet them. Farmani quickly explained to Weidner how matters stood—why the truck needed to be given a makeover and why it would not be safe to use it on the journey ahead. He told the man that there could be a lookout for the truck.

Weidner was a shrewd man who had survived long in the game with the Nazis only owing to his foresight and proclivity to take the right action at the right time. He gave directions to his men, and they quickly changed the number plates of the truck and unloaded it of its contents—both the artwork and the people. The fake artwork in the truck would be burned in the incinerators and furnaces of the factory. When the Germans came searching for a truck delivering artwork between Paris and Lyon, they would find no trace of it.

He assured Farmani that they would not use the same vehicle for the journey to Collonges-sous-Salève. As for Farmani and Cohen, Lyon was as far as this mission took them. Their job had been to deliver the men and women to Weidner, and from there, he would take it up.

Farmani and Cohen shook hands with the fifteen people who were in hiding during the journey up to here. Glad to be out in the sun again, the men and women who had been cooped up in a hidden compartment beneath the apparent floor of the truck thanked Farmani and Cohen profusely for having brought them out of Paris as far as the unoccupied zone. They knew that their travails were far from being over and that they had a long way to go still, but they were glad that they had made the first stretch safe and sound.

Farmani and Cohen did not have much time. They took a brief rest with Weiden, who provided them some much-needed food and water, before changing their guise again and undertaking the trip back to Paris. This time, they assumed the identity of Weiden's employees, going to Paris to bring back a shipment of textiles. They used a truck that was apparently registered under Weiden's name and bore the company logo. The return journey was filled with no real challenges. At every halt, they were stopped for papers which they provided. They took special care not to take the route on which they had encountered Müller.

When they saw the familiar sights and sounds of Paris, the two men could not help feeling a sense of peace and comfort settle over themselves. This passage had gone off well. The consequences of clobbering a lieutenant of the Reich could be dealt with later.

Chapter 18:

Parting of Ways: 12 October 1942

The time for parting had come at last. Eva Klein had heard from her old aunt in Lausanne. She said that it was perfectly fine for Eva to come over and stay for as long as she deemed it necessary. Eva would use her new alias during the journey so that if there was a lookout notice for her in France, she might evade attention all the better. As far as they were aware, no arrest warrants had been issued in her name, but they could not be certain that the Gestapo or the French police force had not been issued private orders to keep tabs on her movements. There was no harm in being as cautious as one could be.

They still had no news from or of Richter. But Farmani was wary. He did not want to relax his guard and find himself cornered. Instead, he took double the precautions as before in all aspects of his work and was now careful more than ever not to leave a paper trail of evidence behind him. Whenever he was part of missions that required his physical presence, he was careful to use a disguise and false identity papers. He also ensured that messages between himself and Toni were delivered in a more circuitous route so that, inadvertently, he did not end up giving away Agent Étoile. The idea was that no activity part of the Resistance could be traced back to him.

In particular, he wanted to ensure that Eva was granted all comfort possible during her seven-hour journey by road to

Lausanne. Though it was hard for Jews to settle down or work in Switzerland owing to the country's non-tolerance toward asylum seekers who were under threat by virtue of their race, the Swiss were more lenient toward those who sought refuge because of their political activities. While applying for her transit visa, she mentioned that she was a Resistance fighter who was being persecuted by the Nazi government. Her permit was almost instantaneously approved. There weren't any real obstacles to her staying with her aunt for the duration of the war now, save one.

The only obstacle that Farmani and Eva saw was that their time together had definitively come to an end. It would be impossible for him to keep traveling to Switzerland, and her safety would be compromised if she were to visit Paris or even write to him. There was no telling when they would meet again. If the war ended, assuming he was still in Paris, they might be able to renew their acquaintance. But for now, the future was vague and hazy. Happy as Farmani was to be seeing Eva go to a place she could call her home and be with somebody she could call her own, he was also sad that he might perhaps not see her for a while. He was also anxious about dangers that could befall her on her journey—especially if one of the personnel were to get wind of the fact that she was not who she claimed to be.

He, therefore, ensured Toni Laurent looked into her papers. He also got external expert advice on ensuring that her papers would look authentic enough so that chances of rejection would be minimal. All this work kept them in a flurry of action during the last week of her stay in Paris. When everything was put in order, there were only three days left. It was almost an anti-climax that everything had been settled so quickly. Neither Eva nor Farmani could decide how to bid each other farewell now.

***

Originally constructed under the reign of Napoleon Bonaparte I, the Pont des Arts was a nine-arched bridge across the Seine connecting the Institut de France with the Quai des Tuileries, where the Louvre Museum stood. Napoleon was inspired by the architecture of the British Empire and wanted a cast iron bridge reminiscent of the one built across the Severn. He had asked for hanging gardens, arches with flowers, and benches built on the bridge—a magnificent spectacle for his subjects. People who loved walks could rest and take in the scenery of the Seine. When the bridge was first opened, there was even a token entrance fee charged for every pedestrian who wanted to use it. Pretty as it may have been, it wasn't the grand success that Napoleon had imagined it to be, especially in one aspect. The nine arches of the bridge made it difficult for barges to pass through them. There were quite a few mishaps involving boats and barges crashing onto the pillars of the bridge. By the 1940s, the bridge was no longer the stunning monument it once was. With the ravages of the Great War and the ongoing one, the bridge was in shambles. Even so, it was often chosen by couples who wanted a quiet stroll over the evening. If the bridge could talk, undoubtedly, it would reveal to you the number of professions of undying love that it had witnessed. Perhaps it was the scenic beauty of the Seine or the breeze that constantly blew across the bridge; there was something romantically breathtaking about the quaint little thing.

It was here that Eva and Farmani had decided to meet for the last time. She had only a day more in Paris before she started her journey to Lausanne. They walked along arm in arm on a quiet, cool afternoon in October. They were at a loss for words. Now that they were on the cusp of saying their goodbyes, neither of them wanted to initiate it. Instead, superstitiously, they seemed to want to prolong the moment. Each of them took in the splendid view of the river silently with the other by their side, perhaps hoping that not saying it would make it more tolerable. So, they walked on and on without sharing much more than general observations of the place and the weather.

Finally, it was Eva who broke the silence on the subject. She said, "Well, how much longer are we not going to talk about it?"

Farmani slowly, unwillingly, turned his gaze from where it was fixed on some faraway spot on the river to her face and said with his crooked smile, "Will saying it make it any easier?" He tried to be buoyant and merry, but it was evident to her that his smile was tinged with sadness and longing.

They had met intermittently during her stay at a safe house near the Sacre Couer. He had deliberately intended not to seek her out because he worried that once he met her, he would not be able to stay away from her presence. He had not pressed Toni for Eva's whereabouts either. But on one of his missions, he met her by pure chance. That was when he suddenly understood why Toni's letter about Eva had contained so many mentions of the word "heart." Sacra Couer was French for "Sacred Heart." After having met that first time, he had no real break from his work. He had been quite busy working on the transportation of the Jews. Except for the occasional general banter when they met, they had hardly spent time in each other's company since she had gone into hiding. This made this last meeting all the more poignant. Who knew when another such rendezvous would happen and how they would have each changed when that day came?

She stored away every bit of his face in her mind's eye—his kind dark eyes, his hair, which now tousled by the breeze, lay across his thick brows, his stately nose, determined chin, and most of all that generous, crooked smile that now nearly broke her heart. Finally, she said, "Well, I suppose not. But it would break this excruciating silence."

It was his turn to take in her pretty little figure clad in a calf-length coat and trimmed at the throat and cuffs with fur. Her pale golden hair, now cut short, was held back in a hair band, but stray flyaways floated around her face like an aura. Her face was undone and yet flawless in its beauty. Her cheeks were pink from the persistent chilly breeze. Her almond eyes held his gaze steadily.

He said, "It would have been excruciating with most anyone. But not with you, Eva. We know how things stand between us without having to break the silence. You know my heart. Or at least that is what I believe."

She laughed, "How flattering. But tell me that you will not fall into dull and depressing ways after I leave. I couldn't bear to be the one woman who broke your heart."

He said, raising his eyebrows mock-seriously, "Oh no! I will be more dashing and charming than ever. I mean to have several dalliances with mysterious women who will simply fall swooning into my arms. Hopefully, I will also have the honor to play the knight in shining armor and save a few more of them from the clutches of evil villains."

She laughed so much that tears were rolling off her cheeks, and she was gasping for breath. Finally, when she was more in control of herself, she said, "Oh! To have found one such as you and now to be leaving!" And suddenly, her tears started falling more rapidly. She unlinked her arms from his and said, trying to blink back the tears, "There! Stupid me to have ruined a wonderful moment like this with unwarranted sentimentality. I'm so sorry."

Farmani pulled her into an embrace, and as her body effortlessly fit into the crevices of his body, he said, "Why do you apologize? It is not stupid at all. If it is some consolation, I feel exactly what you feel at this moment. You have been braver than me in voicing it is all."

For a while, they did not speak at all and just stood there on that cool afternoon, deriving strength, warmth, and comfort from each other. They could feel the beating of each other's hearts and felt a momentary veil of peace envelope them.

She asked wistfully, raising her face to look up at him, "When do you think we will meet again?" She did not want to voice the other question that was eating her—whether they would meet at all.

He said gently, "I don't know. But be assured that I will try my hardest to find you when this madness is over and as soon as I can get away. I just don't know when that will be, Eva. I wish that we did not have to part. Believe me, I have thought of it from every angle possible. This is the best way for you, me, and for the cause."

Eva sighed, "I can wait. I guess writing is out of the question?"

Farmani gently released her, held her by the shoulder, and looked into her eyes, "It would not be wise, Eva. If you happen to be on their watchlist, then that would jeopardize my work and the people I work with too. I am sure Richter will already be working behind our backs, trying to think up a new game. We still don't know what plan they are hatching. If we kept up correspondence, then that would just give him another excuse to alert authorities and have them check me. Perhaps that is why he is holding onto that letter, waiting for the right time. I wish we had that letter in our hands—your identity may have remained uncompromised. For now, let us just lie low for a while until we know that it is absolutely safe."

Eva nodded. She knew that what he said made a lot of sense. She had been prepared for as much. She knew what they were up against and the stakes they were playing for. She did not want him to take unnecessary risks for her sake, but the thought that they would know nothing about each other for the foreseeable future was depressing.

He asked her, remembering something, "Have you heard from Miriam after the radio communication you had?"

She said, "She is still in the south somewhere. She hasn't written, but I heard from Toni that she was doing fine. They aren't as harsh on the Jews in the Free Zone—at least for the present. Toni said that Miriam wanted to leave for Israel eventually, but for now, since France is landlocked by Axis powers, she is planning to wait a little longer. I think her brother has made his way back to France as well. I am not sure about that, though; it was just something I understood from Toni's words, and she wouldn't elaborate."

Farmani knew that it would be hard for a Jew to live in Switzerland, which had been very stringent about the admission of Jewish refugees ever since the start of the war, especially those from Germany and France. There would be no point in Eva asking Miriam to join her in Lausanne. The Swiss did not want to anger the Germans more than necessary. Being a small country, they feared a full-blown German invasion. They were hell-bent on preventing what happened to France from happening to them. One could hardly blame the Swiss for playing it extra cautious.

Again, there was a lull in the conversation as neither of them did not know what more to talk about. Every topic surrounding their impending parting seemed either too frivolous or too serious. Neither of them wanted to spoil the mood or talk about subjects merely to fill up the quiet.

The afternoon was slowly turning into a cold evening. Clouds scudded across the sky, their reflection in the golden waters below, looking like a scene out of some beautiful painting. The breeze that blew now picked up so that there were larger ripples across the surface of the river beneath them. It was so peaceful where they were that it was hard just then to imagine a full-fledged war raging on around them. The juxtaposition of the beauty before them versus the ugliness of war, death, and destruction was harder to digest than ever. It seemed impossible that a world that could contain so much beauty, joy, and happiness should also be one plunged into despair and darkness at the same time. That love should coexist with hate and goodness with evil were lessons that these young people were learning in full amplification.

Farmani said, "So, this aunt of yours. You haven't told me anything about her. I never even knew you had family outside of France."

She said, "Well, we have Dutch ancestry. Aunt Fleur is my father's sister, who fell in love with and married a Swiss archeologist after the Great War. My father and his father were against the match. I suppose they believed that women ought not to be allowed the freedom to make up their minds about such things as their futures and life partners. Anyway, she was determined not to marry anybody but him. Uncle Lucien was a good man and the threats of him turning out to be a wife-beating drunkard turned out to be unfounded, to say the least. They had no children and were a couple devoted to each other until his death a couple of years ago. Together, they built the small, comfortable house in Lausanne where she lives now. Of course, I have had only snatches of communication with Aunt Fleur over the years, and a good part of what I say is more conjecture than knowledge. But I remember that people who knew her always spoke of her in high regard and there was more than one who said that she was a kind and generous person. If her life has been happy, then she seems to surely have deserved all of it."

Farmani smiled, "Then, with her is exactly the place that I would wish for you. At least you will be taken care of and will have someone to talk to. Hopefully, you may even find a space there to hone your talent. Who knows, perhaps you will become the next operatic sensation in Zürich, Geneva, or Bern."

Eva smiled and said, "I do detect somebody trying to mock me. But yes, I do hope to get back to work there. The months that come will be long and dreary, no offense to Aunt Fleur. If I cannot correspond with you, then at least I can find some solace in my career. For now, I only hope to find some rest and peace."

Farmani wanted to keep up the levity and wouldn't let go of the subject, "Maybe one day you will notice among the crowd a certain gentleman who will be applauding you more than anyone else, and you will remember a poor consul who brought you flowers at the Paris Opera House after a fantastic performance and how you cold-heartedly blew him off. Of course, by this time, you will be so famous that you will have bodyguards protecting your celebrated persona. The poor man will not be able to approach you except if you were to allow them to let him pass."

Eva was laughing again at this description of their future reunion. She then said, "Or perhaps you will become such a larger-than-life figure, renowned for having saved so many lives that you will forget a poor opera singer you had once saved. I may have to show you the signet ring you will give me now to jog your memory."

Farmani said following along with her joke, "Alas, fair maiden, I don't own a signet ring. I wonder how I will remember you." When they finished sharing a hearty laugh over the joke, he said more seriously, holding both her hands in his, "I can never forget you, Eva. Not even if I wanted to. You know that. One day, we will be together again. I don't know how yet. But we will find a way."

She looked at him and whispered, echoing his words, "One day—"

For the briefest time, their lips met in an undying promise to find each other after the war. They just stood there afterward, holding hands, fingers intertwined, looking at the sun setting into the Seine, absorbing the orange splendor of the scene around them.

When they finally broke their embrace, Eva took out an envelope from her coat pocket. She smiled as she said, "This is for you to remember me."

Farmani opened the envelope. It was a portrait photograph of Eva, probably one that was taken just before her debut. On the backside, she had written—*To K.M., With love, E.K.* He carefully put it back into its cover before tucking it safely in the breast pocket of his coat. He could only muster the words, "Thank you. I will treasure this."

Chapter 19:

The Summons: 8 November 1942- 9 September 1943

It was soon after Eva's leaving that things seemed to start hurtling toward closure for Kameron Farmani. First came the news that the Allied forces, in what it called Operation Torch, had conquered parts of Northern Africa—Morocco, Tunisia, and Algeria, which had hitherto been loyal to Vichy France. The fighting lasted for only a week from the 8th-16th of November that year. Even the USA, which had refrained from taking part in the war thus far, sent its air force to assist what was otherwise a wholly British and French enterprise. The armed forces in Africa, under its commander-in-chief François Darlan, did not require much of a push to capitulate and join with De Gaulle's Free France against the Axis powers. Of course, this news was not broadcast or circulated in occupied France because the Reich did not want to admit that the tide was turning against them. However, those who had been secretly tuning in to the radio broadcasts pouring in from abroad knew the lay of the land and quickly spread it by word of mouth.

However, optimistic as this may have sounded, things took a turn for the worse within France. In retaliation to Operation Torch, a few days later, the German and Italian forces took over full control of France and conquered the French state of Vichy in Operation Anton, which lasted from the 11th to the 27th of November. The erstwhile Free Zone became

Germany's occupied South Zone of France, and Pétain's puppet government lost even the token freedom they claimed to possess. The armed forces of the French State were disbanded as German troops were stationed throughout France. Some of the demobilized would later go on to join the Free French Army or Resistance groups within the country.

As far as Farmani and his team were concerned, their work got tougher than before. Operation Lifeline now had no "Free Zone" to send its refugees to, even for temporary respite or halts. They and the French Resistance would have to treat the whole of France as hostile territory for their work ahead. With the complete annexation of France to the Reich, even crossing over to Switzerland would become much harder. For a minute, Farmani interrupted his thoughts to feel grateful that Eva had already left and probably reached Lausanne safely.

There was now no doubt about what was shortly going to happen to Iran-German relations and, by extension, his office in Paris. Farmani kept waiting for his summons with a mixture of dread and anticipation. On the one hand, he had already done so much for both Persian and non-Persian Jews here in occupied France. The urge to return to his country was pulling at his heartstrings now more than ever. He had his home and his family there. After Eva's departure, nothing was holding him back here in France.

However, he also thought about being in Iran occupied by the Soviets and British. He knew that the images of luxury and comfort that he carried in his mind of his home were from former days when Iran was free of foreign rule. He had not really kept up with the news pouring in from his homeland, but the snatches of information relayed talked about severe food shortages as the country's produce and stock were being diverted to the war effort. In fact, he heard about severe famines in parts of the country and unarmed uprisings against the government that the new Shah was being forced to smother under British-Soviet directives.

His family still lived in relative comfort, but he was not sure what he would do there if he were to return. He would be too inconsequential a person to help with governmental processes or issues. He would still only be a junior diplomat waiting for a new posting as far as the Iranian government was concerned. In fact, if reports were to be believed, the Shah himself had little say in what was happening in Iran. For the most part, it seemed that the Shah liked nothing better than to join his Swiss advisor and friend Ernest Perron in penning French poems all day long while the British and Soviets made all the decisions for the country.

Farmani thought that he might practice law and earn a living from it. After all, he was a qualified lawyer. Even as he thought about it, another voice chimed in, *Who am I kidding?* He had developed a taste for adventure, and Farmani was not sure that he wanted to live just a comfortable, peaceful life until retirement anymore. He knew himself to thrive best on action and a touch of the heroic.

Put simply, Kameron Farmani knew that if he wanted to achieve something that he could call his legacy to the world, it would only be here, acting in the interests of his people. When he said "his people," he included every person who belonged to the Middle Eastern belt of countries. It did not really matter to him from which particular country they were or what their religious affinity was—Arabs, Jews, Persians, Mesopotamians, whoever they were, all of them deserved a free and equal life. Here in Paris, there was a chance that he could do something to help them win their lives at least.

Back at home in Iran, his hands would be tied several times over from taking any real action. There would also be endless pressure from his family not to do anything that might jeopardize their public standing or mark them out as enemies of the state. His parents were conservatives at heart and would not appreciate him speaking out against the Germans when the Shah himself seemed to be undecided about where his loyalties lay. Government officials would not take kindly to him if he were to directly gain an audience with the British or Soviet administration. He would merely tire himself out in the endless bureaucratic procedures.

He thought long and hard about the pros and cons of the choices before him. He kept turning over in his head what he should do with himself. No matter which angle he looked at it from, the answer was crystal clear to him. He would not go back—not even when the official summons came. He would stick it out for as long as he could in Paris and help the Resistance in saving as many lives as they could. This decision, he knew, would come with its own repercussions. He would have no salary from the government, and neither would he have diplomatic immunity if things were to go wrong. If he should be captured by the Nazis, Iran might wash its hands off him. However, being captured or killed was a lesser evil to him than not doing his duty.

Briefly, his thoughts turned to what would happen to him after the war. After all his efforts here, he wondered if he would be hailed at home as an icon or a villain. He wished he could turn time forward, look into the future, and learn how posterity would remember him—if they did remember him at all. But he shrugged the thought away because deep in his heart, he knew that it did not matter what people thought of him. What would happen would happen. He could not forsake his responsibility to his conscience and to people who depended on him, even if it meant public censure and persecution later on. He did not exactly believe in God and divine retribution and such, but he definitely believed that righteousness would prevail eventually and that a clear conscience was better than all the riches and comforts that life could offer him. He was willing to embrace the consequences of his actions willingly and contentedly when the time came.

And so, Kameron Farmani continued his work. He created new documents and helped Toni Laurent in as many ways as he could. Though he came close to being captured once or twice, there was no lasting damage to his person or legacy.

***

Sometime in December, as another batch of Jews were moved from their safe houses in the city, Farmani received a letter. It was not signed, but the minute he saw it, he knew it was the answer to the question he had been asking himself for a long while now. The letter was terse. It said:

> *What you have is a Pyrrhic victory. The worst is yet to come. Brace yourself and watch your back.*

Though it could have been from anyone, it bore the indelible mark of Richter. Reading over the letter again, Farmani understood what it meant. He knew that Pyrrhus was the king of Greece who had foolishly challenged the Romans and even defeated them in two battles in the third century BC. However, he soon realized that his victory was meaningless because he had lost so many men that his march into Italy was only a temporary win. When he comprehended that while fallen Roman soldiers could be replaced in the blink of an eye, his own men would remain irretrievably lost, the contrite king hurried back to Greece before the Romans could recoup and attack them.

Farmani understood what Richter was getting at. He was warning him that Farmani's moves would be watched and that at the next opportunity, he would strike. He had expected nothing less. He thought of the man who had let them save Eva, only to be duped again in proxy via Müller's episode. He could understand the rage that goaded the German into writing the letter. He also wondered if Richter had received a reprimand from his commanding officers for his blunders. The thought brought a smile to his lips. That might explain the man's absence all this while.

Anyway, it was clear that the old enemy was back. In a way, Farmani was pleased that he had a challenge to rise to. He hoped that he would soon meet his arch-nemesis at one of the social functions that the Reich or the French administration might organize. It would be fun to beat Richter at another round of bridge, if nothing else.

However, Farmani was experienced enough not to underestimate his foe. He knew that despite his shortcomings, Richter was clever, persistent, and ruthless—a combination that could wear out even the strongest of his enemies. By comparison, Farmani recognized that he would never reach the heights of deception that Richter was a master at.

***

Though he expected it every day, it was September 1943 before Iran finally declared war on Germany. With the announcement, also came Farmani's summons back to Tehran. Though it came a lot later than he expected it, giving him time to be a part of several more missions in the meantime, the dreaded letter finally arrived. It came on the official letterhead of the state of Iran and bore the official seal of the Shah. It was not a long epistle, but he had to read it thrice for the magnitude of its implications to sink in. The letter said—

> *The state of Iran has declared war on the German Reich as of September 1943. It, therefore, wishes to cease all further governmental and diplomatic functioning in Germany and German-occupied lands. This is a summons for all employees on the rolls of the Iranian state to return home from Germany or German-occupied lands at the earliest. Iran assures its personnel*

that adequate measures will be taken for their safe return to Tehran. Details of the return journey will be intimated to them at a later date. Failure to adhere to this summons could have financial and legal repercussions for the individual.

It was now or never for Farmani. He could no longer continue to work in an official capacity in France. He, however, had passports, as yet unissued with the official seal and stamp of the country in his locker. His next steps would determine the outcome, and there were only two possible choices: either compliance with his country's law in defiance of his conscience, or compliance with his conscience in defiance of his country's law.

David Cohen heard of the news and came to Farmani's office at once. He did not waste time but asked, "Have you heard?"

Farmani, who was writing a report, did not take his pen off the sheet in front of him. Without breaking stride, he said, "Yes, I have. The offices here will close by the end of this month."

Cohen asked impatiently, "And?"

Farmani looked up smilingly, "About how many missions have we worked on approximately now?"

The other man said, "Oh, God knows Farmani! I would say twenty or perhaps more missions in all?"

Farmani said, "In the light of our acquaintance so far, what do you think my answer to your question will be ?"

David Cohen laughed jovially as he made up a limerick on the spot in reply, "There was a man from Iran, Who refused to follow the plan, Through hardship and strife, He persisted in life, And proved he could do what he can."

Farmani looked up at him and said, "I'm impressed, Agent Monk," Farmani said using Cohen's name within the ranks of the Resistance. The surname once referred to the priestly classes among the Jews. This is why they had picked this name for David when he started working with more Resistance members. "I did not know that the next Omar Khayyam walked among us."

David Cohen and Kameron Farmani clasped their hands in a firm handshake as they laughed over their joke. They knew they still had more work, tougher than what they had handled so far, ahead. But for now, there was this shared camaraderie and peace that they could depend on.

Epilogue:
Nottingham, 11 March 1980

Here, Kameron Farmani suddenly chose to end his story. As I saw it, where he paused was only still the prelude to his wartime service for humanity. For reasons best known to himself, he thought that this was all that he could force out of himself for the present. My curiosity was killing me. I was impatient because I had so many burning questions to which I arrogantly thought I deserved an answer. If I had given it more consideration, I would have realized that though he could have chosen so many people to tell his tale to, I was the lucky one who finally heard it. At the time, of course, I never saw it like that. When the man fell mute, almost as if he had put to rest all possible discussions on the topic, I felt the urge to prod him into speech again.

To make him continue, I said, "That's utterly remarkable! To actually have been a part of the Resistance in France!"

I must have looked at him with something bordering the awe and admiration I felt, for he retorted immediately, almost irritably, "It wasn't glamorous. A lot of it was just mundane, boring paperwork. You must also remember that I had a team putting together those papers for me. I did a lot of the coordination work, I'll admit. I was never officially a part of the Resistance. I used their help because I did not have the resources or the manpower to hide people or help them across the border. I don't want you saying things about me that are factually incorrect. This is partly why I refused to talk to others before. As a researcher, I thought you would be more careful in the way you word things. Some others have no notion of the complexities of war and espionage. I have no intention of making myself out to be some larger-than-life messiah. I hope you will present me with more humanity. I had a chance—an incredibly rare opportunity to do something, and I did what was my duty. That is all."

I asked, "But you stayed back? Despite the official summons? Against your country's orders?"

"I did," he said simply. As an afterthought, he added, "To be frank, I am not even sure that it was a wise move. But when you are young, you have so much energy and spirit that it is hard to curb it. I stayed on till the end of the war in Paris. I witnessed the Allies headed by De Gaulle marching into the city in 1944. It was such a wonderful moment for all of us."

I tried and failed to imagine how it must feel to fight against injustice for three whole years and then see your efforts bear fruits. To know that you have contributed something and that your actions have changed the destinies of many.

"Did you never return to Iran?" I asked wonderingly.

Farmani said, scrunching his eyes together, trying to recall, "Much later, in 1952, if my memory serves me right. I was called back because, finally, somebody had decided to initiate action against people like us who had *disobeyed* orders during World War II."

I asked incredulously, "So many years later? Why?"

Farmani looked at me deep in thought and shrugged, "Search me. I really don't know why it took that long. Maybe somebody had something to hide, and this was a fine way to divert attention from themselves. Or perhaps somebody who had always meant to complain got somebody's attention only at that particular time. Whatever the reason was, I was called back, and there was a trial of sorts."

I asked curiously, "And then? Were you convicted of misconduct?"

Farmani waved away my question, "No, no. Nothing as severe as that. It dragged on for three years, as officials things generally do, but I finally got to reestablish my reputation in 1955. I could have worked a couple of more years with the embassy. But by then, maybe I had enough of it—I was tired. I decided that it was perhaps time to retire. I will admit that I was angry. I knew I had disobeyed orders by staying back. But I had hoped my country would see my intention in doing all that I did. To be hauled up like a common wartime criminal and interrogated was humiliating, even if I could clear my name in the end. That's how I washed up here. One of my nephews had a place in Croydon, and I came here. I like the quiet life here. The anonymity helped too. Here, there aren't people who run up to you, expecting you to play the part of a hero or a double-dyed villain. In this countryside, they just know me as a quiet Iranian ex-diplomat, and somehow, it suits me."

I nodded and then asked him, "So what now? Will you never go back to Iran?"

He looked at me sadly this time, "I doubt such a day will dawn. The Ayatollah regime has confiscated a lot of property and wealth that belonged to the people of royal descent, such as the Qajars. Even if I did go back, there would be nothing left there for me. No land, no home, no money, and very likely no honor."

I suddenly remembered that there were a couple of years unaccounted for. I asked him, "Your story takes us only to the beginning or middle of 1943. What happened between '43 and '45? Were there many more you saved during that period?"

Farmani hesitated and then plunged on, "That, my friend, would be a story for another day. Those final years of the war

243

seemed to fly by in a hurry. You must remember that by then Operation Lifeline was established, and a running network was in place. We just kept using it to help whoever came to us—Jew, Non-Jew, Iranian, non-Iranian, it did not matter. But if I were to talk about those years—the exact numbers we were able to save and so on—I need to jog my memory a little. I don't want to provide you with inaccurate facts and numbers. I want to sit down, remember them, and perhaps even write them down in sequence before I talk to you."

"What about Richter? Did he pursue you? Did the man die? Is he alive?" I asked impatiently. I couldn't fathom why Farmani would stop his tale where Richter had just sent him a threatening note.

He said, "I don't know. All through 1943–45, the man was relentless in his efforts to have us arrested. And then, after the war, I can't say. There was a massive witch hunt against the Nazis right after the war and even through the last decade. Eichmann, for instance, was captured in 1960 in Argentina, where he was in hiding, flown to Israel, tried, and executed. Several of the others who weren't caught right after the war met with similar fates. If a few of them escaped capture, I can only hope that they repented for their sins. I can only hope that Richter met with a fate that was nothing more or less than exactly what he deserved."

"Hmmm," I was thinking about something. I caught sight of the sepia photograph again and asked, "What about Eva Klein? Were you able to trace her afterward?" I hoped that there would be a second meeting. But even as I asked it, I knew it couldn't be possible. It did not fit with the fact that Farmani had never married.

He said, "After the war ended, you mean?" I nodded.

He said, "No, David. I tried searching for her, but I couldn't trace her in Lausanne. Some people—their neighbors—told me her aunt had moved to Bern. But that's as far as I got. After the war, I got an official posting in Brussels, and I had to move there. So, even if she tried to contact me later, I might have missed her communication. Though the war was over, we had livelihoods to get back to, and I'll admit I was tired of France. I wanted a fresh start, and then time just slipped away, I guess."

"Is that why you never married?" I asked. It was a personal question, and I am ashamed to admit now that the inappropriateness of it never struck me then. I was a research student doing what I loved most—researching. I only wanted the facts, even if they hurt the subject. I know I can be insensitive at times like that. I swear, it is a habit that I am working on now.

I have to give Farmani credit here for not losing his patience and for remaining calm when he said the next few words. "We are trained to search for neat conclusions and happily ever afters in stories, but alas, life is not like that." His eyes took on a dreamy glaze again.

Finally, I asked the question I had been meaning to ask since the beginning, "Why me?"

Farmani's eyes snapped back to the present, but he looked confused. He asked, "Meaning?"

I said, "You told me there were others. You told me you had met tens of individuals wanting to ferret out your story. Even our hostess said that you clammed up every time somebody tried to ask you questions about the war. Why did you agree to talk to me?"

Farmani said, "I suppose because it is time the world heard my side too. Or, maybe because the moment seems ripe now. Or maybe your persistence reminds me of another David who worked untiringly and ceaselessly with me—a man I consider my brother."

I said, a little flattered, "You mean David Cohen?"

Farmani smiled as he said, "I think now we have covered everything that should go into your book. Let us leave it here for the present. I am not saying this is the end of the story. But for now, this is all I have the energy for. If you leave your number with me, I will call you when I remember more, or rather when I feel confident of the chain of events that happened next."

And so ended what was to be the first of a series of interviews with a man I considered to be a modern-day Robin Hood. Robin Hood had merely distributed riches among the poor. But here was a man who had gone out of his way to save lives at a time when he could have died for it. To me, there was no greater definition of heroism, even if he chose to look at it only as a duty to be rendered.

Printed in Great Britain
by Amazon